Katy Evans's *USA Today* and *New York Times* bestselling The REAL series strips away everything you've ever believed about passion—and asks the dangerously enticing question "How REAL is what you feel?"

"Sweet, scary, unfulfilling, fulfilling, smexy, heartbreaking, crazy, intense, beautiful—oh, did I mention hot?! Evans [takes] writing to a whole new level. She makes you FEEL every single word you read."

—*Reality Bites* on *REAL*

"Edgy, angsty, and saturated with palpable tension and incendiary sex, this tale packs an emotional wallop. . . . Intriguing."

—*Library Journal* on *REAL*

"I have a new book crush, and his name is Remington Tate."

—*Martini Times*

"I loved this book. As in, I couldn't stop talking about it."

—*Dear Author* on *REAL*

"Remy and Brooke's love story is one that has to be experienced because until you do, you just won't get it . . . one roller-coaster ride that you'll never forget!"

—*Books Over Boys*

"Seductive, wild, and visceral."

—Christina Lauren, author of *Beautiful Bastard*, on *MINE*

"Steamy, sexy, intense, and erotic, *MINE* is one that will have you hanging off the ropes. And begging for more."

—Alice Clayton, author of *Wallbanger*

"Getting inside Remy's mind is one hell of a ride. . . . You may love Remy now, but after you read his side of the story he is going to consume your heart."

—*Book Angel Booktopia* on *REMY*

"Completely mind-blowing . . ."

—*RT Book Reviews* on *ROGUE*

"Apart from being one of my most scorching reads of the year, the 'realness' of the love story took me totally off guard, and held me captive until the very last word."

—*Natasha is a Book Junkie* on *ROGUE*

"[An] amazing, beautiful story that pulls at your emotions and makes time disappear. . . . I have a whole new level of awe and amazement for the talent that is Katy Evans."

—*The Blushing Reader* on *ROGUE*

Praise for Katy Evans's Manwhore series

"Talk about addictive. This book consumed me from the very beginning to its pulse-pounding end. If you're looking for a book that is just fun, super addictive, and sexy as hell, this is the book to pick up right now."

—*Vilma's Book Blog*

"A soul-searing romance, *Manwhore* seduced every one of my senses, weaving its way under my skin in an unforgettable way. An absolute favorite of mine."

—*Angie and Jessica's Dreamy Reads*

BOOKS BY KATY EVANS

THE REAL SERIES

REAL

MINE

REMY

ROGUE

RIPPED

LEGEND

THE MANWHORE SERIES

MANWHORE

MANWHORE +1

MS. MANWHORE

LEGEND

Katy Evans

G

Gallery Books

New York   London   Toronto   Sydney   New Delhi

G

Gallery Books
An Imprint of Simon & Schuster, Inc.
1230 Avenue of the Americas
New York, NY 10020

First Gallery Books trade paperback edition February 2016

GALLERY BOOKS and colophon are registered trademarks of Simon & Schuster, Inc.

For information about special discounts for bulk purchases, please contact Simon & Schuster Special Sales at 1-866-506-1949 or business@simonandschuster.com.

The Simon & Schuster Speakers Bureau can bring authors to your live event. For more information or to book an event contact the Simon & Schuster Speakers Bureau at 1-866-248-3049 or visit our website at www.simonspeakers.com.

Manufactured in the United States of America

10 9 8 7 6 5 4 3 2 1

Library of Congress Cataloging-in-Publication Data

Names: Evans, Katy, author.
Title: Legend / Katy Evans.
Description: First Gallery Books trade paperback edition. New York, NY Gallery books, an imprint of Simon & Schuster, Inc., 20016.
          Series: The Real series ; book 6, "Legends never die."
Subjects: LCSH: Hand-to-hand fighting—Fiction. BISAC: FICTION / Romance / Contemporary. FICTION / Contemporary Women. GSAFD: Love stories.
Classification: LCC PR6105.V3495 L44 2016 (print) LCC PR6105.V3495 (ebook)
   DDC 823/.92—dc23
LC record available at http://lccn.loc.gov/2015042851

ISBN 978-1-5011-0154-0
ISBN 978-1-5011-0158-8 (ebook)

To big dreams and the even bigger people who chase them

LEGEND PLAYLIST

"STREET LIGHTS" by Kanye West

"UNBREAKABLE SMILE" by Tori Kelly

"ROLLERCOASTER" by Bleachers

"RESISTANCE" by Muse

"FEELS LIKE TONIGHT" by Daughtry

"GERONIMO" by Sheppard

"FAVORITE RECORD" by Fall Out Boy

"BEAUTIFUL LIFE" by Nick Fradiani

"I WON'T GIVE UP" by Jason Mraz

"MADNESS" by Muse

"BEAUTIFUL NOW" by Zedd

"FIGHT SONG" by Rachel Platten

ONE

SEATTLE

Reese

My mother drops me off at the airport. I'm wearing my favorite pair of jeans and my favorite top. For luck, I guess.

"You sure you'll be all right?"

"I'm sure."

"Reese." She stops me before I can get out of the car, taking my hand. "I love you. . . ."

"I love you too." I smile at her.

She leans over to hug me, and I close my eyes and cling for an extra beat. She smells of lemons. Like home, like everything I know.

"Do you have your passport, ticket confirmation . . . ?"

I nod, and hop out and get my suitcase.

I turn and wave goodbye to her, a pang of homesickness already hitting me as I watch her drive away.

Inhaling, I step into the airport on my own for the first time in my life.

Between boarding and flight times, it takes over four hours for me to arrive in Seattle. The plane circled an extra half hour until the rain stopped and we were authorized to land. It's wet and green. My cousin Brooke meets me outside the terminal.

"Reese!" With a tall ponytail, skintight spandex running pants, and a killer body beneath, she looks like she could've stepped out of *Sports Illustrated*. "So glad to have you." She hugs me tight before introducing me to a tall, curly-haired man standing next to her. "This is Pete."

"Nice to meet you, Reese," he says as he reaches for my suitcase. "Welcome to the team."

"Thank you for having me."

If Brooke has any reservations about having me around for the whole summer, she doesn't show it. She's excited and talkative during our ride, answering all my questions on how I can help her with her three-year-old, Racer.

At the tip of the cul-de-sac we reach their sprawling waterfront home in Lakehaven, with its stucco facade, sweeping rooftop, and manicured lawn.

I'm speechless, taking in the interior of the house with wide eyes as she gives me a brief tour. Smart technology everywhere, five bedrooms, a kitchen fit for a restaurant. It's got high windows and a lot of natural light, with views of Mount Rainier across a glistening stretch of water.

Brooke leads me down the hall to the guest bedroom. The hall has framed pictures of famous athletes, and among them, there's a picture labeled RIPTIDE and I try not to gape at it, because I know Riptide is her widely known husband, former boxer and now MMA fighter. Even people who've never heard about MMA fighting seem to know who he is. Mom says they call him RIP too, because he kills his opponents. Not literally kills. Well, I *hope* not. But he buries them in the ground. Online, the articles say that he's a fighting machine, and the best there's ever been.

We finally reach my bedroom and I am tempted to ask Brooke if she's ever lost her way in her own house. The room's double the size of my bedroom back home, exquisitely decorated in light tones, with a tinge of pastel blue on the curtains and on the bedspread.

"Here's a gym membership card; we buy them by the dozen for the team. You're part of the family now." She winks. "Food in the fridge, clean towels in the bathroom, bed has brand-new sheets. Cell phone?"

"Yes."

"Okay. Your mom gave you my number, right?"

We confirm each other's numbers. It's been a while since I talked to her. I'm normally shy and not very talkative at all. I guess Brooke knows. I'm sure my mom has filled her in on everything that's happened in my life, from birth to now, just as she let me know that Brooke married Remington "Riptide" Tate.

They're a power couple in the wellness and athletic worlds, a power couple in their own right.

My mom thought I'd be invigorated spending time with them and their team as they work the underground fighting circuit this summer. She suggested I come when I asked her to let me figure out what I wanted to do with my life.

And now here I am, trying to find who I am.

I start unpacking, neatly putting my things into a drawer, and after I hang some of my clothes in the closet, I pass the window and stare out at the water as Brooke approaches a tall, dark-haired man hoisting a little kid up on his shoulders. I know it's her husband and son.

I haven't seen little Racer since Christmas, and I've never met Brooke's husband, but he's got a presence as big as his reputation, even from here. Remy Tate is as big as a mountain, and seated on his shoulders his son seems to be on top of the world. Many things have been said about the famous Riptide, *hot* and *masculine* prevalent among them. Racer is pummeling the top of his father's head, and Remy is holding him by his little feet, staring out at the long dock and toward the water as Brooke comes up and puts her arms around Remy's waist.

I smile when I look at them. They travel so much due to his fighting schedule, I don't see them that often, but we're family. They look at peace, and happy. Racer starts squirming over his dad and pointing out at the water as if he wants to get on a boat.

Racer. My ticket out of town. Someone to worry about other than me.

I think of Miles and a prick of pain hits me. Maybe being away will make him miss me. Being away will make him realize he feels something other than friendship for me.

We communicate, but not as much as I'd like.

Hey I got here safely

Good. Enjoy yourself, Reesey

Thanks ☺ I'll be good

I wait to see if he asks me anything. He doesn't. I curl up in bed, staring at my phone, then text my mom to let her know I'm in Seattle.

TWO

SEATTLE

Maverick

Not in a million years, kid.

No.

NOT INTERESTED.

Get the fuck out of my face!

Four cities in two days, and more doors slammed in my face than I can count. I sling my backpack over my shoulder, pick up my duffel bag, and scratch another name from my list.

Hopping onto a bus and hopping off thirty minutes later, I scan the mix of both commercial and apartment buildings down the block, then knock on my last door.

"Coach Hennesy?"

He's a tall man, his hair like salt and pepper, clad in sweats, with a yellow timer hanging from his neck. He gives me a questioning look.

"I'm your next champion."

He laughs, but then he must see something in my face. In my stance. Thirst, resoluteness, guts. Maybe I'm wearing my balls in my eyes. He falls sober and swings the door wide open. "Come on in."

He doesn't ask for my name.

Guess with one look, he knows he'll find my name in the dictionary, right next to "determined."

He leads me to his garage. "Where'd you train before?" he asks.

"Self-taught. I watch videos."

He scoffs, then shrugs. "Okay, let's see what you've got."

I eye the equipment across the room. The heavy bag hangs from the ceiling, the leather worn from other fighters before me. There's a boxing dummy in the corner. Speed bag. Weights. A whole private gym set up here. I drop both my bags, then unzip my backpack and start to put on the gloves without bothering to remove my hoodie.

"Take that off; I need to know what you've got. Need to see your form," Hennesy says.

I clench my jaw. Slowly unzip my hoodie. Take it off and glance past my shoulder, shifting to keep my back from the coach's view. The guy is clearing the fighting area. Good. We can get down to business. He walks to me when I face him.

"Give it over." I hand over my hoodie and he tosses it aside, then crosses his arms and looks at me. "Speed bag first."

I inhale, position myself before the speed bag, and hit. *Wham.*

I keep on hitting, lightning fast, my fists making the bag fly.

I would have warmed up first, but I've been doing this for days, and I won't stop until I've got myself a coach—and not even then.

I've got momentum now, and I pick up speed, my arms moving back and forth, working the speed bag until it's moving so fast you can't even see it.

I'm starting to sweat; it's stuffy in here, but I can't stop. I need him to take me on. I need one yes to get me in the ring. Just one yes and I'll do the rest.

"Time." Hennesy stops me. He signals to the boxing dummy and the heavy bag. "Let's see you pound the bag."

I swing out and slam my knuckles on the bag, putting everything into my fists. *Thack, thump, thud.*

Hennesy's composure starts to crumble with excitement. "Holy shit, boy!"

I'm getting into it. I'm in the zone, where it's just me, the leather brown bag, my fists, and nothing else but slamming the spot I'm looking at.

"I've seen enough." He stops the bag from swinging. His eyes are glassy. "Fill this out."

I pull off my right glove and grab a pen as he slaps a piece of paper onto a desk at the corner. I bend down to fill out my name and contact information and realize, too late, that I exposed the tattoo on my back.

"You're his boy."

I freeze midsignature.

A second ticks by. Then two.

I slowly set the pen down and take one last look at the paper. I might not get to fill it out after all. I turn.

His face has paled.

I wait it out for a few beats. Maybe he's different. Maybe he can deal with it.

He tosses my jacket at me. "Get out. Nobody wants to see you fight."

I frown fiercely as I catch my jacket in my fist and edge forward, equally mad now. "That's too damn bad. 'Cause I'm fighting anyway."

I keep my eyes on him as I pull off my left glove, shove my arms into my hoodie, and zip up.

I walk out and the door slams behind me. I clench my jaw and shove my gloves into my bag and spot the old, black gloves inside too. I push them down into the bottom of the duffel bag and zip it up.

The season starts in a week and a half. No coach? No fight. I can't even get into a gym.

But I won't let anyone or anything keep me from the ring.

I pick up a penny from the ground.

And I spot a girl in workout clothes across the street, tying her shoelaces. She's a step away from the gym door. I straighten, pull my hoodie over my head, and cross the street, following after her like I belong.

THREE

"HE'S WITH ME"

Reese

Today is the first day of my very own personal boot camp. One day spent with the Tates and the good news is, there are no tempting Snickers bars in sight. Only green food with organic labels on them. All fresh. Fruits, lean meats, all I need to finally—finally—lose the ten annoying pounds I've been carrying with me for the past few years. They come with feelings of insecurity, dissatisfaction, and frustration. They are proof of me having absolutely *no* willpower against my hunger pangs or my cravings. A reminder of why I didn't go to dances, or—despite my love of the beach—head out in a swimsuit to take in some sunlight. I plan to work out like a fiend.

When I get back home, I'm going to walk into a crowded room with a great smile and sans my Himalayan butt, looking so pretty Miles Morris is going to drool in his mouth at the sight of me. He'll admit that it's always been me and only me for him, and he was too blinded by our friendship to notice.

And I'm going to sleep with him—the first time that I will ever sleep with a guy—and I'll do it with no insecurities about him seeing me naked because I'm going to look beautiful and slim and, most of all, sure of myself. So sure of myself I'd do it in broad daylight for him if he asked me to.

Pulling my T-shirt a little lower as it rolls up my hips, I start panting and drop the treadmill speed a little bit. If I don't, I'll have to crawl my way to day care to pick up my little package and, carrying him back home, I'll be trailing my tongue on the sidewalk. No, thanks.

I'm on a healthy living boot camp.

Brooke says I look like Jennifer Lawrence and that she envies my hourglass figure. It's like my torso was cinched with a corset since I was born. Curvy. But I'll take Brooke's athletic physique any day. Genetics made my hourglass figure, but athletic physiques take more than genetics; they take hard work and I admire that.

I press the treadmill speed a little bit faster and survey everyone inside the bustling gym. But my eyes come back to the guy who slipped into the gym after me.

He's at the far end of the room, pummeling a heavy bag. He looks totally concentrated. He's the only fighter here who's not talking to anyone and not with a trainer.

I'd say he looks friendless, but it's more like he doesn't want to be bothered and doesn't need friends: he's got his fists.

The beautiful boy is getting attention from everyone in the gym by now. Maybe because he's really working out the heavy bag, causing the chain holding it to rattle. But I think, for the most part, it's because he crackles with passion for what he's doing. And looks *sooooo* good doing it too.

To my right, I spy one of the front-desk attendants walk into the weights and cardio area. A second one joins her, speculating. "No membership," I hear.

One heads back to the desk, the open-plan concept making the reception area visible from my treadmill, and she picks up the phone and hangs up just as quickly. "They're coming," she says when the second attendant joins her behind the desk.

I keep walking, now focusing on the guy. He's a badass. I've never seen someone hit a bag so hard, and he's not bothering anyone. Nothing seems to exist to him except that bag he's hitting.

I'm watching him when a pair of uniformed security guards appears inside the gym.

The lady by the entrance points to the young man. He seems to sense them, and he lifts his head, frowning. And then, he slowly starts walking forward. He stops a few feet away from them and stands there in the cockiest, most challenging way I've ever seen. Almost as if he's *waiting* to be kicked out.

"We need you to come with us and confirm membership at the front desk," one of the guys says threateningly.

I stop the treadmill and suddenly step down. "He's with me."

The guy and the security guards turn in my direction, and I nod quickly. "He came with me." I pull out my gym card. The guards come over to look at it. One of them brings back a lady from the front desk.

"Have him sign in next time as a guest," the lady tells me with a scowl.

I nod.

The guards ease out, and I realize the guy is looking at me. Like, really looking at me. He wears sweatpants and a hoodie and an attitude. He stands motionless, the drawstring sweatpants hanging low on narrow hips, revealing a bit of skin on his abs and the sides of his hips, the start of a muscular V. He's got a head full of black hair and eyes the color of steel that could melt the same metal they seem to come from. He's got the most quietly intense gaze I've ever seen.

And it's latched to me.

I'm uncomfortable.

And self-aware.

I'm wearing a fuchsia workout top and tight workout pants, my honeyed hair tied in a ponytail. I'm nothing special, not among the girls in the gym, and not among the girls out in the world. As he looks at me, I feel the hairs at the tip of my ponytail brush my back and I shiver like I've never done before.

I find his stare really unnerving, so I shoo him away. "Go back to what you were doing," I say.

He doesn't move.

His face is young and tanned, all chiseled planes and angles, with eyebrows that are sleek and low, like two angry slashes, a nose too perfect to belong to a fighter, and a jaw that looks unbreakable.

Bewildered by his attention, I head back to my treadmill.

The guy's eyebrows lower a little more in obvious puzzlement. I lift my own at him in challenge, my look saying, *Are you going to keep staring?*

He smiles a little, an unexpectedly gorgeous halfway-there smile.

"Go train," I say.

He gives me this cocky nod in a way that makes it seem like he's saying thank you, then heads back to the gym bags, lifting his gloves. He hesitates for a few seconds, frowning thoughtfully as he stares at the bag, as if puzzled about something. He shakes his head to clear it, glares at the bag, and in a flash—*pow, pow, boom!*—hits the bag three times and sends it rattling on its chain.

I notice people are glancing in my direction speculatively. Some appear concerned, others seem to be wondering if he's really with me. They remind me of my mother a little bit. *Reese, promise me you'll take care of yourself.*

Mother, I'll be careful. Let me go. Give me wings! I've earned them, haven't I?

I begged for time by myself.

Today is the first day of the new and improved me.

So I put in my remaining half hour, then I go gather my stuff and hurry off to the day care for my little package.

This whole time, never once has the guy looked away from his bags again.

"HOW DID YOUR day go?" Brooke asks later that evening.

"Good."

"Just good?"

I nod, smiling. I'm not very verbose, and I'm naturally shy and uncomfortable around others. I think this is genetic because, though my mother is chatty, my father is a hermit and mostly keeps to himself aside from the occasional fatherly question like "You okay on money?" or "Your mother told you about curfew?"

I like being with my dad most. He doesn't make me talk, like my mother does.

We're the kind of people who appreciate silence.

I feel that sort of bond with Brooke's husband too.

I met him last night—gorgeous, blue-eyed, strong and quiet, he's a gentle beast—and after our hellos and a brief smile, he's comfortable enough with my presence that he ignored me this morning while I had my breakfast and he had his.

I spoke before we finished.

"Why don't you train in the gym with some of the others?" I blurted out, thinking of the guy I met.

"I concentrate better on my own." He lowered his iPad, where he'd been reading something. "You can come train with Brooke and me if you'd like."

"No!" I quickly protested, for a reason I still can't fathom, and when he looked at me in a rather fatherly, curious way, I added, "I love the gym. Thank you."

Tuesday, I'm so sore I need to crawl into bed. Wednesday is no better. But I feel energized, am sleeping divine.

By Thursday, I'm perfectly comfortable living with the Tates, and super comfortable with my daily routine. Racer has breakfast early with Mom and Dad, while I shower and get ready for the morning. The Tates drop us off at day care, and I head to the gym a few blocks away. Later, I pick up Racer, play with him in the afternoon, swim, call my mom and a few friends, or spend the evening with Pete or Riley.

I've learned that Pete, the guy who drove us from the airport, is Remy's personal assistant.

Then there's lazy, friendly Riley, his coach's second.

Remy's coach is named Lupe; he's bald and he's got a thing for the last member of the Tates' team, the motherly Diane, Remington's nutritionist and chef.

All in all, I'm feeling a lot more settled in than I expected to be at this point. There's this great family vibe with the Tates and their team. I feel like I fit in, they treat me like one of their own.

It's cool this morning, so I cover myself with an extra layer and wonder if I'll see Mr. Mysterious from the gym. It rains sometimes, even during the summer. Soft, quiet rain that I'm able to sleep through all night. Some nights, Brooke steals away from Remy when he's busy talking to the guys and we spend a girls' night talking about things. I'm very interested in learning how to take care of my body now. It's something that had never interested me until now.

Brooke told me what to eat after a workout, depending on what I want to accomplish. Fat and proteins for weight loss or muscle building. Carbs for energy. I've also been getting frequent calls from Mom and Dad. My parents are loving, and I'm their only child. I never lacked for love or anything I wanted. I never wanted to leave home; I was too comfortable there. Felt safe. But then I realized: I counted so much on my mom and dad, I started letting them make decisions for me. What college? What career? I know my mom and dad have a valid reason to worry about me and a valid reason for wanting to make these choices for me, but I wanted control of my life, so I finally asked them to let me choose on my own. They said fine. And I was shocked to discover, I didn't know. And as the last decision I let my mother make for me, she called Brooke and asked if I could come.

My mom has a plant nursery. She once told me that whenever a plant is moved to a new home, it can't be watered immediately or it dies. For two weeks it needs to be stressed, its survival tested, and only after those two weeks pass will it be ready for the water it needs to grow.

I didn't expect coming here to be easy. But I am ready to grow. I needed a change. I'm almost twenty.

"Sure you're okay?" Mom asked.

"Yes," I said last night, when she called. And for the first time in a long time, I meant it.

I've also learned about the Underground. Last year, the final fight was between Remington "Riptide" Tate and Parker the Terror, who was a real nightmare all around. It was a close match, but the Terror lost and later was hospitalized and kept from fighting due to being in intensive care. An older nemesis and opponent, Benny the Black Scorpion, apparently disappeared this year and no one knows where he is or if he's coming back. Some people think Twister is a contender. And apparently Spidermann—who left Oz Molino, his former trainer, and went with a new one—is rumored to be in good shape too.

Parker and Scorpion used to give Remy a run for his money, but they wore themselves down. It takes discipline for longevity,

Pete tells me. Not just the fight itself but the lifestyle you build to support yourself in a positive way.

I'm embracing the lifestyle with gusto.

The guy—Steel Eyes—has been in the gym every day. He speaks to no one. You'd think it was too much effort to do so, effort he seems to prefer laying on the punching bag. Straight from those eight-pack abs and to the punching bag with a dull thud. He's new in town, I think. Nobody knows. He keeps earbuds in to shut out the rest of the world. I recently snuck a peek at the log page where we sign in; he signs his name as *Cage*.

Caged is the way I felt when he looked straight at me on our second day.

Recognition flared in his eyes when he saw me in my exercise clothes, and something like excitement kindled in his eyes too. In that stupid moment I felt as if it was excitement to see *me*. He's got eyes the oddest color I've ever seen—metallic, really, a shimmering steel—and he was standing outside the gym door as if waiting for someone. I saw him, felt an odd little prick of nervousness, then pulled out my card to get in. He started after me, pulled his hood up a little higher to cover his face, and eased into the gym when I did.

I stopped before we got farther than the desk. "He's with me," I told the ladies, and he grabbed the pen by the log and signed his name.

"Thanks," he said under his breath as we headed into the gym area.

I nodded, and suddenly it felt as if I'd had butterflies for breakfast for some reason.

It's been like that every day now. And every day, I've caught him looking at me as he trains. Every day a little longer.

The guy punches hard. He doesn't stop. Other gym members,

especially some of the ones training near the bags, seem threatened and keep talking about him.

He's got a chip on his shoulder, that one.

Who the hell does he think the bag is?

Who pissed off the kid?

He's not a kid. He's a 195-pound-plus, six-foot-plus *man.* At least a few years older than my twenty. Maybe . . . twenty-three?

He plays around a lot with the bags. He teases and bounces around them, and hits like he lives for that punch. But when someone speaks to him, the playfulness is gone and he puts up a wall that has pretty much kept everyone away for the past few days. The air he exudes is implacable. Determined. And way too intimidating for anyone to miss. Way too intimidating for anyone to call him out on using me to enter the gym. Nobody questions him. They let him be and keep on training, all while shooting covert glances his way.

I'm getting ready to leave for the day when he stops the bag and approaches.

"Hey."

My eyes widen when I hear his voice clearly. A deep, male, dark-thunder voice.

Oh no, buddy, you're not breaking our unspoken code of silence, I think in alarm.

"What's your name?" he asks me, eyebrows low as he studies me.

"Reese."

He nods, and thankfully walks away. I'm left feeling a little funny, uncomfortable. I've never felt so discomforted by a guy. I exhale, turn around, and head outside, briefly noticing that Cage is taking off his gloves as if he's getting ready to leave too.

♥ ♥ ♥

RACER CALLS ME Ree. Just Ree. Though he can't really pronounce the *R*s well yet, so it sounds like Wee. Which is adorable. And embarrassing.

He can speak better than that, but I think it's his pet name for me. The little bugger loves me. The one lone dimple on his cheek pops out whenever I appear. I straddle him on my hip when I pick him up after the gym. "Did you have a good time today, Racer?"

He just nods and looks at me, with the dimple.

"What?" I pretend I don't know what he's waiting for, then I go, "Ooooh! This?" I pull out the Popsicle.

He reaches out one chubby hand.

"Give me a kiss or you don't get it." His kiss is wet and sloppy, but it delights me to no end. Almost like my dog Fluff's kisses.

Brooke wants to get pregnant again. I know that with the lifestyle of the fights, she'll find it hard to watch over two babies. But Racer is older now, and smart. And very, very mischievous.

We stop by the park, where I always sit down to give him some lunch. Riley, one of the team, meets me with the stroller.

"Hey, stranger," he says.

"Hey."

"Borrowing babies to pick up guys?"

"That's right. But there's none to pick up around here. No good ones."

Like Miles, I think.

"Here you go, little man." Riley sits Racer in the stroller and they bump fists.

"I can't believe he does that."

"Yeah, you can. His dad would bust a vessel if he didn't know how to bump fists by now."

"What does he have in store for him next? Shadowboxing at the age of four?"

He laughs and heads off.

"Thanks, Riley."

I feel a prickle in the back of my neck and turn to see Steel Eyes looking at me. He's doing push-ups on the ground, army-style, quick and sleek, his head raised to look straight at me. Straight at me with such intensity and confusion, I catch my breath. He stops the push-ups and eases to his feet.

He looks at Racer, then at me.

He looks confused.

"Wee, my fut!"

"Food. Right. You want to get to the fruit bears, don't you?" I turn to open the container of food as well as a bag of healthy dried fruit nibbles, and when I look at the spot Cage occupied, he's gone.

I search the park and see him hit the running path. People pass by on rollerblades. Others throw balls. There are people walking and running, and couples on blankets making out or having lunch.

And Cage trotting and punching the air like his life depends on it.

I narrow my eyes and look at his profile a little more closely.

He gives me this rebel vibe. Like he'd rather say *I'm sorry* than *may I*, and maybe not even the "sorry" at all. There's a fierce passion in his features and a kindled fire in his eyes. I admire passionate people. People who burn out everyone around them, they're so passionate, they want so much, they crave so much.

Drops of moisture cling to his forehead, and not for the first time, I find myself wondering about him, things I shouldn't admit to wondering about. Even to myself.

I stare until he disappears into the trees around the trail, and then I notice Racer has handily climbed out of his stroller. The little bag of dried fruits is right there, where he used to be eating. My heart turns to lead in my chest at the sight of the Racerless stroller. And then the dread slams into my midsection.

Leaping to my feet, I scan the park. Racer is already running a thousand miles an hour after a Labrador that's chasing its own tail and then chasing some phantom shadow, running from one end of the field to the other like it's never run in its whole life.

"Racer!"

I can't put the blanket and everything back into my bag fast enough. In fact, I don't. I just leave everything there and run after him the moment the dog spots Racer and *charges* after him. The dog is off a leash and three times the size of Racer.

I see a familiar figure leap up to a nearby tree branch and grab what looks to be a tennis ball stuck between the leaves. He tosses it to the ground.

The dog grabs it and scampers off, fast as a bullet.

Racer starts after him with a giggle of delight.

He doesn't get very far. Cage scoops him up under his arm and brings him over. "You lose something?" he asks as he sets Racer on his feet before me.

Did I lose something? I think dazedly.

My breath.

My head.

Part of my soul just now, to be honest.

My heart is a kettledrum, still.

I could've lost Racer in the park!

The dog could've mauled him!

Brooke told me he was restless and irreverent toward dangers, but I never thought looking after an adorable little kid like him could actually be *hard*.

But it wouldn't have been hard if I'd been paying attention to

Racer rather than the guy standing two feet away from me, and far too close for comfort, now.

Cage watches me struggle to compose myself. "Thank you," I tell him, then I drop to my haunches in front of my charge. "Racer." I look at his happy blue eyes and feel my body tremble. "Don't do that again. If you want to pet the dog, I'll go with you."

"Why?" he challenges, eyes bright and twinkling.

"I couldn't see you, and I was scared you'd get hurt."

He tilts his little head upward and eyes the guy, squinting beneath the sunlight.

Cage is looking at him too, and then at me. He looks fascinated all of a sudden. And that face of his is so distracting that I have to force myself to look at something else, so I stare at a spot past his shoulder.

"Wee's my fwend!" Racer says proudly, extending out his arm to Cage. I quickly realize Racer is giving him his fist.

"He wants to fist-bump," I hastily explain to Cage.

Cage takes in Racer in his Superman tee and his perfect little jeans. "You're a cool little dude."

He makes a fist—his huge and tan, Racer's white and plump—and their knuckles bump.

Cage lifts his eyes and then looks at me. And I make the mistake of being caught blatantly staring at him when he meets my gaze. His dark, intent stare is a little hot and confusing.

Obviously he and I are not going to fist-bump, and for the life of me, I can't draw anything but a blank from my brain. I seem to have forgotten how to speak.

The pheromones are in the air and my body is acting funny. Why is my body acting funny?

I'm not talkative, but this guy is *worse*.

"Did you grow tired of the gym today?" I ask him.

Geez. Could you come up with a duller question, Reese?

He still looks a little fascinated, but there's a subtle difference in his expression when I mention the gym. Grows a little darker for some reason. "No sparring partners. Too full."

I nod. "I can be your partner," I blurt. "Tomorrow."

Sable eyebrows go up. "You spar?"

I raise my chin a little tauntingly and nod. "I'll learn."

Suddenly I feel really energetic.

I sweep Racer up in my arms. "I'll see you tomorrow," I say, and turn back to the stroller and our stuff, walking quietly. I think I feel his gaze on my back, so I distract myself with Racer and fish the dried fruit from the stroller seat. "Do you want more of these?" I ask Racer, showing him the bag.

He shoves my hand away and tries to run off again. "I want to find the dog."

I sweep him up with effort. "Okay, but hop in here and I'll push you real fast."

He stops squirming to get free and obeys and lets me sit him down, grinning over my shoulders at something.

Or someone.

I turn back to Cage, who's watching us with a half smile on his face that does more for me than anything halfway should do, and I smile wanly and feel his eyes on my back as I push Racer down the path.

"That's not fast, Wee! Fastew!" Racer says.

Shit. Really? My ass is going to bounce like crazy.

I lean over to him. "When we round the corner, please, enough embarrassing Reese in front of a boy for a day." I ruffle his hair and then look ahead in search of the Labrador.

FOUR

KNOCKING

Maverick

The hotel business center has a dozen dormant computers save for the one I'm using. Surfing the net for trainers in the Seattle area. Writing a new list. I started at the top and am at the lower tiers now as I write down the second name, then scan for another half hour. Fuck, I'm quickly running out of options.

I log out, tear the page off the hotel notepad, and stare at the two names I've got on the list. I rub my jaw and reread the addresses and locations.

I fold the page, shove it into my jeans pocket, grab my bottle of water, and head out to the bus stop.

I make two stops.

Two more doors closed in my face.

I plant my hand flat on the last one, gritting my teeth and slamming my palm into it.

"Come the fuck on, man!" I yell.

No response.

Jesus.

Motherfuckers.

I drop down on the sidewalk and lean my head back against the wall, scowling.

I've got three days to find a coach. Three days to make fighting even possible.

I dig into the front pocket of my jeans and pull out the penny I found outside Hennesy's. I curl my palm around it, willing it for a change of luck or something even better—a goddamn chance.

I GREW UP with my mother in Pensacola. Near the beach. She wanted me to enlist in the army. Turns out, I was never good at being disciplined. "When I named you Maverick, I didn't know you'd take it so to heart," my mother playfully chastised when I left the corps.

We'd agreed when I turned twenty-one, I could see him. My father. "He travels due to his work, Mav. I don't know if you should see him."

"I'll travel with him. I want to learn. I'm his son, aren't I?" I think I imagined a connection between us. I couldn't wait to get out of Florida.

My dad used to send me a pair of boxing gloves every birthday.

"He was a good man," my mother would say when I asked about him.

"I want to see him."

"He *was*. A good man." She emphasized the "was."

I didn't get it. You weren't good, and then bad, that couldn't be. Could it? I was too young and too fucking stupid.

On my twenty-first birthday, she gave me his contact information, and when he never answered his phone, I went looking for him on my own.

My father—the one I envisioned as big, powerful, and one who had noble reasons to leave my mom and me—was helpless in a hospital bed too small for his body. There was no warning. Nothing to tell my mother and me that his life was going to change ours forever. It was pure daylight, a day like any other. But I was in a city I'd never been in. Alone.

So I sat there with no tears to cry.

Just him and me.

A stranger whose blood I share.

The doctors said they were trying to get his brain to cool down after the accident. They induced a coma. He hasn't wanted to wake up. His coma is real now. It all depends on his will to live, they say.

"My father fights; that's what he does," I told the doctors. It's all I know about him.

"He may not have any fight left in him."

I looked at my father; he was scarred, banged-up, beat-up. Not the guy my mother has a picture of.

Don't stop fighting, I wanted to say.

But I didn't say it. He's never heard my voice. I still don't know if I should call him Dad, Father, or the nickname they gave him as a fighter.

Instead, I said, "I'm going to make you proud."

I flew back home, showered, and changed, remembering the doctors when they told me it didn't look good as I took out my boxing gloves. I found my mother in the kitchen.

"I'm not coming back home."

She cried softly. I put my arms around her and I held her. Six years before, I outgrew her in height and she felt small in my arms and fragile.

"I love you, Mav." She grabbed my jaw and kissed my cheek. "Let me know where you go. Stay in touch."

"I will."

"Maverick. You're not your father. You don't have to do this."

"No. But I'm half of him. And half of you." I looked at her. "I want more than what I have here." I opened the door with nothing but a duffel bag, my saved money, and my backpack. "I'm going to prove him wrong to believe I was never worth a moment."

On the bus, I pulled out the last gloves my father sent me a birthday ago. He didn't send me new ones, he sent me old ones with a message: *Since you never use the ones I sent and clearly don't plan to, sending ones a real fighter's used.*

The gloves are so old, they're taped at the wrist with silver duct tape. I slipped my hand into one glove, and then the other, and realized they fit me.

They fit me.

FIVE

SPAR WITH ME

Reese

How's the high life?

Miles finally texted last night. I was already in bed when my phone buzzed. I peered at the screen and jolted upright.

I should've probably waited a minute to answer. It's not good to seem anxious or anything, and to be honest, I haven't been. But he's one of my closest friends and one of the few people who knows everything about me and likes me anyway.

Good! I texted back.

Thinking of visiting and meeting your new friends.

Was he using that as an excuse? I frowned and wondered. But we're friends. He doesn't need an excuse; he could say he misses me and that's it. Maybe? Hesitantly, I typed, Sure. When do you want to visit?

Not certain yet, maybe to semifinals? Can you introduce me and the guys to RIP then?

I read the message, then eased out of bed and looked at myself in the mirror. By the time he comes I'll look amazing, be exuding so much self-confidence, and have a clear direction in my life. So I **wrote:** I'll see what I can do but I'm sure it'd be fine.

I DON'T HAVE that many friends; I value the ones I have because it's always been a struggle to make any and keep them.

I show Brooke the text in the morning. "Hmm. I don't know," she says thoughtfully. She shows my phone to Pete since we all have breakfast at the Tates' large kitchen table.

"Nope."

Riley looks at it next. "Definitely friend-zoned."

Remy stares at the phone before passing it back to me. He lifts his gaze and looks at me with beautiful blue eyes, just like Racer's, and shakes his head somberly. "Get a man with balls, Reese."

I tuck my phone away. "Men with balls scare me."

"Not a real man. A real man hands them over." He leans to the side of the table with a dimpled smile, chucks Brooke's chin, and kisses her on the mouth. My ears grow hot, yet I can't stop staring at that dry but hard, possessive peck on the lips they give each other.

Once I've got Racer's picnic bag from Diane, we head out to day care in one of the SUVs. I start getting nervous as we drop off Racer and I walk to the gym.

What possessed me to tell Cage I'd spar with him? I can barely trot on the treadmill with my head held high for an hour.

But it's a boot camp, a physical and spiritual and mental one—a whole lot of new Reese to discover and nurture—so I'm giving myself the boot. Or letting Cage do it.

Disappointment hits me when I don't see him outside the gym. I scan the block to see if he's late, but there's no sign of him.

The doors open halfway and one of the admission ladies calls me inside. "Reese?" She waves me forward. "We let your friend in; we know he's with you." She grins at me, sheepishly and knowingly.

I want to explain that it's not what it seems. That we're just friends. But I spot Cage through the glass doors of the gym and I feel helplessly tongue-tied.

I keep my eyes on the jet-black hair on the back of his head as I wander into the bustling gym area, the sound of weights slamming down and padding footsteps and background music around me. My eyes trail the suntanned skin on the back of his neck. Add to that sweatpants that hang low on his narrow hips and give new meaning to sexy.

Why is he so damn *intriguing*?

He's taller than I am. At eye level, I'm staring at the middle of his chest; his defined pectorals, to be exact. His nipples that are sometimes hugged by his damp-with-sweat shirt. His impressive muscles. His body is lean and corded but muscular, like fighters' bodies usually are, and a dangerous rebel vibe radiates off him.

He's jumping rope, with his earbuds in.

"Hey."

I'm about to tap his shoulder when he stops jumping and turns. Eyes that are quiet and remote fix on me. My gaze drops, just a little, admiring his beautiful lips and the angle of his jaw. . . .

I take in his neck, the fit of his shirt on his tapered torso, and by the time I take an impulsive, reckless visual trek down the rest of him and back up to his gorgeous face, his brows quirk up. Those electric steel eyes pierce me, sending a strange buzz through my body.

His entire attention and focus is on me now, not on the gym. His eyes are not moving, and my heart strains as he takes one step forward with predatory grace, closing the distance between us. This guy would be a panther in the fighting ring. . . .

My eyes widen in surprise when I suddenly realize he heard me greet him.

He's wearing his earbuds, but I said hey and he spun around, and now he continues staring unabashedly at me. He most definitely heard me.

I realize he's not listening to music.

That he uses the earbuds to keep people away.

I have an odd understanding of that too.

He pulls out the earbuds and shoves them into the pocket of his sweatpants—and yes, he didn't stop the music at all. Because he wasn't listening to music. He was, like a predator, paying attention to his surroundings without alerting the prey.

"Hey," he says, and the muscles rippling under his shirt quicken my pulse when he starts coiling the rope around his wrist.

"You're not listening to music," I say. "You're using those earbuds so people don't talk to you."

He shoots me a skeptical look along with an amused twitch of his lips as we both start to glove up. "I'm not here to make friends." He scans the crowd dismissively. "Way I see it, one day I'm going to face them in the ring. Easier to smash their faces in if I don't know them."

Holy god, the *look* in his eyes.

I've read novels with vampires, where the terms "bloodthirsty" and "bloodlust" are used. I have never, ever seen bloodlust in anyone's eyes. Until this heartbeat, this second, this crowded gymnasium. When this guy's eyes glow red with it.

"You can't smash my face in, I'll have headgear," I tell him as I reach for the headgear.

He frowns, then there's an exasperated clench of his jaw. "Look. You said spar, not chat."

"I don't like talking or hearing myself speak either, but you make me want to talk." I frown at him. "I don't even know why I offered to spar when I don't know anything about you."

He sighs and leans on the ropes as we both climb into the ring.

Sending him a wary look, I drop down on the edge of the ring and slide my legs under the ropes to let them hang to the side. I won't gain much, sparring with this guy. I know for a fact he'll spar like a *pro*. I'll gain more from talking—I'd gain information.

And I'm intensely curious.

He sits beside me reluctantly. He's tall and strong and wide-shouldered. A person shouldn't occupy more space than their body actually occupies—but this one person does. I've never felt a presence as strongly as I do his.

I'm uncomfortable, too acutely conscious of this male, extremely attractive person sitting warmly next to me, his body so hot from the exercise and exuding such powerful warmth and energy, I feel the strangest urge to edge away.

I don't though.

I stand my ground, or rather, park my ass on it, and try to act chill.

"What's your name? Is it Cage?" I ask him.

He seems to consider the question as he looks at me, almost as if he's deciding whether to tell me.

"Maverick," he finally says, frowning a little and staring out at the room as he seems to consider some complicated puzzle.

"Maverick? Like *Top Gun*?"

"Minus a Goose." He grins and it's irresistible. I can't help a feeling of losing hold of myself.

"So what's your story?"

He's quiet. As if there's no story to tell, and there's no way there's no story behind those steel eyes.

"You from around here?" he asks me instead, leaning back to look at me. I get a squeeze somewhere. I don't even know where it's at, it's so alien. I clear my throat and try to use the same tone I'd use when talking to my girlfriends.

"I'm traveling for the summer. For the season. With my cousin." I don't tell him that I'm trying to push myself, trying to better myself, even trying to find myself. "Are you fighting?" I ask him.

"Not yet."

"But you will?"

"Yeah, I will."

"You're good?"

"We'll see." He bites the Velcro wrap of the glove around his wrist and then pulls it off with the opposite elbow, and when he does the same with the other glove, I notice his hands, long-fingered and strong. His knuckles are impossibly bruised.

"I need a coach for the Underground to accept me," he says.

"So get one."

"They're booked. They suspect I'm not good at taking direction."

"You're a bit of a rebel, Maverick? *Who would've guessed?*" I grin.

He almost smiles back at me.

His muscular arms are bare and flex again as he sets his gloves aside and reaches out to remove mine.

"So get a coach who doesn't coach."

He laughs. A pleasant laugh that surprises me. When he tugs off each glove, I wrap my arms around my midriff. "I'm serious."

"Someone to just sit in my corner?" he asks.

"I guess."

"You available?"

Oh.

Is he serious?

I don't know a lot about him—*Maverick*, god, I love his name—but even when *Maverick* is near, I want him nearer.

There's a low hum in my body now and it's impossible to shake off.

I shake my head ruefully. "No, I can't go to the fights."

"You travel for the season but don't go to the fights."

Now he's teasing me. And it's making me smile.

"Because I'm *working*. I don't get to go on a soul-searching vacation without earning my keep for it too."

"If I get into the Underground, will you come watch me fight?"

"Can't, I'm working."

Something like hope dies in his eyes. He clenches his jaw. "Yeah."

"You can try Oz."

"What?"

"Not what. Who," I specify. "Oz Molino. He's retired. I heard . . . nobody wanted to use him 'cause he just sits there, drinking or hungover. His wife left him."

He nods then. "I'll look him up."

We run out of things to say. I'm reluctant to leave because, with him, it feels as if I've known his voice and *him* for more than the few days it's actually been. I like this feeling so much but I can't even determine its source.

His gaze feels so probing all of a sudden; he looks at me as if he's been waiting for me for a long time. I feel like *I* too have been waiting for him for a long time.

It makes no sense. It's just a look, and just a feeling.

You never know what really lies under a look and you can't

apply reason to every feeling. But it's all there. Tangible, palpable. As though there's a string between us, one end in him, and the other end in me.

As we settle into a long silence, there's a shuffle behind us. We glance simultaneously over our shoulders to realize the ring is being taken.

"Oh, drat," I say, mock-scowling at him. "I'm going to have to show off my awful sparring abilities some other time."

I'm not sure, but I think I detect a flash of disappointment in Maverick's eyes.

Unexpected warmth floods me to the marrow of my bones.

"I'll go get Racer early, I guess."

I slide under the ropes and hop onto the floor, and he slides from under the ropes and smoothly stands as I shoot him a smile and start to leave.

"Hey, thanks," he calls back at me.

Our eyes hold for the most intimate pair of seconds I've ever lived. Inside my sneakers, I swear my toes are curling.

"'Bye, Maverick." I hurry away.

Then I join the day care pickup line and try to regroup, but my brain isn't in the game. It keeps replaying our talk. Him in the park. Him piggybacking into the gym with me.

I'm so relieved when Racer is led out of day care—so I can stop thinking about Maverick now—that I drop to my knees and engulf him in a bear hug, smacking a kiss on his dimple. "How's my favorite guy in the whole wide world?!"

"Hungwy," he says moodily, scowling.

I laugh and take his hand in mine. "I'm hungry too."

SIX

THE GREAT OZ

Maverick

It's evening. On the second floor of an old extended-stay hotel, I head down the hall to 2F and knock on the door.

It opens an inch, a bloodshot eye peering at me through the slight crack the chained door allows.

Well, there he is. The great Oz.

"A word," I say.

"Busy," he replies.

He tries to shut the door in my face, but I've got some experience now, and I quickly stop the door with my foot.

"A word? Please."

He narrows the eye. "Ease off on the foot, kid, and maybe we'll talk."

I clench my jaw, debate with myself silently, then ease back on the foot.

"Who are you and why are you here?" he demands.

Behind him, the place is a mess of empty bottles and pizza boxes.

"I need a trainer."

"I need more vodka." He slams the door in my face.

I grind my molars and raise my arm, prepared to bang, but the flat door staring me in the face really fucking bugs me. I'm so sick of staring at doors, I'd bang my fist straight through it if I thought it'd get me anywhere. I head to the stairway exit and stalk down the stairs instead, taking several at a time.

❤   ❤   ❤

THIRTY MINUTES LATER, I knock again. He opens the door, with the same bloodshot eye at the crack.

"You," he says in disgust.

"That's right. Me."

I turn around and jerk my hoodie off over my head. He might as well know now before he asks for a little private show. I wait, letting him get an eyeful of my tattoo, then I turn around to find the bloodshot eye wide open, regarding me.

"I need a trainer," I repeat, and I lift the vodka bottle I bought. The door shuts.

Then I hear the sound of chains. And for the first time—for *real*—the door of opportunity swings open for me.

❤   ❤   ❤

BY THE NEXT morning I've figured out the love of Oz's life—before the booze replaced all his other loves—was named Wendy. When he calls people cowards, he calls them Wendys. "They're fucking Wendys, the whole lot of them. Wendy's my ex-wife. She couldn't take me."

"Maybe she had her reasons," I said.

"Yeah. I worked too hard, and now I don't work at all!"

I was prepping up my gloves, but he came over and yanked them away from me.

"We're signing you up to the Underground today. No training."

He stalked into his bathroom to change, and now he takes a swig of vodka, straight up, and tucks the flask into the inside pocket of his blazer as he readies himself to leave.

Exasperated, I drop my head on the back of the couch I've been sitting on while the lady readies herself. "Oz, it's seven in the morning," I groan.

He hunts through the mess for his key card until he finds it and pockets that too. "I'm an all-around-the-clock kind of man. Morning's just an extension of evening."

Oz guzzles alcohol like a regular person breathes.

"How come you were in town?" I ask him as we head down in the rickety elevator.

"Habit dies hard. I've always been in the city for the Underground inaugurals; I wanted to go watch and feel sorry for myself."

Guess Oz is as unwanted as I am.

When we reach the Underground sign-up location—an old warehouse building set up with a pair of tables—he notices the silence. It catches like wildfire the moment we step into the room.

I start toward the lines for the sign-up tables when Oz's voice stops me. "Hang back. We don't know if there are any nukes hidden anywhere."

Giving everyone in the line a lethal look, I lean against the wall and watch as Oz dutifully stands in the back. I've seen most of these fighters in videos, though the big ones—like Tate—sign up later in the day. Their spots are guaranteed anyway.

We're the early birds, so we manage to get signed up in a half hour.

"If it isn't the Wizard of Oz, this kid's ticket *home*," a group of three older fighters cackles.

I walk next to Oz, toward the exit, ignoring them. "They're not making fun of you, they're making fun of me."

"Oh, they're making fun of me all right." He eyes me sideways. "I know who you are. Some of my competition might be looking for their golden boy. But my golden boy found *me* 'cause those dickheads were too scared to take him on."

"Why did you?" He was drunk and I could see that. But still. I *did* let him get a fucking eyeful of my tattoo.

"Nothing to lose. Nothing left to lose." He slaps my back and gives me my schedule. "That's your first night. How do you feel about that?"

I scan the paper, verify that I fight at the inaugural. And I see what he's dubbed me.

I laugh. "You're so fucking dramatic," I say, smacking him on the back of the head.

He smacks me back. "Really. Now live up to the name. Let's bring some excitement around here. Show them what happens when two nobodies pair up—two nobodies against the world."

"Hey," I growl, taking exception, "we're not nobodies. We're somebodies. Everybody's somebody."

He takes a long swig from his flask as we step out into the sun. "Somebody's not enough. Let's be the champions."

SEVEN

PARK

Reese

I t's midweek already, and I'm halfway through my workout when I get a text from Brooke:

> Hey! Huge line at the Underground registration, might pick up lunch on our way back home. Don't wait for us - lunch home w/Diane

> Got it ☺ Will take Racer to park and meet you home ltr

I set my phone aside and scan the gym again. Some otherworldly impulse has me walking past the weights section. I cross the treadmills, bicycles, toward the mats at the end and the boxing bags. I scan the area where Maverick always works out. There are several guys at the bags now. None of them are as big, or mysterious. Or hot.

He's gone.

Disappointment washes over me. I wait a bit, checking the time. Five minutes to leave for Racer.

Reese, you're acting stupid.

"You're looking for your friend? The one you come in with?"

"I . . . ah . . . yeah."

"He hasn't come in."

"Right. Thanks."

I head to pick up Racer from day care, meet Pete there with the stroller and our snacks, then sit Racer inside and push him to the park. There's this spot I like under the shadow of a tree. I head there. "How was day care, Racer?"

"Okay."

He's scanning the park for dogs, I know.

"This is nice, isn't it?"

I pull out his fruit bears and open them. He dives in.

"Racer, I ran extra hard today and I'm suddenly hungry. If I tell you an extra story tonight, would you give me one of your fruit bears?"

"Two stowies," he negotiates.

"Okay, two stories, for two bears?" I shoot back.

He hesitates, then nods and lets me pull out two bears, examining my hand thoroughly. I let him open my palm.

"See? Two?"

He grins a dimpled grin that I could eat up, and then continues eating.

I shove them in my mouth and start to set up my blanket and stop in my tracks when I spot the figure doing pull-ups on the tree.

His T-shirt is riding upward due to the lifted position of his arms, and I can see the concrete-like squares of his abs perfectly.

His extraordinary eyes blaze and glow when he spots me a few feet away, not far from the tree. He drops himself to the ground, lithe as a cat and surprisingly quiet, and as he stretches to his feet from the crouched position he landed in, his eyes are direct and interested and warm. No, not warm. *More.*

There's a flip in my stomach when his lips curl a little. He ambles over and I have the oddest sensation that he was waiting for me. But . . . was he?

"Maverick," I say softly to myself.

"Mavewick!" Racer repeats—embarrassingly loudly—and puts out his fist.

He bumps fists with Racer. "Dude. Cool cap."

He taps Racer's Yankees baseball cap. Then his eyes lift to meet mine.

My stomach feels unsettled, but it's not from hunger, more like from nerves or something like . . . anticipation.

"Didn't see you at the gym today," I say.

He shakes his head. "I talked to Oz."

"You did?"

He gives me this quiet, perfect smile and simply nods.

"That's great."

"Yeah."

We smile for the most delicious few seconds.

"So you're fighting during the inaugural?" I ask excitedly.

He pulls out a page from his jeans back pocket. "That's me."

I take and scan the page. It indicates his accepting the Underground terms and rules of engagement, states his coach's name, and then his name. A dangerous little chill runs down my spine when I read:

Maverick "the Avenger" Cage

And Maverick "the Avenger" Cage is watching me read this paper, studying my reaction.

My palms are sweaty all of a sudden. "Well . . . wow."

My stomach is quaking upon seeing his name; I don't know why. Maverick Cage. His name is a conundrum. Maverick means "rebel," and cage . . . But it looks like this maverick is coming out of his cage.

He tucks the page back into his jeans. "I had to tell some-one."

"And you came to tell me?" If I sound bewildered, it's because I *am*.

He stares into me, a liquid look coming to his eyes. "It wouldn't be happening if it weren't for you."

"That's totally not true."

He glances down at the stroller. "I wouldn't forgive myself if I didn't tell my buddy here." He fist-bumps Racer again and Racer giggles at the attention.

"Mom and Dad are busy, so I get to keep him for an extra while," I tell Maverick.

He stares at me. He has a very stubborn, arrogant face, but when he smiles, pleasure softens his granitelike features. And he's smiling right now. *Dear me.* "So he's not yours," he says.

"God, no. I wish!"

I can't think straight when he looks at me. I feel naked. As if he knows that I've missed him. As if he knows that just looking at him makes me feel odd. Odd and oddly sensual inside. Respond-ing to *him*.

I open my blanket and bend over to smooth it on the ground. Then I realize my butt is sticking out, the Himalayas of butts out there for him to see. In tight exercise gear. Fuck.

He sits on his haunches at the edge of the blanket and opens his hand. "Share the blanket with me?"

His knuckles are still scarred. I can't decide why I keep look-ing at them. I get a gut squeeze of empathy every time I see the bruises. His hands are *huge*. He plants them on the blanket, then shifts to lean back on his arms, stretching out his legs before him. Other couples are nearby on blankets. It feels intimate when I set my stuff down, and I feel myself go hot when I sense him watch-ing me settle down next to it.

He spreads out just a little more and squints up at the tree, then looks at me in silence.

I search the picnic bag. "Want some . . . kid food? Or I've got . . ." I pull out my emergency Snickers bar, which I'm proud not to have touched yet, and I hand it over. "Plus one water and a drinking cup with a lid."

I pass the drinking cup to Racer and hand Maverick the water. He takes it. "I'm good." He opens the water bottle and hands it to me.

I shake my head. I'm not hungry, really. Or thirsty. My stomach feels full of butterflies again and it makes no sense, since I don't even *know* him.

He shifts up higher on his arms, the flex of his torso's muscles visible through the cotton of his shirt.

"I almost thought you'd arrived to the gym and got yourself kicked out," I try.

"Not yet. There's still tomorrow." He smirks.

And there's a tinge of merriment in his eyes.

"Wee, and the ducks?"

I jerk my attention back to Racer and my pending business with him. "Right. I promised we'd feed the ducks today." I quickly pack our stuff and then push the stroller toward the lake. Maverick walks beside me.

I feel him watching me as I stop at the dispenser to fill up a cup of duck food.

"Mavewick, get me out," Racer commands.

Maverick sweeps him up and sets him on his feet.

"Don't go in the water, Racer, just stay on the edge, and don't let them bite your finger. Do it like this. . . ." I show him how to cup his hand. "Or throw it in the water and watch them pick at it."

He nods and starts throwing all over, sending the ducks after the nibbles.

I sit on the ground, the scent of damp grass surrounding us as Maverick sits beside me.

"Hey, I want to do something for you."

"What?"

I can't remember how to breathe.

I give him a moment to explain, but he's not helping me out, only smiling. His face is open, friendly, his smile captivating. But his eyes are guarded, careful. I try to keep my voice indifferent.

"You mean for the gym?" I ask, a puzzled frown on my face. He nods. "For that. And Oz."

"Oh." I shake my head, laughing softly. "It's nothing, really."

When he looks at me, he looks curious, and unsatisfied somehow. But a genuinely appreciative smile touches his eyes. "Trust me. It's not nothing. It's something, and I appreciate it."

His open gratitude makes me so *warm*. He makes me feel impulsive.

"I'm in a healthy-living boot camp this summer. You're meeting the new Reese," I hear myself blurt out.

Wow. Did I just spew it out like that?

I'm so desperate for him to share bits of himself that I'm just totally baring myself to him without his even asking. Thank god he takes it in stride with an attractive little dance in his eyes.

"What was the old one like?" he asks easily.

I shrug and shake my head, not really wanting to get into that.

When he does nothing to fill the silence that settles between us, it leaves me with nothing to do but look up at him. I lift my lashes, and he's staring at me with a look of total intrigue in his eyes. Wisps of hair tease my face, and I push them away, feeling really restless under that stare.

"Help me kick my own ass, and we'll call it even," I suddenly suggest.

He shakes his head with playful stubbornness. "We're not even. I still owe you." His eyes grow thoughtful, and he reaches into his pocket and extracts something. "Open your palm."

He looks so intense that I open my palm and watch him drop something in it. "What's this?"

"My IOU."

I stare at the penny in my palm, then look up at him in confusion.

His voice sounds a little more harsh and textured all of a sudden. "I don't have a lot right now, but I got this."

"For a rainy day?" I ask.

"For any day."

He sounds somber and he looks even more somber, if that's even possible. His eyes are gloriously intense, and I am utterly dazzled and confused by this *feeling* of being utterly dazzled.

I don't understand why he's giving me this. My ears hot, I look down at the penny, then up at him. What I did for him was nothing, really. It looked like he really enjoyed working out, and I could tell he had talent.

But his eyes are roiling with something forbidden and almost pleading. . . .

He needs me to take this penny.

He needs to know he can pay me back in some way.

I realize he's got a pride as big as he is.

My chest aches a little. Nodding, I curl my fingers around the penny because something tells me Maverick "the Avenger" Cage never takes back what he gives. He looks like a guy who doesn't budge, who doesn't give in easy.

"I can get in after hours to the gym with my membership," I hear myself say, surprised by how impulsive he makes me. "Do you want to come? When I go back home, I want to buy a new dress, one size smaller than what I wear."

He looks at me, stays silent, and tightens his jaw, then stares out at the water. "I'm game."

And we sit there, watching Racer giggle and try to pet the ducks as he feeds them.

And I like being here.

I really like being here.

❤ ❤ ❤

WE MEET AT the gym at 9:00 p.m. I had dinner with Racer, left him with his parents, and told Brooke I'd be back by eleven.

That night, the gym is completely empty. An odd something is in the air. It crackles between us. Around us. The silence only seems to magnify it.

Maverick unzips his hoodie and then, unexpectedly, takes off his shirt. He waits a moment, then walks to set his T-shirt aside. I stare at the body art on his back, transfixed by it. The lights are dim, but I can make out the shape of an open-winged bird. A bird with another symbol or letter or number I can't make out on its back.

There's something about tattoos, body art, that's magical and intimate. A piece of art on your body that identifies who you are, what you believe in, even what you mock.

He turns and looks at me.

He seems to be waiting for me to say something.

But I can't.

He's beautiful in a way beautiful had never had a visible image for me except for things that felt surreal and perfect. He is perfection in an all-male way. He is surreal, like from a different species, exuding an air of a rebel and of someone implacable who will not be stopped.

He lifts his brows, as if he's genuinely surprised I didn't say anything at all.

"That's beautiful body art."

He frowns a little, thoughtfully. Then he smiles to himself and turns around.

What? Am I missing something here?

He throws me a set of gloves. I put one on, and then struggle with the other one. "Here. I'll do yours," he says.

I'm nervous when we stand so close. I could touch him from here. His hands wrap the glove around my wrist, and I'm vulnerable and feel like rambling, even though I don't like to talk a lot.

He's watching me.

He turns away, exhales softly, then stalks to the bags. I see his tattoo again, amazed by how much of his back it covers. A massive bird with its wings outstretched spreads out toward his shoulder blades, the tail trailing down Maverick's spine. Some sort of ominous black shape sits on the bird's back, while fire consumes the tips of the bird's feathers.

I feel as if he's giving me something. A glimpse of something no one in the gym has ever seen. I stare at it, thirsty for it, my eyes taking in every inch of that tattoo while the muscles of Maverick's back work beneath it.

He's punching.

He seethes with energy, mounting with every hit.

It's just me in the gym.

And Maverick.

And my dirty thoughts about Maverick.

I hate the thought and scowl at myself.

But there is no extra space in the whole gym. It seems like he takes up more than his body occupies—a world more.

When he shifts to hit the bag on the other side, the bird's

wings flare with every ripple of his back muscles as he slams the punching bag. *Pow, wham, pow.*

I decide to test myself against a speed bag, all the while wondering where he gets the force that drives him.

I work out on the bag for about half an hour, then come settle down on the bench closest to him and lie down on my side and sigh, close my eyes in exhaustion, and hear silence.

I open my eyes, and he's staring at me with the most puzzled expression. He looks away and exhales.

When he starts back up, his hits become fiercer. I'm feeling agitated. My brain fixating on the way he moves. The lock of hair that falls on his forehead when he slams. The way he braces his feet and swings. The look on his face that makes me imagine him being this concentrated doing something else.

Doing something to me.

Oh god, this is not what I meant when I signed up for a Summer to a Better Reese.

I get up on my feet, surprised that my body feels as substantial as liquid. "I'm going to leave, I have somewhere I need to be."

His eyes slide to me in surprise, and suddenly, blatantly, his gaze dips downward and he stares at a spot of sweat under my throat, above and centered between my breasts. He scans my chest and then jerks his eyes upward, with a flash of frustration sparking in their depths. "I'm staying until I'm worn."

Did he just check out my breasts?

Right *in front* of me?

"Okay. I'll . . . see you. I guess. Teach me how to remove the first glove with both on?"

I walk over to get him to show me, but oh. Mistake. He smells delicious. Of sweat and guy. Like he just took a shower and now with the heat of his body, his soap and shampoo smell strongest.

I inhale deeply, looking at his face to see him staring at me.

God, did he notice?

For a moment there, I think I see heat in his eyes.

He speaks then, his voice low. "Use your teeth on the Velcro. Tuck the glove under your other arm and pull your hand free."

I try it, tightening the glove under my arm as I pull, and manage to succeed. "Oh. Neat trick."

I go hang up the gloves and hear him start punching again as I leave. I step out of the gym and look inside, but the windows are frosted, blocking him from view.

EIGHT

COMPULSIONS

Reese

I once read that external inconsistencies create compulsive actions. Performing the same action and getting different results, a positive and a nil or a negative, causes people to more compulsively perform the acts in search of another positive.

This must be why I'm compulsively spending time at the gym. At the Tates' home there's a pool, tennis court, sports court, and home gym. But have I used any of that? No. I keep telling Brooke it's because of the sun, but the truth is, I have an odd compulsion every morning to go to the gym.

And look for him. At the door, waiting for me. Inside by the speed bag, the heavy bag, the ring. But nothing.

Today, I've run five miles. I've sweated buckets and need to leave for Racer in ten minutes, but I compulsively wait at a side bench, drinking a sports drink, wondering if I will never ever see him again.

Wondering why the thought makes me so sad. Like I lost something.

I'm finishing my drink when a tall fighter with a shiny shaved head and a chest of bloated muscles comes over. "Hey."

I smile and pull out my phone in the hope he goes away.

"I'm Trenton."

He seems to expect a reaction.

"Twister," he adds finally.

Once again, I smile dismissively but worry I'm being rude, so I end up offering, "Reese."

"Reese, I like it. How come I've never seen you before?" he asks, stepping forward.

He starts telling me he thinks I look Southern and that he lives here and fights in the Underground, and I'm nodding, which seems to encourage him, and he fills me in on how many years he's been training when I feel a prick on the back of my neck, and then I feel something—someone—sit down right next to me.

A pair of jeans, a black crew-neck T-shirt, and a whole lot of Maverick Cage.

I try to ignore the feeling of his thigh against mine. His shoulder against mine. It's impossible to concentrate on the conversation now. How can this guy sit here, without saying anything at all, and grab my attention more than all the noise? His quiet, his presence, and the way he's staring at Trenton with a frown makes a bubble pop in my stomach.

Trenton's voice trails off, his eyes flaring a little in annoyance when he spots Maverick, who's taller, with a more compact body, but more intimidating than you'd imagine.

"We haven't met," Trenton says flatly.

"No," Maverick says, just as flat.

"I'm Trenton," the guy says proudly.

I don't hear an answer. I steal a look at Maverick's profile and he just sits there with a look that clearly emits the message *Get lost.* He's staring unabashedly at the guy.

The guy narrows his eyes, but Maverick keeps staring him down, even when he's sitting and the other guy is standing.

"Yeah, right. Well, nice to meet you," he tells me in a tone that says he's actually not so happy that we met, and he turns around and carries his balloonlike muscles to the other end of the gym.

Maverick is looking at me, and I'm such a coward, I can't seem to find the courage to look at him just yet. I'm still . . . processing him. So near.

He doesn't say a word to me, but I can feel him. He's all I feel. *Everywhere.*

And I wonder if he can feel me. If he's aware of me, even if in only a fraction of the way that I am aware of him. I turn and catch him staring, and the impulse to look away and pretend I just hadn't checked him out is acute. But I don't, so I stubbornly hold his gaze. Forever passes, and neither of us looks away. What is he thinking? And is it true the one who looks away submits?

"Where are you staying?" I ask in an extreme effort to sound casual.

"Just across the street." He gestures to the hotel at the corner, and I nod. He leans closer, so it feels like we're alone in a bubble, him and me. "You?"

"At my cousin's house."

Why do we want to know where the other is staying? Living? Sleeping?

I asked because I selfishly wanted to picture him, because wondering where he is and what he's doing is driving me out of my mind. Maybe, once I know, my mind will *stop with these constant thoughts about him already.*

We stare at each other a little longer, almost as if we haven't ever seen each other before. His eyes seem starved for my face. I feel starved, but not for food, or anything else. For something I can't name. And I have never wanted before.

He ducks his head closer to me, his voice dropping an octave.

"During a fight . . . you can gauge someone's next move by look-ing at his eyes," he says softly.

"We're not fighting."

"No. We're not." He looks at me, so deep I feel found.

But I'm not found. Because his eyes are watching me as if he's trying to figure me out.

"Maybe your opponent's move depends on your move," I say, voice getting raw. Ask me out. Or to the park. Or just tell me maybe, during the season, I'll see you again. We leave in three days and I get the sense I might never see him again.

"Just any move?" he asks with a teasing note in his voice.

"Not any move."

"You know, Reese"—he leans forward on his elbows, his shoulders straining the shirt covering those muscular shoulders as he looks sideways at me—"I've got moves," he cockily informs me.

"You've got limited moves and they all relate to punching. So I don't believe you."

"Believe me." He nods with exaggerated meaning.

"Show me," I dare, smiling.

He smiles too and straightens in his seat, but his eyes darken a little as he shakes his head. "Not here."

There's an odd look in his eyes as he looks at my lips for a beat. My ears get a little hot, and I drop my gaze to his chest. I'm frightened. I'm exhilarated. I need to change the topic, fast.

I flick my eyes back up to find those metallic eyes watching me. "How's Oz?"

"Waiting for me." He stays put next to me though. Doesn't leave. Instead, he begins to frown and then is jerking his hard jaw in the direction of Twister. "I'm going to fuck him up at the inaugural this weekend, so don't get too attached."

I laugh and tsk under my breath. "You're full of yourself."

He smiles wider, but narrows his eyes warningly, his voice dark and raspy. "Laugh all you want. But I'm going to bust his nose, his jaw, and the rest of his face. Don't get attached to any of those assholes. I don't want to break your heart."

"No way! And my heart is behind steel walls, promise." I lift my fingers, crossed.

"Yeah right." He mock-scowls, and then he just scowls. "Really. Don't grow attached to any of these guys."

I'd think he was jealous if he wasn't so obsessed with fighting, plus I'm sure his jealousy is purely professional. He wants me to root for him, and a little part of me does, enough that I don't want to tell him that I can root for no one but Remy. He's part of my family.

So rather than promise, I frown and push him away as we both head to the exit. "Go away, you bully. Go bust your bags."

With a curl of his lips, he holds the door open for me, and once outside, he turns to leave.

I feel puzzled and uncomfortable in my skin as I watch his back retreat and realize it's because I don't want him to go.

I watch him cross the street to his hotel, fighting the urge to call out his name. Maverick briefly glances back at me as he hits the opposite side of the street. He lifts his index finger in the air and circles it, and I realize it means—*tomorrow.*

Feeling a kick in my heart, I lift mine and do the same move, suddenly excited.

Tomorrow.

NINE

PENNY FOR YOUR THOUGHTS

Reese

Though I spent another sleepless night, dreaming of birds and sweaty male flesh with rippling bird feathers, I'm super motivated the next day. As if I'm being fueled by something other than sleep. Something like . . . anticipation? Excitement? Whatever it is, *go, Reese.* My whole life I've been wanting to change but resisting the effort to do so, maybe. Or maybe fearing who I can become. I'm changing now. It's always been within reach, but I never wanted to become her until now.

Maybe it's the penny.

Finding a penny is supposed to be lucky. But if there's anything that feels luckier, it's being given a penny as a blank check.

I look at the little copper coin in my palm with a happy prick in my chest.

"What is that?" Brooke asks.

"I found it," I lie. I'm embarrassed to tell her that I met a guy. She'll ask about him, who he is, and I don't know anything, and it's not like that. Not like that at all.

♥ ♥ ♥

WE MEET UP outside the gym entrance. My heart speeds up when I see him leaning against the gym windows, in dark sweatpants and an electric-blue hoodie, waiting.

He lifts his head, and under his hoodie, I see his eyes light up a little when he sees me.

We smile. And I swear this smile of mine comes straight from my heart.

"Ready?"

That's all he says.

It's only one word. One word in that deep, dark, deep, thunderous voice, which activates all my brain receptors and other, more embarrassing ones.

I nod, and when we walk into the gym, our shoulders brush a little and my receptors flood with something warm and hot and uncontrollable.

The sparring ring is busy, so I head to the treadmills and he heads to the mats. Determined to sweat, I walk and run at intervals, and I look at him—the only person out of dozens of sweaty people in here who I actually *see*—and I can't get over the fact that he keeps looking every few minutes at me.

When I finish and go gather my things, he comes over. "My first fight is Sunday." He looks at me with a wry smile and a happy gleam in his eyes. "I've got two days to train, I'll be training with Oz."

"Okay."

He looks at my mouth and starts back across the gym.

"Hey, I guess I won't see you again," I call out, stopping him. It's disappointing, but I don't know why. "Good luck, Maverick."

Good luck, Avenger. . . .

Our eyes hold for forever and a half. Then Maverick gives me that slow, cocky nod of his, like he did the first day I met him, a nod that seems to mean *thank you*, and when he smiles at me with those lit-up metallic eyes, I smile and duck my head when my ears get a little hot.

I turn around and walk away, feeling happy for him and unexpectedly sad for me.

❤ ❤ ❤

THERE ARE CHANGES happening in my life. Good ones.

Miles texted recently. He wants to come visit. Maybe he's been missing me. Taking me for granted and now missing me.

My body is absolutely sore from all the exercise I've been doing.

I have more energy and I'm losing a little bit of butt and I'm happy.

But it's *he* who wanders into my thoughts tonight, when the house is so quiet I can hear the soft patter of rain on the rooftop as I lie in bed and wonder if I'll see him again.

I was in private school. There were a total of 460 students enrolled, from middle school to high school. Every year was littered with circles, circles that I never quite fit into. I craved connection, but being shy didn't help. Being quiet didn't help. They mistake shy with uninterested or boring. Quiet with having nothing to say, and equating that with having nothing to feel. They saw me, quiet as a lamp, so I *was* a lamp to them. I never thought of myself as a lamp, maybe the lightbulb. But I never managed to find the switch until now.

I never thought there was another human who could be quiet enough that I feel like he can hear me. I never thought anyone else could help me find the switch but me.

Is that why he's so intriguing to me? Why he's a stranger and feels so familiar too? Why he makes me so aware? Of him? And me, my body? My heartbeat, my breath, my . . . sex! He hijacks everything.

It's like my body's not mine; it runs away from me. It's re-active to every glance or smile or the sound of his voice. What's wrong with me?

Miles and I would work. But Maverick is just so manly, and *this is what happens when you don't give out your V card by senior year, Reese.*

It's like being on a diet and craving what you can't have. Exactly. This is why I'm so . . . warm lately. Maverick Cage oozes sex, and I've lived a sexless life. He's like the Snickers bar I haven't had in weeks.

And there were plenty of opportunities for sex before. In junior year. Sophomore year. Even in freshman year, and definitely in senior year. Some guys have wanted to sleep with me, Lex Kent, and Julian Parrish at senior prom. They wanted to sleep with me, on different occasions, of course, but I didn't want to sleep with them.

They kissed and touched me and I felt a little bit used by them, and I didn't want to be used.

I wanted to be understood, and I wanted to be known. And I wanted to be loved.

FOR THE NEXT two days, the team is packing and getting ready for the first fight. Remy is hardly home. Brooke keeps texting me during the day: How's Racer?

He's fine! ;D We're playing with the trains

Oh him and his trains. Hug him for me. I'll try to be home before bedtime.

When Diane starts making dinner, she, Racer, and I are the only ones home. I've learned that she's been with the team for over a decade, and she's got such a warm, earthy vibe; she's like everyone's mother.

"You're a quiet one, aren't you?" Diane says as she shuffles around the kitchen and I help her chop the vegetables.

I smile. "I guess."

"Reserved with strangers or just quiet?"

"Quiet."

"Please stop me if I'm bugging you."

"You're not. Tell me about all this." I signal at the kitchen island full of bright-colored food and vegetables and over half a dozen prime-grade rib eyes she's marinating inside zipped bags.

"Remy gets more protein in a day than a normal person gets in a week. He trains all day and his nutrition is as important as the training," she says as she takes out a tray and sets slices of sweet potato in two perfect lines, then drizzles them with olive oil and a dash of freshly crushed herbs.

The entire kitchen smells like a mix of rosemary and peppers, and I like the way it makes my lungs feel clean when I take a breath.

"Everyone is so close," I say as I watch her slide the tray into the oven, and then I go crush the basil for the zucchini pasta dressing she's making.

"We're like a family. With all its ups and downs, I guess."

"What downs?"

"Remy is temperamental, but he'd never hurt anyone. He just has his moods. Brooke can handle him well though. He'd do anything for her."

"I can tell," I admit.

"What about you? A boy back home?" she asks slyly, eyes sparkling as she sends me a woman-to-woman smile.

Miles.

"Maybe," I say. Finished crushing the basil, I then go wash my hands and towel off.

"What does 'maybe' mean?"

"He's a friend, but I think I want more. It's hard to be friend-zoned and then make the change. I can't seem to get him to see me in a different light."

"You're a beautiful girl. Just don't settle until you find the real thing."

The real thing.

Everyone talks about it as if it were black and white, but how do you know when it's real? I believe in making things real. In making a conscious effort to make things happen. Which means that maybe, right now, I should be texting Miles and finding out why he really wants to come.

But just maybe, he should miss me some more. Maybe he should be the one to text me. I'm all for fighting for what you want, but I don't feel like a meaningless texting ping-pong game with messages that don't say anything at all.

Instead, I pull out Maverick's penny and turn it in my hand, wondering what he's doing, willing to give a penny for his thoughts right now.

TEN

TRAINING WITH OZ

Maverick

We're training in a garage, boxes to one side, the bags in the middle of the room. No one watching. No one interrupting. No one distracting me.

First, jumping rope, forward, backward, sideways.

"Time."

I stop, dripping in sweat, and go take the speed bag.

Flashes of my father. I see him in the hospital bed.

Flashes of my mother. Her, at the door when I left home.

Flashes of the coaches before they shut their doors on me; *You won't ever be good enough.*

I'm shadowboxing.

Sparring.

Running.

Weights.

Planks, push-ups, pull-ups, ab work.

And flashes of her. *That's beautiful body art. . . .*

Flashes of her. *Good luck, Maverick. . . .*

Flashes of her. Light blue eyes looking at me, pink lips saying, *He's with me.*

"Get personal if any of the fighters get touchy," Oz says.

I'm doing sit-ups, exhaling through my mouth.

"And if you get to Tate, don't let him wear you out. He's got more endurance than anyone's ever seen. Right after he swings, he is invisible; one second there, the next gone. You never fucking take your eyes off him, you hear me?"

We take a forty-minute lunch break, and Oz plays a few tapes on an old portable TV. Tate in his crimson-red robe, heading down the concrete walk leading to the arena and the ring.

Clad in yellow, Apocalypse follows.

They touch gloves.

The bell goes.

Apocalypse jabs. Tate moves his shoulder, evading.

Apocalypse jabs again, high. Tate swings at his head, frowning. Tate throws a left, a straight jab, then a right that cracks on jaw.

The blows stun Apocalypse. He starts blocking, backing away.

Tate's clearly the aggressor. He goes after Apocalypse until he's got him against the ropes, dishing out multiple hits to the body. Ribs, gut.

"Somebody needs to teach Tate how to fall the fuck down and stay down," Oz grumbles, forwarding to another point when Tate's got Apocalypse against the ropes. Tate's fist loops out. One last hit. Apocalypse is about to fall.

It's the end of the round.

Tate backs off and takes his stool and gets a spritz of water.

Apocalypse takes to his stool too, bloodied, shaking his head at his coach.

He's not getting up and spits out his mouth guard.

The announcer starts yelling out the victor. "Riiiipti—"

Oz turns off the video, and I start suiting up with my gloves again. "More often than not, when Riptide fights, he leaves with no mark on his face. He's the greatest ever seen."

"I'll be greater."

"You're cocky." He comes over to tighten my gloves at the wrists, then he slaps me on the back of the head, sober enough to glare. "Save the cock for the girls."

"Fuck, I am."

"Really?" he says, suddenly interested. "What girls?"

"One girl. Just one."

"What's her name?"

I shake my head and aim for the heavy bag.

Sorry, Oz, but she's all mine.

ELEVEN

THE UNDERGROUND FROM AFAR

Reese

I'm wondering a lot about the Underground from my room tonight. The Tates wanted easy access to the inaugural fight, so they booked us at a five-star hotel downtown.

Apparently there are many fighting circuits. In this one, it's fought by seasons, two a year, winter and summer. Spring and fall are for training. The fights take place at different sites—starting with the inaugural, happening tonight in Seattle, up to the final fight, which is in New York this year. During the season, fighters drop out due to injury or losses. Every night, if a fighter wins, he has the opportunity to fight another opponent, and then another, until he steps down or loses. This means the best fighters fight last; otherwise, others won't have an opportunity to get very far. The good rookie fighters can climb their way up to fight the top dogs. From what I've heard, there's only one undefeated one for the past three years. Remy Tate.

The suite is eerily silent as the whole team except for Diane, Racer, and me has gone to the inaugural fight.

I almost fainted when Remy came out with his duffel and his sporting gear. He swept past like a beast and I'm stressing about

the pounding Maverick could get from him and other more sea-
soned fighters like him.

I'm nervous for Maverick.

I've tucked Racer into bed. I read him a book about trains,
and then I even went and searched for some sugary treats—the
kind that are not available in the Tates' suite kitchen. I try to
watch TV.

I set the remote aside and stare at the window when, hours
later, I hear the team shuffle back into the suite.

Usually I don't know what they're talking about, I'd rather
play with the trains and giggle at Racer's smile, his eyes shining.
I want to eat his dimple and take his chubby cheek along with it
too. But tonight Racer's asleep already, and I'm way too curious
to go to my room yet.

Remington is soaked as he stalks straight to the kitchen to
guzzle and hydrate.

He's quiet and satisfied, and Brooke doesn't look frazzled at
all. So I'm sure things went well tonight.

When she goes to check up on Racer, I hang around the men,
wondering if I should ask.

"Lots of new guys. With Scorpion out and Parker the Terror
still in the hospital, they're all thinking they have a shot at the
final match this year."

"They're a bunch of dumb shits," Coach Lupe says.

"What did you think of the new star, Coach?" Pete asks
curiously.

"Can tell he's been provoked in his heart and his spirit. He's
got anger locked so tight, his muscles practically seize with it."

Maverick?

"Got some fire. You think he thinks he'll get to fight Riptide?" Riley asks.

Coach scratches his bald head. "He'll have to go through dozens to get a chance. Rookies don't fight the champ unless they're kicking some serious ass."

"Oz was just snoozing behind the ropes." Pete shakes his head in disapproval.

Ohmigod. They *are* talking about him. They are talking about my Maverick.

My Maverick?

No, not mine. At all. But my friend.

Maybe my friend.

"What do we know about this guy?" Pete then asks, taking out his phone as if making notes.

"Confirmed?" Coach asks. "Nothing. You saw his mark?"

"Couldn't mean what we think it does. Rem's not worried," Pete counters.

"'Cause it's *my* job to worry for us," Coach growls.

I touch the penny in my pocket. I get a horrible pang for chocolate and vanilla ice cream. I head to the kitchen in search of something to fulfill my craving. "You need anything, Reese?" Diane asks.

"I'm looking for something to snack on. Dietetic!" I specify to Diane. "Definitely not chocolate or ice cream."

"I've got almond milk vanilla ice cream. It's pretty good, lower calories than the normal kind. One scoop? Or two?"

Oh god. "One," I say, but lift two fingers.

She laughs.

I carry it to my room and then just stare at the ice cream and think of him. *Maverick.* Cage. Maverick is outside the box, but cage is as if trapped. I think of his tattoo of the bird and picture fingers tracing it, and guess whose fingers those are? Mine.

And then lips are pressing against it, and guess whose lips those are? Mine.

And he tastes better than this vanilla ice cream, and it sud-

denly feels like the only thing that will satisfy this endless craving
he's started in me is him, and I'm pretty sure I can't have *him* just
like I can't have normal ice cream.

I hold the bowl in my hands but actually strain my ears to
hear more of the talk out in the living room.

Remington Tate is the king of the ring. Undefeated for years.
He trains like his life depends on it, and he fights like he lives
for it. He's an icon of the Underground and a master fighter.
First a boxer, kicked out because of his unruly temper, he's now
made a name for himself in the Underground to rival that of any
heavyweight, welterweight, or middleweight champion. He fights
mega-fights, which draw mega-crowds, and between his cocky,
dimpled grins and the way he beats his opponents to a pulp, the
sensational fights he creates are cause for a lot of money and a lot
of fans.

Maverick, however, has never fought in his life until tonight.

I wander back outside and stay by the fringes as the four
men—Coach, Riley, Pete, and Remington—sit on a couch, bent
over something. Brooke stands nearby because Remy's arm is
around her waist and she seems to have no other choice.

They're watching the fights on Coach's phone. Evaluating all
the fighters.

Maverick?

My eyes hurt with the need to see.

"First fight. Not enough to see real weakness except he lacks
patience," Coach says.

"Play it back," Remington says. He watches. "Huh," he says,
impressed.

"Yeah. You might just get a challenge."

Remy mumbles something, stands, and walks away, patting
Brooke's butt all the way to their bedroom.

"What did he say?" Coach asks the other two.

"He said, 'About goddamned time.'" Pete exchanges looks with Riley.

"If Oz tries to stitch the poor kid's open cut, the kid's going to lose an eyeball," Coach declares as he gets up and grabs his jacket.

My heart turns over in my chest.

"He's got some chip on his shoulder."

Coach shoots them a grave look. "If his old man is who we think he is, of course he has a chip." He spots me and for a moment seems confused as to why I'm here. "Reese, right?"

"Yes." I smile at all three of them. "Congratulations."

"Come with us next time," Riley says. "I promise you it's quite the experience."

"Can't. Apparently Racer's on an I-need-Reese-to-sleep phase. I'm his new blankie."

I quickly shuffle back into the kitchen, ask Diane for a cooler bag to fit a pint of ice cream, then go knock on the door of the master bedroom. I hear shower water in the background when Brooke opens the door with a towel clutched to her chest. I force myself not to look inside because when I'm around them, I almost feel like I'm intruding on the incredible chemistry they share. "Can I go out for a walk? Racer's tucked into bed. I want to burn some calories."

"Sure, but . . ." She glances into the bedroom as if to check the time.

"I'll be fine," I assure, dipping my hand into my bag. I take out the pepper spray she gave me.

She grins. "Okay, then. You're set. Be careful, Reese. One hour back here or I'm going to bust your phone."

"Yes!" I cross the living room and head outside.

TWELVE
FIRST AID

Reese

Twenty minutes later, I'm at the lobby of his hotel. I pretend to be his girl, the dumb-wit who forgot the room number, just got into town, and wants to surprise him. Because I'm young and seem sweet, the staff falls for it and dishes out the room number, and three minutes later, I'm a mass of nerves knocking at his door. "Just do it," I hear, a low growl.

Even through a door, the guy's voice makes me shiver.

Why are you here, Reese?

"Maverick." I knock again, then say, "Maverick, it's me."

There's total silence to the degree that I wonder if I made up the sounds I just heard coming from inside the room.

He swears and three heartbeats later, the door swings open. Maverick Cage stands before me, utterly still. Tall. Sweaty. And intimidating. I inhale, because, hello? *Intimidating.*

One eye is closed, bleeding at the eyebrow. The eye beneath it is swollen and bruised, and the power in his other eye's stare is so absolute, it would thrust me backward if I weren't so determined to get in there and help.

It takes me a moment to realize that while I stand here and gape, he's been checking me out, head to toe.

Heat pops up all over my body, quickly following his stare.

"What are you doing here?" His voice is about as raspy as sandpaper. There's a world of frustration in his expression, and his throat is so tanned and thick and he's bleeding and shirtless and he is so *ripped.* And glorious. Every muscle of his chest is chiseled and rock-hard, covered in the smoothest, most golden skin I've ever seen. His nipples—

You are not staring at his small, pointy, brown nipples, Reese!

"I can sew," I blurt. "I mean, shirts and stuff but . . . my cousin insisted I learn first aid and more when I came to help for the summer."

His one eye once again runs over me and he waits a beat. It's such a long beat, in my mind I have a chance of leaving the building before he opens the door farther. "Come in."

He's reluctant about letting me into his space, and I'm suddenly just as reluctant when I step inside. If I thought by coming to his room, I'd have a clue as to who he is, I was on another level of fantasy. The place is as bare as a clean hotel room gets—except this room is littered with fighting gear. A duffel bag by a chair in the corner. Water bottles and electrolyte drinks. Plus a first-aid kit open and full of material that seems to have been shuffled around as something was extracted.

Seeing the bed he sleeps on makes my chest feel so weird. Like somebody punched *me* there. There's a pair of black boxing gloves on the nightstand next to a similar pair of older gloves. Those second gloves look old; they're worn and torn around the wrists, taped haphazardly with a silver tape. They're the kind of gloves one doesn't keep around for fighting purposes. They look older than Maverick is.

In the center of the Spartan room, a middle-aged man stands holding a shiny little needle with a slim blue thread running through it.

The man has a belly, has clearly been running his hands through his white hair in frustration, and his eyes are bloodshot and confused as he scrutinizes me as if he's not sure if I'm really in the room or maybe in his head.

"Hi, Oz," I say.

He squints. "And you are?"

"You don't know me, but everyone knows you."

He huffs. "Is that right? As the has-been, right? I'm making a comeback, just you wait and see." He drinks from his silver flask. Maverick smirks at me and goes to pluck the needle from Oz's grip.

When he walks up to me with the needle, I suddenly don't know what possessed me to come to his aid. I've sewn pillows, not warm, living flesh.

"Do your worst," he says, raising his good eyebrow, challenging me.

"Has it been sterilized. . . ?" I ask, trying to focus on the needle he just handed to me.

Not on the fact that Maverick is too close.

Not on the fact that Maverick is watching me with more interest than he's ever watched me with.

Pulling out the nightstand drawer, he grabs a lighter, turns it on, flickers it over the needle, sterilizing it with the flame, then he walks to a bag of ice and sticks it inside to cool it immediately.

"I'm impressed."

Our fingers brush as he passes the needle again, and then he sits down on the chair by the window. I try to keep my pulse steady as I clean the wound. "No hospital for you, huh," I whisper.

"Don't want to go there to heal and I don't want to go there to die." His voice is low but adamant, and so close his breath fans over my face—and it feels so warm.

I stop smiling when I see him looking at me and feel that strange flip in my tummy.

Be strong, Reese.

If he can take the gash, you can do some needlework.

You might even take his stare.

I stand between his parted legs. He's in shorts and . . .

Oh.

God.

His thighs are massive and bulging like rocks. He's sitting down, his hair gleams under the yellow room lights, his knees scraped. His legs are hair-dusted and tan. His chest is soaked with sweat. I'm standing, and his face is eye level with my neck. Every inch closer, I get nervous. My hand shakes a little.

I know it's going to hurt, but there's no concern in his gaze. Almost as if he's immune to pain.

"Lower your gaze," I say.

He drops his gaze. And it *doesn't help.* I can't concentrate because whatever it is he's staring at now, my lips are tingling. Tingling.

Is he looking at my *lips?*

I can feel his eyes on me—in me—like he has X-ray vision. I set my fingers on Maverick's forehead. He doesn't react to the touch at all, but touching him is making me feel funny. But this is not a funny moment, so *you should just get down to business, girl!*

Inhaling and holding my breath, I pierce his skin with the tip of the needle, wincing inside. He doesn't move. He watches me in silence as I ease the needle out. And then pierce his skin again.

"You'll have a scar," I whisper ruefully.

He reaches out and curls his wounded hand around my waist as if to steady me, and I can't stop my body's instant quiver in reaction. *Body, behave!*

My hand has stopped stitching as I assess whatever it is that's unsettling me to the core.

His pinkie somehow stole under my shirt, the others over it. The pad of his finger is a little rough. His fingers grip me a little tighter as he draws me closer. I catch my breath, then realize he's steadying me so I can finish. And I won't be able to finish if I keep focusing on the fact that *my boobs are right in his face!*

I pierce his skin again, this time quickly, trying to sew as tightly as possible so that it heals better. And as fast as possible, so I can get out of here. He inhales sharply.

I pause. "I'm hurting you."

His head tilts and his eyes flick up to mine and there is so much heat there, the kind that I have never seen in anyone's eyes when they look at me. Not *me.*

"Are you done?" he asks, voice textured, his eyes roiling with frustration all of a sudden, as if he can't wait for me to be done. But his fingers are clutching me closer, until my knee is up against . . . his groin.

I purse my lips and focus on piercing his skin again. I do a total of twelve stitches. Even while my heart is running like Seabiscuit in my chest and I pray he doesn't notice how fast my chest rises and falls.

"There. You'll live to fight another day."

I pull away and then put almost half the room between us as I search for something to say. "I brought ice cream to celebrate. It's your first fight at the Underground. *Tell* me!"

Back to the business of celebrating, I bring out my ice cream pack.

He leans forward, elbows to his knees, watching me in curiosity. "It was nothing special." He curls his fingers into his palms and watches my profile intently.

Then Oz says, "It was spectacular! He KO'd three!"

Maverick's eyes flash on Oz, a spark hot enough to melt steel. He growls angrily, shaking his head. "Not enough."

"Better than any starter fighter I've seen in a long time. You broke Twister in one round." He stares at Maverick, who's staring at me.

"Twister?" I ask, impressed.

"I'll get you a cab so you can go home, Oz," Maverick tells him. I notice how meaningfully Maverick's eyes slide toward the door.

Oz's eyebrows fly up.

So do mine.

Maverick looks unperturbed.

I have the strangest feeling that he wants to be alone with me.

A kernel of panic settles in my gut.

And two of excitement.

Three of lust.

"Boy, I've been taking care of myself before you came along, so fuck off. I can get my own cab." Oz slaps the first-aid kit closed and carries it under his armpit as he sips from his flask and grabs his coat.

"'Bye, Oz," says Maverick, and when the door slams shut as Oz grumbles, Maverick looks at me and smiles.

I take out the ice cream.

Please god, let him not smile at me like that ever again.

We're so alone, and it's so quiet, and he's so . . . bare-chested.

"What are you doing here?" he asks, still smiling.

"Plastic spoons," I say, like they're the best invention ever. I purposely ignore his question and make a big ceremony out of studying the spoons—as if there's a difference between them— and finally I hand him one.

He watches me and takes it between his thumb and forefinger. I almost feel connected when we're both holding the spoon at the same time. Which is ridiculous.

"It's dietetic," I say as he slides the spoon into the bucket of ice cream. He jams it into his mouth. I watch him, uncertain. "It's good?"

He takes another spoonful and frowns, as if considering.

"Tell me about the fight."

"Why?" His voice is rough and dry, unlike the cool ice cream he's eating.

"I want to know. How did it feel?" I ask.

"Why are you not eating?"

"I . . ." I stare at the ice cream.

He lifts his spoon to me.

My eyes widen.

My lips part. And as he moves the spoon forward, I let the ice cream trail on my tongue. I suck it back and grab my own spoon and nervously gobble down another bite.

"Tell me about the fight," I say again. "I bet you already have fans."

"Sorry to disappoint."

"Oh, come on. You must notice girls."

"Oh, I notice." He grins, his eyes twinkling. "A distraction I don't need."

I didn't expect this admission from a guy as young and blatantly hot as him. But then, Maverick is so focused on his career that I can believe getting laid is not a priority. Getting laid, for him, must be something easy and accessible any time he wants it. But fighting in the Underground at the level he wants to fight is not.

For some reason, I feel a new connection with him and I hear myself admit something I'd never even told Miles.

"I'm a virgin," I whisper.

His eyebrows shoot up, and the surprise mingled with respect mingled with something unnamable I can't decipher on his face makes the tips of my ears go hot. He opens his mouth as if searching for words, a puzzled frown creasing his forehead as he finally says, "Why?"

"Insecurity about my body, I guess. Wanting it to mean something, not just . . . feel good."

"What's there to be insecure about?"

I shrug.

"Seriously, Reese?" he asks softly, disbelieving.

I laugh nervously, nodding with a smile. "Seriously, Maverick."

I'm talking more with this guy than I've ever talked to anyone. Because I want to listen and make him talk to me too.

Listening takes on a whole new meaning with him.

Talking too.

Words.

Looks.

Tones of voice.

A *whole* new meaning.

He holds my gaze with his, and then he says very quietly, a little huskily, "I think that's cool, Reese."

We hold stares for an eon. The room shrinks in size, and his hands spread out over his knees and he drums his thumbs restlessly on both.

I just don't know what to do with my hands, with my eyes, with myself.

For the first time in my life, I'm aware that in the deepest part of me, I hurt. Then Maverick glances around the room with a frown and rubs a hand restlessly across the back of his neck. "Sorry about this place."

"Oh no, it's good. Cozy."

"I used all my savings to help my dad."

"I . . . I'm sorry. What happened?"

"Shit, I guess."

"I'm sorry, Maverick."

His eyes meet mine, and I detect a strange look on his face when I call him Maverick. It's such a puzzled look that I pause and immediately want to retract.

"Would you rather I call you Cage? You . . . stiffened when I said your name."

"I'd rather you tell me about you," he says, shifting forward in his seat. "What are you looking for?"

"What do you mean?"

"You're here at night. What is it that you're looking for?"

"A friend."

"I'm not a friendly guy."

"But what you see is what you get with you, and I like it."

"You get nothing from me, that's what you get."

"That's fine. I got a penny. And at least I can eat ice cream without you telling my mother."

We eat a little more. I spot the old, worn gloves by the nightstand and get up to touch them.

"Those aren't mine. These are mine." He leans back to grab the others, hands me the pair of new gloves, and sets the old ones aside. "The old ones were my dad's."

I glance at the gloves. Well, he must've given quite a few people a very good beating with those. "He must've been good."

When he talks about his father, there are clouds in his eyes, and something inside me makes me ache to remove them. "I never watched him fight, but I've seen a few videos online. In the early days he was good. But not the best."

"And you want to be the best."

"I want to be a legend."

"Ambitious, are we?"

He laughs softly.

My phone is ringing. "I need to go. I only had one hour." I answer the call. "Hey, I'm on my way, I'm fine." I hang up, then steal one last glimpse of him. "Sorry. It's annoying; my mother asked my cousin to keep a close eye on me."

"Don't apologize, it's nice they give a shit."

The honesty suddenly makes me realize that when I leave, he's alone in this room. I compare it to the bustle of people at the Tates' and shake my head, stunned.

"Don't you have anyone?"

He shrugs and slips on a shirt. "I'll take you home."

It's the most tense cab ride of my life. Maverick and I are both silent as the cab heads toward the Tates' hotel, but we stare at each other every couple of minutes. Each time our eyes meet, we smile. But inside me, other things happen. My body squeezes in places and I ache between my legs.

I glance at the skin I sewed above his eye and feel somehow really possessive of him.

I notice, as he hops out of the cab to walk me across the lobby toward the elevators, that people stare at him as he walks next to me. There's something about him that just calls your attention. Even from a distance. The confidence, the stride, his carriage, his body, his face, and his *eyes*.

I don't want the team to see him though. So the moment we hit the elevator bank, I spin to face him even before I press the Up arrow. "It's fine. I'll go up."

Just then, my phone buzzes again. I'm suddenly concerned. What if it's Brooke already sending the cavalry, aka Pete and Riley, to look for me? I glance at it in dread.

Instead, I read Miles's name on my phone screen. I tuck the phone quickly away.

Maverick lifts his brow, his eyes smiling down at me.

"Your cousin?"

"No. A boy back home."

And Miles *seems* like such a boy compared to Maverick. Maverick is a bit boyish sometimes but so manly, so grown-up and mature. I wonder what made him mature so fast. The kind of tragedy that gives you that look in your eyes, the one that warns people not to get close. That tells them they will never be able to get close.

As if deep in his own thoughts, Maverick looks upward speculatively and then back at me. "Next time, I'll get a nice place like this."

"Next time?"

"Next time you come over." His eyes flick down to where I hid my phone, and then up to me. Was that . . . jealousy?

"We're leaving to the next location tomorrow."

He nods. I don't know where he plans to work out, but it's the only place I get to see him. I blurt out, "I'll be at the Body Factory Gym in Denver. I can get you in there too."

His eyes flood tenderly. "Some people might easily take advantage of how nice you are."

"I'm not nice on the inside."

"You're nice all over." His eyes run over me, and my toes curl as his eyes reach my feet, and then he catches himself, clenches his jaw, and looks up at me, sincere and strangely puzzled.

"I don't want to be nice," I blurt out. "I want to be un-nice. Badass and special and unforgettable. People mistake nice with weak, and I'm not weak." A man as hard as Maverick should despise weakness.

"I don't think you're weak. It takes strength to be kind," he says in a haunted tone. But his eyes gleam in approval of me.

I want him to say what he thinks of me, but maybe I'm not ready to know. If it's bad it will funk me out, and if it's good I'll be gone. I'll be gone.

"I won't make it until at least three days from now. I'll see you there." He walks away.

Don't watch him walk away, Reese.

Don't look at his inverted-triangle back and his fine ass, Reese.

I am looking at both when he swings the door open, and my heart does an odd little flip when a group of guys comes in and he looks over his shoulder at me. He remains there, watching me until I board. Just as the doors start to close, I watch him turn away and lift his hand to touch his wound.

A stolen moment. That's what just happened with him and me. But I want more than a moment. And I don't want to steal it. I want it to be ours.

I see Miles's text again and I tuck my phone away without answering.

❤ ❤ ❤

THAT NIGHT I have a dream of us eating ice cream. "Do you want to know something?" Maverick slams the spoon into the bucket and then uses that hand to touch my mouth. "I want to kiss you right here."

"Why here?"

"Seems like a good place to start."

And when he sets his lips on mine, I wake up, as if it's too incredible a reality, it can't even happen in my dreams.

THIRTEEN

FIRST PAY

Maverick

I haven't called my mother. Haven't wanted her to think I couldn't do it. Now we're in Oz's messy hotel room after picking up our pay and I stare at my first check for 18,005 dollars.

I slip it into an envelope and write a note.

My first check. It's all yours.
Maverick

"You sure you don't want to keep some of that?" Oz asks dubiously.

"Nah, she needs it more than I do."

"Plan to send her all your checks?"

"As many as I can, yes." I eye him narrowly while Oz rests his head on the back of the couch and eyes the ceiling.

"When you get to fight Tate during the season, we're talking that check will have six, possibly seven, digits, not five."

"Next one's for me. I'm setting us up in a nice hotel like the big fighters do."

"So you can invite her over?"

"Yeah, so I can invite her over."

He sighs. "Good girls don't date fighters."

"Fighters have good wives."

"*One*. One does: Riptide." He raises his brows challengingly. "All the others are divorced like me." He shakes his head, then adds, "When you fight for a living, it's like your whole life is at war; it bleeds into your personal life."

"Like my father's."

He stays silent, then cracks open his flask and takes a long swig.

"What do you know about my father?"

"Oh no you don't." Oz cackles and stands to leave, the fucking coward. But before he heads off, he slaps my back. "You don't pay me for that." He eyes me. "And you don't want to know."

"Actually, I do."

He sighs and considers it for a moment. "Got all fucked up after being in the fighting world too long. He became a . . ." He searches for words. "Terror."

"Drugs?"

He snorts, takes another swig, and midswig he frowns at the flask and turns it fully upside down to realize it's empty.

"He fought dirty; I've seen the tapes," I tell him.

"You don't fight like him. You've got more good in you than he ever did. You fight better than him. That's all you need to know." He finds a half-drained bottle nearby and refills his flask.

"Oz, fuck, man," I say.

He lifts his flask at me in a toast. "I'm taking my baby to bed, let it nurse me into a good mood."

I sigh, then I flip the envelope and add my mother's address.

FOURTEEN

GREYHOUND TO DENVER

Maverick

Two days later we're in the back of a bus, on our way to Denver. Oz is snoozing. I have my earbuds in, watching my father fight Tate in the ring. I've watched the videos so many times. Studying for weaknesses. He has none. He's fast; my father has trouble staying balanced when he catches a hit.

If I withstand ten fighters next fight, I can get to him. Face-to-face. I get to fight him. I get to see exactly what he's made of.

Hell, I get to see what *I'm* made of.

I sigh and turn off my phone, then I set my forehead on the window and stare outside, not really seeing anything but her.

She's in my head. She said *He's with me* and now, somehow, *she* is the one who's with *me*. She's there when I go to bed, there when I wake. I rub my thumb over my cut.

Her eyes as she stitched me up.

Her lips closing around the spoon and licking off the vanilla ice cream.

My mind goes in all directions but it ends up in the same place: her.

Her watching me fight.

Her in a nice room with me.

On a nice bed.

And me, kissing her in a very un-nice way. Hearing her make noises that are the opposite of nice.

She huffs when she exercises and makes a certain noise when she makes effort, almost a moan, and then she sighs as she catches her breath, and she's the sexiest thing I've ever seen inside a gym or out of it.

She's got a tiny waist I could encircle with my hands and the most delicious butt. It bounces when she runs, and so do her exquisitely delicious breasts. She's a sexpot, made to fuck. I can't look at her without imagining what she'd look like under me.

Dragging my hand over my face, I pull my phone back out and try to focus on the man I need to beat.

And still I think of that nice girl who doesn't want to be nice. A girl who wants to be unforgettable, and doesn't realize she already is.

FIFTEEN

WE MEET AGAIN

Reese

The next few days we spend in Denver. The weather is fabulous during the summer. Everything is green and the breeze is fresh and clean. It's been five days since I last saw Maverick Cage, but less than one second since I last thought of him.

Every moment of the day he's been in my mind's eye. I'm confused about my fixation on him, why I'm so aware that he's not near. I live with the curiosity of wanting to know what he's doing and a fierce body ache that's been growing exponentially as my days without seeing him keep adding up.

It took a full day to get Racer into the perfect Denver day care, mainly because Brooke wants him to interact with other little kids and wants something close to both her and Remy's training area and the team's gym.

I'm at the Body Factory Gym now when I see *him* walk in. He hands over a card at the entrance and I realize he's got himself a membership.

I'm almost disappointed that he doesn't need me anymore. I look away from the entrance, drag in a breath, and turn to him again, waiting for him to glance in my direction.

He tucks his card away, signs his name, and I see the lady try to flirt with him, and Maverick . . . oh god, Maverick smiles at her. Then he walks inside. He hasn't seen me but is scanning the treadmills—where I used to be. But today I'm on a Pilates bed. I sit up and stand uneasily to my feet.

And then his eyes find me.

And I'm . . . *found*.

And alive.

And nervous. It's been an eternity.

Forever and ever since you looked at me.

And when he does look at me, he seems to stop breathing. He takes me in for the tensest second, and then he drinks me in with one rake of his eyes over my body. My breasts feel his gaze. So does my sex. And my tummy. And my heart. His fingers seem to flex at his sides and he jams them into his drawstring sweatpants pockets.

I want to act cool, but I can't.

I'm possessed by my happiness.

I'm possessed by *him*.

I head over, my smile hurting on my face.

"Maverick Cage," I breathe excitedly. "I missed you."

Jesus, Reese, you didn't just say that!

My eyes widen instantly when his eyes flare in surprise too. I drop my gaze and search for something to say when I realize—

You're staring at his crotch, Reese!

"Fuck," I say.

"What?" he asks.

I jerk my face up to his, burning in embarrassment, to find him wearing this really male smile, and I turn around and start heading to the treadmills.

"Hey," he says, taking my wrist.

I slip my hand into the front pocket of his hoodie to fetch his iPod shuffle and earbuds. "I really need these more than you right now," I say apologetically, and then I stick the earbuds into my burning ears and hop onto a treadmill.

My treadmill faces him.

He's standing there, looking at me in amusement.

I don't know what kind of pull he has, or what kind of power over me. I want him for my birthday and Christmas and it's always the best things at Christmas and oh my god, what's going on with me?

He's like the world's most perfect sight and feel and smell and I can almost taste him in the air.

I don't want to like you, Maverick.

I don't want you to turn around, Maverick.

He turns around, and I do like him, and I don't know what to do to get him to like me. He's all hard to my softness. I feel extra voluptuous 'cause he's so hard.

As he moves around the training area, he jerks off his hoodie and the T-shirt beneath rides up a bit as he does, revealing every concretelike square of his abs. And yeah, I feel so voluptuous right now—I just don't know why I can't look more like Brooke. I stopped eating a little bit when Miles pulled a Mr. Darcy on me. *Reese is nice, but I like them on the slimmer side, though she's totally fuckable.*

Nice.

Sigh.

Though I've lost a few pounds since the day in his hotel room, I'm just not hungry. I've lost my appetite. I've grown a new addiction and obsession, and it's more dangerous than food could ever be to me. More dangerous than any addiction I've ever had.

And I stare at this addiction of mine, feeling things that are definitely very un-nice, and I notice he sips his drink and watches the other fighters beat up the heavy bag as he waits for his turn. He's absently stroking his thumb across the cut I stitched up.

He sets his drink aside and then grabs his hoodie again, as if he's just made some decision. He comes over.

"Let's get out of here," he says. "There's a walking trail nearby."

"But . . ." I'm shocked. "Your punching bags?"

"I fight tomorrow. Today's my recovery day."

I power down the treadmill and hop off. "In that case, how are your legs? You're going to need to catch up."

We head outside and I watch him from the corner of my eye as we take the trail, the noon sun blazing high above us for the minutes it takes us to wander into the shelter of the trees.

"I like spending time with you," I mumble.

"Me too." He smiles at me sideways, and I feel that smile in every sexual place of my body.

"Wow, look at this view." I stop and take in all the green slopes on the horizon. We've been hiking up the trail for twenty minutes, and it'll take most of that time to hike our way down. "I only have twenty more minutes or Racer will get restless."

"How's he liking Denver?"

"Good. He's obsessed with the mountains. So do you hike when you're not punching?"

"Not really. . . ." He mysteriously trails off, then shoots me a studious look before he adds, his voice soft as the breeze, "I wanted you all to myself."

I stop. "What? *Why?*" I choke on a laugh.

He's not smiling, just looking amused and honest and so much like a *guy*, his eyes a little dark. "You know why."

"Do I?" I shake my head in consternation. "Maybe I just want to hear you say it."

"Why?" His lips twitch a fraction.

"Because . . ." I search for a reason, trying to regain my breath. "Maybe I like your voice?"

Suddenly he's in my space, backing me up, his gaze intent.

My Himalayan butt hits a tree and I gasp when he props his arm against it. He pins my body between him and the bark. All my breath goes when the front of his body makes contact with the front of mine. My nipples react so strongly they hurt.

I'm suddenly smelling forest and earth and Maverick Cage.

Maverick looks at me for a moment, his face harsh in concentration, the leaves of the lush surroundings rustling with a breeze, thankfully hiding my rapidly quickening breath. Maverick lowers his eyes so they are level with mine, not touching me with his hands, only his body keeping mine in place. "I want to spend the twenty minutes you have left kissing you, Reese," he says, his voice—so deep, so textured, and so irresistible—running thick and heady through my veins.

But it's the look in his eyes, asking for permission, that slays me.

"You're attracted to me?" I ask disbelievingly.

He says, as if it's obvious and not easy for him to stand, "Very much attracted to you, Reese."

"I . . ." I look away, acutely aware of how hard every inch of his body is, contacting mine.

I did not see this coming.

I'm blown away.

In cinders, right here, on this trail, I'm leaving a part of me *right here*.

He leans his head forward slowly, and I turn my head instinctively away, just an inch, scared to feel his lips on mine. Scared of what it'll do to me.

He brushes his lips across my jawline instead. I hear a moan rip out of my throat. He exhales and eases back, looks at me for a moment.

The weight of his gaze feels like sex on my face, then he dips his head and sinuously, heatedly, drags his lips along my temple, up to my forehead, where he sets a kiss there, his soft, firm lips pressing into my skin in a kiss that lasts for about ten perfect, frightening, thrilling seconds.

My throat is tight, and I want to beg him not to stop when he inches away and studies me with eyes that shine with jealousy and possessiveness. "Is it him?"

No. It's you. You make me reckless.

I like it.

But I'm afraid.

"Maybe," I say instead, swallowing. I'm leaning against the tree, struggling to get my knees to work.

"What's he like?"

I can't even remember Miles, and it stresses me. I put even more distance between us as we start walking again. "He's . . ." I search for words. Miles.

"This guy back home," he says with a suddenly vicious, happy sparkle in his eyes.

"I know who we're talking about, Mav." I roll my eyes, and he laughs softly—happy that I don't remember? "He's . . . not like you."

When I met Miles, I was alone in the college cafeteria and saw this guy, clean and wholesome, call two guys and a girl, his friends, over to him. They followed him to my table. "Mind if we sit down?" he asked.

And I nodded, and when he said, "I'm Miles," I thought that at last someone got me. Somehow someone wondered if there was more to me.

I'm ashamed to tell him I'm this easy. This charmed by something so simple. A name or a penny, or a look from silver eyes and a guy who's so upfront he tells you he wanted you alone so he could kiss you.

He pulls off a leaf from a tree we pass, cuts it thoughtfully, and tosses it aside with a frown. "Meaning."

"He's more polished."

"You mean he has money." Jaw visibly clamped now, he grabs another leaf and just tosses it completely aside.

"No. He's . . . not primal. He wouldn't be caught dead in a fight."

"'Cause he'd lose."

I smile and watch my feet as we take the trail down.

"Do you trust him? Does he care for you like you do?" he drills on.

I look at him, wide-eyed. "What is this?"

"Just gauging competition," he says simply.

"There's no competition," I lie. "I've known him forever and I just met you. I can't like you more. I don't love him, if that's what you mean. But I've always thought that we could have more and it would work."

"How often does he call?" He's been frowning ever since I said there was no competition and I can't believe how easily the lie slipped out since I'm so uneasy myself right now.

I stop in my tracks and face him as he—hot and big—turns and does the same.

"He doesn't call . . . often," I admit.

Not ever. Only text, now that I think about it.

Maverick exhales, his eyes darkening even more, and then he starts forward, in three steps closing the distance between us. God.

His walk.

His talk.

His *stare.*

"I think of you." He reaches out with his bruised-knuckled right hand and touches my face. All of Maverick Cage's fingers are *on my face.* "I think of you a lot." He searches my face and his thumb caresses my chin so briefly, but so powerfully, my knees feel like overbaked cake. "I think of kissing you," he says.

I feel like he's kissing me now, with his metal eyes. Kissing me and making me fly.

His lips are so beautiful, I can't take my eyes off them all of a sudden.

I tremble, and when he notices and his eyes flash a little predatorily, I drop my gaze and then start taking the trail down with a vengeance.

We're silent as we hit the end of the trail. All this time, Maverick has been smiling to himself. Did he dismiss Miles as competition? Why is he looking so smug? Because he saw me tremble?

"Maverick?"

"Reese?" His lips curl.

I want to erase his smirk of superiority against Miles. I lean up, resting my arms on his shoulders—hard as rocks—and kiss his jaw. "That's all the kisses you're going to get." I punctuate my next words with a few more kisses. "On this . . . very hard . . . jaw."

I've never been so bold before. It took all of me to follow the impulse to do that, and I don't have anything left to look back at him with as I walk away, but I stop and close my eyes when he calls my name.

"Reese?"

I pull myself together before I turn, and when I do, Maverick eye-fucks my lips. His eyes stroke them so leisurely, time stops. My breath catches. Maverick's eyes wandering over my mouth, my lips, top to bottom, corner to corner. My knees feel wobbly by the time he looks smolderingly back into my eyes.

Holding my gaze with an intensity that makes my whole body shiver, he retraces the space between us in three long steps and ducks his head to me. "Give me a real kiss, for luck."

"What?"

He's staring down at my lips again, fiercely so.

And he just spoke to me in the hottest voice anyone's used with me.

He grabs my hips and pulls me close. "Kiss me for luck, Reese." I watch his lips speak—nearly growl—the words, his beautiful, perfect bow lips that some asshole can crack open tomorrow.

Feeling a huge anxiety settle in my gut, I stare at his mouth with a reckless urge to kiss him there. What will he taste like? Feel like? He's got so much fire I'll be in cinders upon contact alone.

I edge a little closer, my heart pounding, fear choking me.

His hands are on my hips.

Spanning my waist.

All it takes is a match to light a fire, and He. Is. The match.

Maverick waits, looking down at me impatiently, his chest heaving with his breaths. As beautiful and male as ever and looking at *my* mouth.

And I can't.

I can't.

I just can't.

A guy like him could totally wreck a girl like me.

I take his huge hand, uncurl his tightly curled fingers, and set a quick, almost haphazard kiss in the same place he held the penny. "Good luck."

He curls his hand and smiles at me, and I turn and walk away, smiling too.

SIXTEEN

THE DENVER FIGHT APPROACHING

Reese

The next morning at the gym, he's already inside. I take a tread-mill while I see him gloving up, and I see the girls looking at him and going over to talk. I can't take the way he actually removes his earbuds and talks to them. He keeps glancing my way, curious about something.

And I don't know why I can't hold his gaze.

I dreamed of yesterday all over again. In my dreams things got heated pretty quickly, and I'd actually had the balls to kiss him. On those perfect lips.

I'm scared as he looks at me that he'll see what I'm feeling.

That he'll see what he makes me feel.

I glance away when I feel his eyes on me, but when he actually starts training, I watch him, the heavy bag swinging side to side. He drives his fists forward. I know that he uses the earbuds to block out distractions, and he seems to be listening to the sound of his fists. They make different sounds depending on how front and center he slams the bag. He's testing out hits.

He shifts positions to take on the back of the bag, facing the room, and our eyes catch when the bag swings to the side and his face is revealed.

He's wearing the most bloodthirsty expression I have ever seen.

He stands there, a full head taller, twice my weight—at least. And packed with muscle. My heart beats a dozen times. The bag is hit a dozen times. And he still won't look away. There's something dangerous in his gaze. Making my heart speed up and my body feel out of control. I want to know more about him—all there is to know. But he's more impenetrable than the bag his fists are knocking. He's like a steel wall, with steel eyes. Eyes that pierce. Like knives.

I wonder how he moves in bed.

All hard but fluid.

If he loses control.

I wonder what it takes to make him smile. Not smirk, not a brief smile, a real smile.

After putting in my time, I head for Racer and take him to a nearby park. I brought snacks for us—for Maverick and me—thinking I'd invite him with us, but it turns out I'm a coward and I couldn't. And now I tuck them back into my backpack. I'm so strangely lust-lovesick that I'm exhausted and sleepless, to boot.

Maverick

I ALWAYS KNOW when I hit right depending on the sound I get. I start getting the long, hard, deep sounds, one after the other, and I know I'm hitting right. I haven't been on the mark today because I caught her watching me and got hard.

Something about feeling those light blue eyes, pure as a clean sky, makes me react. I have trouble tearing my eyes off her. I like to stare at her face. I like to trace the oval shape with my eyes, take in her plump, puckered-looking pink lips, and the sleek little nose of hers with a total of three freckles at the bridge. I even like to wonder how many more freckles she'll get if she keeps taking Racer to the park.

Forcing myself to focus, I feel the sweat on my brow as I continue slamming. The heavy bag swings side to side. I drive my fists forward. I keep my earbuds in to block the distractions but she's still in my head.

I clench my teeth and test my hits, frown hard when the bag doesn't make the noise I want.

I shift my arm, pull in from my abs, and there. *WHAM*.

I shift position, facing the room. The treadmill she just emptied. But I remember her walking there. Her eyes catching mine. My dick going wild.

I'm twice as heavy and a full head taller, packed with muscle. She's all girl and woman and it took all my willpower to focus on training and look away. I feel dangerous when I look at her. My heart pumps faster and I want to know more about her, all there is to know. I'm as impenetrable as the bag I'm hitting, but she's as elusive as the air. I could be a steel wall with steel eyes, but the truth is, what I feel, I feel it hard too.

And I want to kiss Reese like I want to win tonight.

I stop punching, and I tell Oz I'm taking an hour.

I head to the front desk. "There a park nearby?"

"Sure. Two, three blocks this way." The attendant points with her finger, and I say thanks and pull up my hoodie, heading to the park.

I spot the stroller by a field, where Reese sits with a book and Racer sucks on a crimson lollipop.

"Mavewick!"

We fist-bump. "Hey, buddy."

Reese drops her book and looks at me, blue eyes wide in surprise. Then her cheeks flush pink, and I shove my hands restlessly into my hoodie pockets. Hell, I want to lean over, take her face in my hands, and kiss her mouth and taste her until she can't remember her name, much less the guy back home.

She scoots over and pats the spot next to her, and I drop down and look at her. Reese is a virgin. I need to take care with this girl. Be patient with this girl. Patience is not my strong suit, but patience wins this fight, and I'm not losing, just like I'm not losing in the Underground.

"Hey." I lean over and brush my lips to her cheek, then smile down at her when she glances worriedly to see if Racer saw. He giggles, watching us. Then I take her hand in mine and just sit there for a few minutes; ten minutes later I'm lying down and pulling her into my arms so she can read her book with her head on my chest. She sets the book aside and closes her eyes, inhaling as if I relax her. "Watch Racer for me? I haven't slept well at all."

"Yeah," I murmur into her hair, and I reach up and cup the back of her head with my hand, keeping her against me 'cause she feels too good here. I rub my thumb over the back of her head and smell her hair. And I stay the hour with them like I belong.

Me—a guy whose own father didn't want him—entrusted with this little boy.

Racer showing me all the toys he's brought with him.

And Reese in my arms, where I want her.

SEVENTEEN

TATE

Maverick

I rub my father's old gloves before the fight so much, I've worn them down as much as the years fighting did.

Everyone knows who I am now. Backstage, I'm in a room of my own. All the other fighters are scared shitless of me. If I see a fighter out in the hall, I can stare him down in a second. And I do. I've got the staring thing down pat.

I like that they're afraid.

They should be.

I'm young but I'm fast, I'm strong, and I've got more to prove than these assholes ever will.

"She might be coming to your fight. Look good. Chicks don't like losers," Oz tells me as we wait to get called.

"That's all you've got for me?" I lift my brows, incredulous.

"Yep. It's the most effective I've got."

I clench my teeth. Is she coming to the fight?

She can't come to my fight.

I don't know what it'd do to me if she ever did. When she walks into a room I'm speechless, thoughtless. High.

She's different to me.

She's not *afraid* of me.

The moment the announcer yells out my name, "Maverick 'the Avenger' Cage!" the crowd outside falls deathly quiet. I finish lacing my boots and kick Oz's ankles to get him to wake up from where he was snoozing big time on a bench.

"Wha—"

"We're up."

I slip my fingers into the gloves and the anticipation to hit the ring starts simmering inside me. A black hooded robe covers me as I stalk out and take the aisle, tapping my gloves as I warm up to the idea of kicking some shit.

Inside the ring, my opponent waits. Hector "Hellman." The fact that he's up against *me* makes him an immediate favorite. There are signs floating with his name on them.

No signs for me.

In every video I saw of my father, he gave the crowd the bird as he came up into the ring.

My father was the most loathed fighter in history. But also the most feared.

I can feel the fear in the air, thick as oil.

Oz heads over to his corner while I take the ring, taking my time to climb the ropes. Swear to god, these people don't even seem to be breathing. I stand in the center and look around. They want to see if I'm going to curse them, spit on the floor, or give them the bird. I smile privately when they keep waiting—and I do none of that.

I'm here to fight.

I'm here to win.

"Booo!" the crowd starts. "*Boooooo!*"

"They hate your ass, Maverick," Oz says, scratching his head as if he's trying to figure out how to win them over.

Bell rings, gloves touch.

He throws a punch. I duck and throw out my fist, hearing it crack into his gut. The crowd gasps. The boos silence.

Hellman's stunned. I loop out a left and hit again. The crowd is silent as a morgue. I can hear the sound of flesh pounding flesh as I have a go at him. They've got no more cheers. I hope they're saving them for their golden boy. Because I want a chance to get a hit on that boy. I want a chance to prove to myself I've fucking got it. Got more than my father ever did.

I knock Hellman out.

I don't take my stool as I wait for the next fight.

The moment the bell rings, I go straight for the kill—jab, straight jab, hook. He wraps an arm around me and then slips away. I back him up against the ropes, jabbing, ducking, jabbing, then I hook.

The hook stuns him.

And he's down.

I start beating them all, a third one, a fourth one, a fifth. My body's producing heat like nobody's business. I'm on fire and so are my fists. I've got long arms, a far reach. My opponents think they're in the safe zone away from me, but they're not. Over and over, I hit. Flesh. Bone. Flesh. Bone. But I'm wearing down. I know it's because I haven't been training as I should.

I was at the park, with a kid and a girl who's driving my head in all kinds of directions, all of them leading to the same end: her.

Her in a bed with me.

Her lips under mine.

Her sweet, round little butt under my hands.

Every second spent with them reminds me of the family that I don't have and desperately crave.

I take the stool at my corner and let my body recharge when the announcer's voice flares through the speakers, introducing my next opponent. "Okay, ladies and gentlemen . . ." He trails off

mysteriously and lowers his voice. "I know you all have been waiting for this," he begins.

The crowd shifts restlessly, and as a chorus of gasps and titters
sweeps across the crowd, I tiredly roll my shoulders. I twist my
sore neck to one side, then the other. Motherfuck me, I need gas
right now.

"That's right, ladies and gentlemen!" the announcer starts to
yell. "LADIES AND GENTLEMEN, our record-holding champion, Remington 'Riiiiiiiptide' Tate!"

I can't even relish this moment; I'm catching my breath.

Worn out. I've taken a few hits, my eye has swelled up, and
my cut is about to bust open and bleed again.

My jaw aches like a bitch. I open my jaw and flex it, rubbing
my arm across the sting as Tate takes the ring.

The crowd goes wild. I glance at Oz while I wait. Oz looks
as fucked-up as I am, snoozing in my corner. He really needs to
back off the booze.

"Hey. At least pretend you give a shit." I nudge him. "Put
some Vaseline on my face or something."

He lifts his head and does as I tell him, then he looks at Tate
as he climbs into the ring and his eyes widen.

"WHAT THE LIVING FUCK?! How many have you
knocked out?"

I shrug, eyeing Tate's size from up close. He's an inch taller,
two or three wider. And he looks fresh as spring compared to my
sweaty, bloodied, beat-up self. I'm not as big as him, but I bet I'll
look pretty big from the ground.

We go to center. Touch gloves. The bell rings.

The screams take over the arena. "REMY . . . REMY . . .
REMY . . ."

I take a hit: a blow straight to my ribs.

I ease back, shake my head.

He comes in with a hook that knocks me off-balance.

I hit the ground.

The counting begins. "Stay down," Oz says.

But I can't stay down, I'm leaping to my feet. I'm fighting this guy. I'm beating this guy.

Dizzy.

I should've stayed down.

I take another hit, then three. This guy comes at me like a bull-dozer, from all directions. My brain is already swimming in my skull.

We get a break.

I take my stool.

"Dude, you're getting creamed out there," Oz says.

"Really? *That* you're awake for? Got something for my jaw?"

"Think not. Maybe." He checks his materials and slaps something on. "There."

This time, I block better. I'm braced for his force and catch a few hits, then start swinging. I open up my side when I hook, and he takes it.

I fall splat on the floor, winded.

The girls out in the arena scream his name. They quiet down when I stand. Sweat dripping down my forehead along with blood and a whole shit-ton of frustration.

Tate leans to me. "Your hook's off." Then he jabs and hooks and knocks me to the ground.

The announcer's voice cuts through the speakers as the ring-master raises his arm. "Ladies and gentlemen. Once again . . . *Riptide!* Riiiiiptiiiiiide! UNDEFEATED FOR THREE CON-SECUTIVE YEARS. The most unstoppable beast this ring has ever seen. RIPTIDE!"

The crowd's sudden, wild roar pulses in my eardrums. I plant my glove on the ground and come to my feet. The crowd quiets. Riptide lowers his arm, his grin fading.

Neither of us looks away from the other as we climb the ropes to get off the ring.

We head down the walkway, side by side, silent.

Oz is wide awake now—and he's pissed. "Why the fuck are you giving my fighter pointers? You want him to beat you?" he demands.

Tate shoots me a look when he speaks. "I want him to try."

"You can fucking count on it!" Oz replies.

Tate stops by his door and turns to face me, waiting for me to say something.

I don't.

I just look him directly in the eye while our teams try to shuffle us into our rooms.

"You have something to say to me?" Tate asks.

"Not yet," I say.

His team piles up on him to usher him inside. It takes Oz a lot more effort to move me.

"You're the only fighter I've ever met who's not intimidated by the current champion, Maverick, I swear . . ." He shakes his head in consternation as he pulls off my gloves.

I look at my fists, curl my fingers in slowly, then squeeze and release them.

It's my first time in the ring with Tate, but it's not going to be my last.

I'M BACK IN my hotel room an hour later, my body in a tub of ice. I've got an ice pack on my temple. Oz sewed up my cut and just dropped dead on my couch. I'm bouncing a tennis ball against the wall of the bathroom, catching and throwing it back. I used it to lay my back on and release any knots, but I just like the rhythmic sound of it now. Helps me think as I replay what Tate said.

I'm getting madder and madder, throwing the ball faster and harder.

Something to say to him?

I might have something to say to the asshole.

Hell, I have a lot to say.

I would prefer my fists did the talking, but those will have to wait for another day.

Catching the ball, I toss it into my duffel, then swing to my feet.

"Oz," I call into the room, tightening a towel around my hips as I storm out of the bathroom. "Oz." I nudge his prostrate form. "Where's he staying?"

"Huh?"

"Motherfucking *Riptide*. Where's he staying?"

He grumbles a hotel, and I shove my legs into my jeans, slip on a T-shirt, and head over there.

THERE'S A CROWD outside the Tates' hotel. I shoulder my way past and through the revolving doors just as Tate and his wife step off the elevators. Gritting my teeth, I stalk across the hotel lobby. "Why are you giving me pointers?"

His brows lift. "Because you need them."

I laugh mockingly. "I don't need your help. Fight me. Privately, you and me."

"I don't fight puppies."

He narrows his eyes when I stay in place and cut him a dark, unflinching look.

"Armor's gym tomorrow. Five a.m. Be there," he says.

He takes his wife by the elbow and leads her across the lobby when the elevator opens and feet shuffle out.

"Mavewick!" I hear.

My eyes fall down to a familiar little grin and there's Racer, looking up at me. He's dressed in tiny shorts and a Batman T-shirt and someone is holding his hand. A female hand with neatly trimmed, soft-pink nails. My chest feels tight, and I lift my gaze.

Reese.

And it dawns on me.

She is with them.

I look at her and search her face to see if she knows who I am.

She knows.

I fought with Tate tonight and he can't not know. Everybody knows by now.

I can see wariness and concern in her eyes, concern for what, I don't know.

It's not concern about me. Can't be.

She glances past my shoulder at Tate and his wife, and I realize, it's concern about them knowing she *knows* me.

Loss.

You can't lose shit you don't have.

But in my mind I had some sort of . . . attachment to looking for her every day. I feel like I just lost a fight I didn't even know I fought.

And I lost it to Tate.

"Mavewick!" I hear again, and I feel a tap on my thigh.

I look down again. "Hey, little buddy." I fist-bump him before I can catch myself. I look at Reese, and she's amused and surprised seeing that. I edge my hand back. A tight black top covers her upper body, and dark-wash jeans cover her legs. It's hard to breathe right.

There's something about this girl. What the fuck is it about this girl? I can smell her, a sweet flower scent, and feel her. She's under my skin. I'm boiling in jealousy that she's with Tate. Jealous she's living with him, holding the hand of his kid. Rooting for him.

Jesus, how come my body always knows when she's in my space?

Her purse slides down her shoulder and I impulsively grab it.

"Oh, it's fine," she flusters.

I sling it over my shoulder reluctantly and signal for her to walk past me. "After you."

"Mavewick, come celebwate."

"Can't, buddy."

I watch her as they walk next to me.

Every inch of my body is beat-up but the pain is gone now. The pain is gone except the new one in my crotch.

I'm attracted to her round little face, her heart-shaped mouth, her firm little legs, the softness she has going on in all the right places. The shade of blue in her eyes. She calls to me on the most primitive level. She's in my fucking veins. This girl.

I grab her waist and keep her close to me as we shuffle out into the crowd.

Her breasts press into my chest. I inhale for control, but my mind's fucking running a thousand miles an hour. The blood rushes south. Impossible to get enough blood supply to my brain. Her hard little nipples press against the flat of my chest. It's impossible to stop thinking of those firm, round breasts and how great they feel. I'm getting all lathered up just thinking of getting my hands on them, squeezing and teasing them with my fingers, tasting them. I'm betting her nipples are as pink as her lips, and I want to softly smother them with my mouth and suck on the tips until my jaw hurts.

My dick is in pain and my balls hurt big time. The fact that she smells great and that I seem to lately be replaying our conversations in my head doesn't help.

The crowd clears and Racer starts running for his dad, who's watching us narrowly. Reese starts after Racer, but I catch her wrist.

"Wait," I softly command.

She looks down at my hand, and I force my fingers to uncurl and let the fuck go. My jaw aches when I clench it but I can't loosen it up, not my jaw, not my fists at my sides, ready to crush something. I don't know what frustrates me more. Who Reese is, or who I am.

I want to say something, but I can't seem to know what. It's Reese who speaks first.

"You're not Parker the Terror's son."

Our eyes meet and hold. "No."

"Your father is Scorpion."

"Yes."

She says nothing after that. As if there's no more to say.

EIGHTEEN

WHO I AM

Reese

"Why did you let him bait you?" Brooke asks Remy.

We're in the SUV on our way back to the hotel and the tension after Maverick hasn't at all dissipated. Pete, Riley, and Brooke have all been sending Remy covert, confused glances, and I haven't been able to get past the moment Maverick took my wrist and stared into my eyes, looking raw and frustrated.

Racer is asleep in his car seat. It seems that she's finally asked what the team has been wondering. Everyone except me, because I'm drowning—drowning—in my own thoughts so much I cannot breathe. I'm just staring out the window at the Denver streets, wondering who sewed up the cut above his eye, which looked freshly open and swollen again.

And remembering what it felt like to have his strong arm around me in the park and lay my head on his chest and smell the soap on his shirt. Oh *god*.

Remy just shoots her a smile with Racer's same dimple, except he has two.

"He's Scorpion's spawn!"

He laughs softly and clenches his hand around the back of her neck. "He's a puppy, Brooke. Oz is not what he needs, and no one else will give him the time of day."

She sighs.

"What did his father do?" I blurt out.

I'm all wound up from what I've been hearing. All I know is that him being Scorpion's son is not good. Pete and Riley threw out words like "corrupt" and "poison" like I've never heard.

And then I saw him in the lobby, his cheekbone a little purple and a cut above his eye, and all I know is that he's the same Maverick from the park.

I'm sad.

I'm sad with hopelessness and helplessness, wondering if this means the end of the bone-deep, soul-deep things Maverick makes me feel.

Remington looks at me with interest after my question. I'm sure he knows I know Maverick, beyond tonight. That Maverick and I have . . . well, I don't know what we have. But it means something to me. Maverick means *something* to me.

"On his ol' daddy's list," Pete says, "there's blackmail, extortion, kidnapping—"

"Drugging my sister, harassing our team," Brooke adds fiercely. "His father is the most *despicable* fighter in history. No scruples, he is pure evil incarnate who would do anything to win, no matter who he ran over, drugged, cheated, blackmailed, or—"

"Brooke," Remy cuts her off gently.

She's looking emotional. She drops her head back and is now staring at the car ceiling and blinking her eyes. Remy takes her chin and forces her gaze to his. "Hey. He's a *kid*," he states.

"Scorpion's kid."

"When you're up on the ring," he says firmly, "you're nobody's kid. You're you, your team, and that's it. With Oz in the state he's in, this kid's up there alone."

Brooke takes his hand, kisses his knuckles. "I trust you, Remy," she says thickly, and when the car stops, she scoops Racer out and stares into the car interior when I try to maneuver myself to the door.

"You haven't had time to have any fun here, Reese," she says, stopping me from getting out.

But I shake my head. "Oh, no, I have a blast with Racer."

"Go out with the adults tonight. There's this party hosted by a huge fight lover. Diane's staying in and she offered to sleep over with the little guy." She smiles to convince me and heads away, and, reluctantly, I sit back by my window.

I look at Remy and he's watching me speculatively. I say, "Thank you. For helping him."

He raises his brows, laughs softly again, and says, "I'm not doing it for him, I'm doing it for me."

"And him," I counter.

He says nothing, simply lifts his brows as if surprised by me, then he hops out of the car to walk his son upstairs with Brooke.

Riley breaks the silence in the car. "A part of him misses Scorpion. No one gave him a run for his money like that man did. He doesn't like his wins easy and that's all they've been lately. Which is why he's leaving the Underground."

"What?"

Pete nods. "This is his last season. The final match of the season will be Rem's last."

NINETEEN

CIRCUIT PARTY

Maverick

The two-story Denver home is pulsing with music inside. Fighters I know and fighters I don't know bustle around with their teams, groupies, and the high-end Denver crowd. I'm not talking to anyone. Everyone knows better than to come near me. I suspect I'm putting out some major back-off waves, and there's a wide radius around me that people are steering clear of.

I watch her in a lounge area. She's with a couple of other women she just seemed to meet. The group is talking, but Reese isn't. I watch her tuck her hair behind her ear, and not for a second do I miss the way her eyes slide over to meet mine. Her breasts coming up and down with each breath. Her eyes escape me again. Then come back.

To find me still watching her.

Every time they do this . . . her eyes, come back and hold . . . I get harder and harder.

I'm stone-hard and still waiting to make a move until she can't take my stare anymore.

She shifts in place, then messes with her hair. I want to mess that hair too. I was taking it slow. But now she knows who I am. And I know who she is.

If I don't grab her now, I'll lose her from my grasp.

I don't want more distance between us when there is already too much as far as I'm concerned.

I've wanted her closer. Every second since she said that I was with her.

She's drinking a bottle of water, meeting my eyes across the rim as she takes a sip. She sets it down and stares at me. My blood is heading south faster than a thousand-ton drop. I'm slammed. I probably look like shit. Oz sewed up my cut, and for sure it'll scar this time around from his hands. That scar brings to mind the girl who said, *He's with me.*

I *am* with her. And tonight, she's with me.

She breaks her gaze, at last goes to her feet, and starts down the hall. I push away from the wall and start forward.

She looks back at me, and her eyes widen and her lips part, and I like that they part. I like that she knows, with every step I take, what it means.

Reese

I COULDN'T SIT there anymore. Avoiding the bar, drinking my water while everybody talked about Avenger. And I felt his eyes on me, giving me a thousand knots in my stomach. I glance back, and he's following me. He's like a legend already. The juiciest, naughtiest word on everyone's lips tonight is "Maverick." The fact that he's Scorpion's son is threatening enough, but the fact that he has amazing talent and caught Remy's attention is just cause for more gossip.

I don't know a lot about his father. Only what I've heard from the team, and before tonight, I hadn't really paid close attention.

All I know is that he was a bad man, and that what I feel when I look at Maverick just now should be bad.

Bad.

I head to the ladies' room, safe. Away from his eyes.

But not away from this aching, throbbing *want* inside me.

No sooner do I step inside than Maverick comes in behind me. I hear a pair of startled gasps from the two ladies by the sink.

Maverick opens the door and levels them with a gaze. "Out," he says, firm and oh so quiet.

My eyes widen and a thread of fear and anticipation unfurls inside me.

He narrows his eyes as the girls quickly shuffle outside, then he kicks the door shut. We're alone. So alone there could be nobody else in the world.

He has a massive presence. He's lean and young but acts old and wise, as if he's traveled to the future and knows exactly what he's supposed to become.

What else does he know?

Does he know he will one day kiss me?

Will he still *want* to one day kiss me? Taste me?

"I'm pissed off, and I'm high on the fight, and you're not making it easy to come down from that high." His voice breaks with huskiness.

"No?" I ask in a silky voice.

I don't know where this voice comes from; I never even knew I had it in me to speak like this to a man.

He exhales. He sounds frustrated. *Is* he frustrated? He drags a hand over his hair and then takes a step, leans forward—our eyes level. "No."

"Maybe it's the sugar from the sports drinks."

"It's not the sugar," he dismisses.

He remains without touching me for a moment.

I'm sad and frustrated about what I learned, and I'm frustrated and desperate and feeling reckless and *I don't know*. It's an inexplicable turmoil of feelings as I look at him.

I want him more than I've wanted anything, and I've wanted things that were bad for me before. But I want Maverick Cage now like a sickness.

I don't move when he reaches out.

His hand moves from the back of my head down to my neck, where he squeezes a little, causing his touch to make me tremble all over. His hand is warm and gentle, both familiar and new. I react so strongly my lips part and he notices.

He inhales slowly, and his eyes start darkening and darkening as he spreads his fingers on the back of my neck and slips his hand into my hair. As he pulls me a few inches closer, I catch my own breath. And the breath smells of *him*, hot and spicy.

He exhales through his nostrils and narrows his eyes. It's as if he's losing some form of inner battle. He lowers his head and every inch of my body—from my head to my toes—grips and squeezes in anticipation.

Oh god. I don't even know what to do with my fingers. I clench them at my sides, exhaling a nervous breath.

I'm stunned by how good my body feels as he pulls me closer. Feels good when his fingers touch it. I feel good when he touches me.

I don't know my name. What's going on between us. All I know is Maverick. Maverick looking at my lips. Maverick opening his hand on the small of my back possessively. Maverick leaning his head down. Maverick . . . about to kiss me.

And I want to kiss Maverick.

I know I want Maverick's lips on me.

So when they touch mine—Maverick's lips on me feel like the most incredible, amazing thing that has ever happened in my life.

He's kissing me. . . .

His tongue, dipping inside my mouth. His mouth is possessive; his grip is possessive; *he* is acting so possessive. My tongue has never given me so much pleasure than when it's stroked, slow and sure, by his tongue.

He shifts me closer, his hand splaying on my waist. And he . . . groans. He groans into my mouth and crushes my body against his. And I like possessive Maverick so much I can't think or breathe, only soften my lips so he takes everything.

There's a change in pressure in his grip that speaks to me on such a primitive level, I'm twisted inside. He takes a ragged breath. His nostrils flare a little bit as he seems to fight for control. He wraps his wounded knuckles around my hips and edges me closer.

My tongue slips into his mouth, and he draws it in deeper.

It's like he's pouring all his frustration into this kiss.

I don't want him to get turned off by my inexperience, so I try to rub his tongue back. He groans. He slides his hands over me as if he likes the curve of my ass, and my breasts squish against his chest pleasurably. He edges back, takes a breath.

So many words I've heard before.

Toe-curling.

Panty-melting.

Heart-pounding.

Breathtaking.

I can apply them all right now. To this guy. This moment.

His muscles tighten, and the warmth of personal contact, of our mouths, our bodies closer than close, the pounding of his heart is the pounding of mine, his breath my breath, our space the same . . .

Placing long, calloused fingers along my back—a rough touch is not supposed to feel this delicious, this feathery, this *good*.

Lust. It's not soft like the touch of a raindrop. It's not easy like floating aimlessly on the water. It's weighted, and heavy, a spark that catches on the forest of your body. A wildfire.

I have never been marked by lust like this.

I can't speak.

Even Maverick's voice is extremely thick right now. "Tate and his wife left earlier."

"Yes. I promised her I'd be careful. I have pepper spray."

He smiles, then scans my face, his eyes as dark as I've ever seen them. "Did you tell them you'd meet them later at your hotel?"

I nod.

"Do you want this like I do?" He looks at my lips, and then into my eyes as he curls his fingers around the back of my neck and gives me a gentle squeeze. "Do you?"

Say no, Reese.

This can go nowhere.

I open my mouth and say, "More. I want it more than you."

He exhales, then he leans his forehead against mine and looks deeply into my eyes. "That's impossible on every level, I'm breaking every existing record."

He eases back and looks genuinely tormented by this same lust I feel, and I say, "Maverick, I haven't done this before."

"I know, Reese, but god, I need it to be me." He presses his mouth to me and groans rather than kisses me, groans and embraces me against him and whispers in my ear, "Please let it be me."

We start kissing feverishly again. I push my tongue into his mouth and grab his hair, suddenly needing him more than he needs me. He tears his lips free, stares down at me with liquid metal in his eyes, takes my hand, unlocks the bathroom, and leads us out of there.

❤ ❤ ❤

MAVERICK SITS BESIDE me in the back of a cab. Devouring me with his eyes. And I sit here. Devouring him with mine. My diaphragm hurts when I try to breathe. He's cloaked in shadows, but some of the lights outside fall on his neck, his square jaw. His lips. As I grow accustomed to the dark, I slowly study the clear-cut lines of his features. He's so handsome with those platinum eyes and a secret expression, dark and brooding. He looks like he just committed murder and is daring the world to come lock him up. No, actually . . .

He looks like he's ready to take a girl to bed and fuck the living daylights out of her.

God, and that girl is *me*.

To lead me out of the cab, he takes my hand.

My hand, in his hand.

I like his touch so much I feel an internal combustion from this alone.

Tomorrow, I won't be a virgin anymore. I wanted to wait for it to mean something. I wanted to feel beautiful and to give it to Miles. And instead . . . I need this like I need oxygen right now.

His grip is strong and rough, like Maverick Cage.

I follow him across the lobby, and his grip is as firm and steady as his stride, and my heart is pounding like a living drum inside my chest, and wherever it is he's taking me, I can't believe how much I want to go.

We take the elevators and he leads me into a room on the second-to-top floor. I step inside as he shuts and locks the door behind me. It's a nice room that I'm sure he's easily affording now, thanks to the fighting money. His duffel bag sits in a corner. It's misleading to think that's all he owns. That everything he is and wants is tucked inside the bag. Because when I turn to look at him, I know he is so much more. I know he wants so much more.

And I want him more than I've wanted anything.

He starts forward. My knees grow weak. I want to take a step back but I hold my ground because I want his touch *more* than I want to take a step back. I hate him for making me feel like this, and I love him for making me feel so alive too. The air crackles between us as he stops a few feet away. Pure anticipation floods me. I stick my chin a little higher, meeting his gaze, holding it.

He reaches out to grab the back of my neck. He sets my nerve endings on fire beneath his fingertips. He never takes his eyes off mine as he draws me the rest of the way to him. I don't miss the meaning. He brings me to him—he doesn't come to me. It excites me and I don't know why.

He bends and nibbles my lip, barely getting started, his head bent to mine. Reason checks out as waves of feelings rush through me, and I feel my hands fill with his hair, my throat close with things I want to say that I have never said—dirty things, sexy things, and intimate things, and just . . . things. I can't. I feel rawer with this man than with anyone.

He walks me to the bed, and when he sits me on the edge, the rough fabric of his jeans grazes my jean-clad thighs; I can feel his hard quads beneath. Liquid fire warms my body, consuming. My heart skipping, jumping, fluttering.

His fingers brush over the tips of my nipples and shoot a delicious shockwave through me. A seductive smile touches his mouth. His fucking perfect mouth.

I shouldn't be here.

I shouldn't want him like this.

But not a single part of me—of the ones that are working right now—cares.

I grab him, and the muscles in his shoulders tense under my fingers, and the air is burning, primal. When we kiss, there's no hesitation or uncertainty. Our lips fit perfectly, his body crushes me into the bed, his erection against my stomach, and as he's kissing me, he doesn't tease, or play, he just takes.

My fingers slide over the back of his neck, and it's warm beneath my fingers, and I want him to touch more, touch everything at the same time. He eases his hand to the small of my back, and I feel alive, the touch firm but achingly gentle, intimate, possessive, and our control starts slipping when he shifts and fits his erection between my legs. I can feel him through my jeans. His fingers skim over my top, then he pulls it off.

I unhook my bra, discarding it.

There's no one else here, just us, and I am a hostage to this, this lust, as he fills his mouth with a breast and shifts again, the move bringing his hips closer, nestling his erection deeper.

My eyelids shut. He handles my breast a little roughly, sucking the nipple. Stars flicker across my eyelids and I convulse from the pleasure. He eases back and jerks off his T-shirt and kicks his jeans aside, and I can't believe how good his skin feels under my fingers.

God, he's so gorgeous, my eyes ache when I look at him. His muscles hard as granite, hot as fire, smooth as velvet.

He's sucking my breasts again, both. Hungrily as he spreads above me. Soon we're all hot flesh and hands and mouths on the bed. And he's prepping me with his fingers. I don't need prepping; I'm so ready I can't see, my vision is hazy, and all I know is how warm and male he smells, how much I love the way he's breathing fast, how totally he melts me in every spot he puts his mouth on.

Then Maverick reaches out and puts on a condom. And I devour him with my eyes, my first time seeing a guy. I will never be able to love the look of one like I love the look of Maverick, naked and hard.

"I'll make it good for you, Reese," he promises as he stretches out his long muscles above me, and I nod breathlessly and touch the scar on his face.

He groans and shuts his eyes, and then Maverick Cage is kissing me. Saying *Reese* into my mouth.

Maverick Cage prodding me open with his fingers again.

Maverick Cage just growled.

He parts my legs wider with his hand. I feel his fingers slide, first one, then two. Then he's plunging deeper and slower. Rubbing my clit with his thumb. I'm so wet I hear his fingers moving inside me as his lips graze my ear. He presses a kiss there and then he looks down at me, heavy-lidded.

"God, Reese." He ducks to lave my breasts with his tongue as his fingers plunge deeper. Maverick eases back again to watch me as he touches me. "Look at you."

He's so hot above me. He's so tender when he touches me.

He looks just as undone as I am.

I come quickly, and while I'm coming, he settles between my legs and I can't breathe.

I feel him there. So hot and so big and so hard.

I tense up in anticipation, waiting.

He hesitates for a painful few seconds, then he scans my face and clenches his jaw. "This is your first time. You should be treated right, on a nice bed with nice sheets—"

I cover his mouth with my hand. "No," I plead anxiously, searching his darkened silver eyes with an ache in my chest and between my thighs.

I should be afraid. I had always been afraid, wanting the right moment, the right guy. *This* is the moment and *this* is the guy and I'm not scared. All I'm scared of is this never happening between us.

He grabs my face in one hand and uses it to open my mouth, and he kisses me, his tongue thrusting wetly into my mouth.

I claw at his skin, down his back, shifting beneath him as I slide my hands down the small of his back to grab his muscular ass and urge him closer.

He nips my lips on a loss of control and watches me as he starts going in. My vision blurs. My body burns, from where he enters and to my heart. It's everything he's giving me and everything he's taking. Every time I said no was for him, every time I wondered about it was for this. "Oh," I whisper in his ear, surprised at the feel of him.

He stops, cups my face in one hand, and looks at me, a little raw and a lot hot. "You okay?"

"More than okay." I nod so fast I'm dizzy.

We're both breathing hard. I'm quaking with need and his body vibrates with self-control. Maverick's eyes smolder, but I'm the one on fire. He sucks one of my breasts, and I buck from the pleasure. There is pressure as he advances, and heat and length and him, pulsing and alive and perfect and male and right now mine. So mine. So wrong. And so, so right.

He braces his arms on either side of my head as he withdraws. I feel my body clutch around him in the most exquisite way when he slowly drives back in.

It feels even better this time, and he goes an inch deeper. "Oh god," I gasp as I rear up, biting his shoulder, clenching one of my arms around the back of his neck.

"Tell me," he gruffs in my ear, caressing my breast in one palm, watching me like he *needs* it to be good. "Do you want more?"

I can't speak; I'm too busy trying to hold back another orgasm, waiting for him to go there with me.

But I nod wildly up and down.

He moves his hips and enters me some more, his jaw tight, nostrils flaring, eyes heavy. I can tell he's trying to take it slow for me and that it's taking every ounce of his willpower to do so.

"How's that?" Taking my face back in his hand, he kisses me wildly. "You sweet, gorgeous little thing."

"Oh god. You feel so good, Maverick."

He's big and wide and engulfing me, breath by breath, inch by inch. I'm dying an exquisite death. My breath rasps in my throat. "More. Don't stop."

He grits his teeth, his eyes brimming with passion as he pushes the last of the way in, his jaw squarer than ever, his neck straining with his effort, every muscle on his torso taut as he takes me.

"Oh god," I say in wonder as my orgasm starts quickly building. I grab his shoulders and press my face into his neck.

When he goes all the way in, I stop breathing. He's inside me and I can feel him inside me, thick and pulsing, stretching. He groans and clutches me to him. "God, hold on to me," he says, starting to slowly move in and out of me.

"Maverick," I rasp, and rock my hips.

He's almost crushing me against his body, moving his hips faster. He watches my face for any signs of pain as he withdraws and thrusts all the way in . . . again . . . and again . . . and again.

"*Maverick*," I gasp, and arch and writhe, rubbing my fingers all over his muscles. We move together, and his breath is my breath, his body is my body, and we're all instinct. I'm only feeling, hazy and raw and alive.

I can't find words to say how I feel, how I need, how glorious he feels, smells, looks right now.

He grabs a fistful of hair and keeps my head in place as his lips come down to fasten on mine. I expected them to be crushing, but when they touch mine, they're achingly hungry and gentle as he moves inside my body. I feel full when he's inside, so full I can't breathe. I exhale when he leaves me. Then I hold my breath and rock my hips anxiously because I want him in me again.

He drives forward, no hesitation now. He's instantly picking up speed, his eyes pools of liquid fire, his steel eyes, and I'm flying. My body sweaty, tinged pink; this man, who kisses me like he needs me, looking down at me. Metallic eyes cut and pierce me.

"Still okay?" he asks.

His voice, so gruff and low, does a number on me.

Pushes me to the edge.

I'm writhing for him, dying for him. "Oh god, more than okay."

He's taking me now, deep and powerful. "Am I hurting you?"

Maverick Cage. The Avenger.

We're a part of each other. No teams, no past, no future.

I rasp out, "Only in the best ways."

He increases speed, stroking his hand over my breasts greedily. I feel his thighs flex as he moves, his biceps, slowing down into a powerful rhythm that pushes me over the edge.

I come. It's violent and fast, taking over me. Causing me to make a sound—a gasp—and to twist beneath him, and to clench and relax, and to lose my vision as stars flicker behind my eyes. And I realize he slowed down to watch me, then he hungrily kisses my ear, presses his nose to the back of it, and comes with a soft growl, his body jerking over me. He exhales and presses a kiss to the side of my neck, then the top of my head, and when he inches back, we stare at each other.

I don't know who looks more intensely at the other.

And he smiles at me. His kiss is wet, hungered, as if I didn't just come in his arms. As if he wants to encompass as much of my mouth as possible. He raises his head and looks down at me.

"How long do you have until you need to get back?"

"A few more hours."

He unwinds one muscle at a time from my deliciously relaxed body, rolls to his back, and then stares at the ceiling.

"Did you know who I was?" He's staring at the ceiling, a muscle in his jaw working fast.

"No. Did you?"

"No," he says.

I swallow. "But you know now," I whisper.

"A part of me wishes I didn't."

I roll to my side to look at him and then slowly lift my leg, and entwine it over his.

He turns his face away as if to get some semblance of control back, exhales, and then pulls me to his side and rubs his jaw against the top of my head. "Reese," he whispers in my ear. "You shouldn't be here with me right now." And then he squeezes me, as if he wants me to be his and is frustrated that I'm not.

"I like it here."

It's raining outside, the sound soothing on the windows and hitting the street and the rooftops.

I want to say something. What are we doing?

Do we know?

I think we don't.

I think we're here because it feels right. Because we are impossibly, irreparably drawn to each other.

I think it won't last.

So I just lie here and make this one moment last.

On impulse, I reach down to my jeans on the floor and pull out the penny, showing it to him.

He looks at it in my palm.

Why haven't you cashed it in? his silver eyes seem to ask as he takes it between his thumb and forefinger.

Because it feels like that's all I'll get from you, this unspoken promise, this blank check, and I don't want to give up all I'll get from you, I think.

I just take it from his hand and tuck it into my pocket, saying silently, *I won't give this back to you. I'm keeping this.*

MAVERICK LOOKS LIKE a gourmet meal on the bed, all male, testosterone-laden, dark, and tattooed. And asleep. I watch him, trying not to make noise as I quietly get dressed—and I try not to remember how good it was. How fucking great it was. I am simply doing my best to get dressed and get out of his personal space and back into the safety of mine. Where I'm not the one dating a fighter, sleeping with a fighter, dangerously close to being in love with a fighter. The one fighter I can't have.

I'm acting recklessly. The other times in my life I've been reckless, I've paid such a huge price, I'm still recovering.

I shouldn't have admitted I wanted this.

I shouldn't have followed him out.

I shouldn't be here at all.

But at the same time, I can't think of anywhere else I'd rather be but here.

I look at the tattoo on his back as he sleeps prostrate on the bed, one arm haphazardly stuck under the pillow, his ass hard and muscled, the backs of his legs dusted with hairs. And my eyes go back to the tattoo, the most beautiful tattoo I've ever seen.

It's a burning phoenix, I now realize, with a black scorpion riding on its back. It almost feels as if the weight of the scorpion is dragging the phoenix into the flames, or maybe the phoenix is the one lifting the scorpion from the fire. Reviving it.

I watch the tattoo and the way it moves, like the feathers of the phoenix, rippling as he seems to sense my gaze and props up on one arm and turns. I step back into the shadows and see him groggily drop his head down, and quietly I tiptoe to the door, making sure I have my penny in my pocket.

A HALF HOUR later, I tiptoe into the Tates' three-bedroom suite and make my way through the darkness into my room. I lock the door to keep Racer from coming in without notice, strip to my panties, and slip into bed, sighing as I hug my pillow. I shove it under my head and stare up at the ceiling, reliving every moment and every kiss and the way his body moved above me.

Did we just do it?

Did he love it as much as I think he did?

I stare at the ceiling, smiling like a dope.

I dream of the phoenix in flames, burning me, and I wake up, sweating, to the buzzing of my phone. Maverick doesn't have my number, but I'm still breathless when I pick it up because he's the first thing I thought of. "Hello?" I ask hopefully.

"I thought of texting, but I really wanted to hear your voice," I hear on the other end.

"Oh, hi," I say, leaning back on my pillow as the reality of the reckless hot sex I had last night comes crashing in when I recognize the voice.

"Well, you don't sound too excited, Reesey," he teases, pretending to be sad. "Have you already forgotten about me?"

It's Miles.

TWENTY

TRAINING WITH RIPTIDE

Maverick

I wake up and do a body check of what hurts. Head. Chest. Arms. Shoulders. Back. Quads. Calves. Inhaling, I turn my head into my pillow. Hell, my pillow smells good. My cock wakes up. I reach to the side of the bed for her, smelling more of the jasmine on my pillow. It's the scent of *her*. The bed's empty under my hand, and I open my eyes and scan my hotel room. Reese is gone.

I peer at the time, then sit up and curse under my breath. I head over to shower and pull out my training gear. If Tate's ready to teach me some lessons, I'll get ready to dish out his. In the ring.

He's waiting impatiently when I arrive.

Tate's an aggressive fighter; he doesn't wait. Neither do I. I've seen his tapes. I know his moves. He started boxing in his early years and his endurance has been unmatched in the Underground. No weakness. No mercy. Fast, strong, and precise. He doesn't waste swings. More than half of his swings always land. My father swung much more, but they were wasted efforts. He would wear out and leave Tate fresh as spring rain, beating him to a pulp. I'm not making the same mistakes my father did.

The gym is vacant save for the three members of his team. His coach, the coach's second, and his PA. I nod at the three and spot Tate by the bags. I know when a guy's ticked, and he's ticked now. Punching the speed bag like he's out for murder.

I shake my arms and shoulders to loosen them up, pull my hoodie over my head. "I'm here."

"Fucking late. I would kick your ass for that alone if I weren't kicking it anyway."

I grit my teeth and scowl. He turns to grab something from the wall and looks at me, scowling too, and tosses me headgear.

I catch it and toss it aside. "I won't be needing that."

"Fine with me. I don't mind busting your nose." He climbs into the ring from one side, and I climb in from the other. "Your father and I go way back," he says.

"It's because of you he's in a piece-of-shit hospital bed."

"Is that what happened?" His eyes gleam menacingly. "He did that himself."

One of his team members comes over to tape up my hands and then shoves the gloves on me.

At Tate's corner, outside the ropes, his coach whistles. "You two get some headgear on. *Stat.*"

Tate's lips curl rebelliously, and he looks at me with challenge in his eyes.

I smile back, a feral curl of my lips.

We tap gloves.

No headgear.

I jab. He swings his arm, blocks the hit, leaps back, and I jab again, blocked again.

We space apart and jump in place, shaking our shoulders, loosening up. I pull my gloves back up, narrow my eyes, and he asks, "You think you're the shit because you're fast and strong? I got news for you. I'm faster, I'm stronger, and I'm disciplined. Your coach isn't doing you any favors."

"He's in my corner, and that's enough for me."

He swings, I duck fast and come up behind him. He straightens and faces me again. "If you settle for that, then you should settle for second place."

"What the fuck. You want me to win?"

"I want a good fight. I like keeping things real. Reminds me I'm a man. Mortal."

"I want to be a legend. Legends never die. Even if they die alone."

He swings again, and I duck, come up, and jab three times.

He blocks repeatedly, then hooks with his right; I deflect. He grins and jabs again. I block, then I duck before he puts me up against the ropes, and I head back to center. He follows.

"To be a legend you need to fall seven times, get up eight," he says.

I remember a final a few years ago when my father kicked Tate to a pulp. "Or not fall at all."

He backs up his arm and then smacks the smirk right off me. "Before you stop falling, you need to embrace the fact that you're going to hit the ground."

I clean the blood from my mouth, glowering.

We take positions again, and he watches me as if waiting for my next move as we start dancing around, jumping, waiting for the other to strike.

"Do you want the headgear now?"

I lunge and start hitting, and he blocks, deflects, blocks. "Fuck you," I grit out.

"Getting angry doesn't help. You control the anger, not let it control you."

I want to prove him wrong, I loop out my arm and aim for his head.

He ducks and hooks, his knuckles cracking into my jaw. I spurt blood and bounce against the ropes.

I shake my head, wipe the blood away, grit my teeth, and straighten, narrowing my eyes. "My turn," I growl, and I swing. My fist connects: a kidney punch.

He blocks my next hit, frowning in thought. "You're cocky for someone who just lost yesterday."

He jabs.

I dive my upper body to the side, evading. "You got to play it to become it."

"I'm the champion, not you."

"You won't live forever, champ."

He jabs three times, then leaps back, flexes his arm, and looks at it.

"Muscle memory. You hit enough times, you fight on instinct; part of your brain works on your assault, the other is focused on the other's assault. Let your muscle memory work for you and consciously stay focused on your opponent's eyes."

I laugh mockingly. "I don't need your pointers."

"Go back home to daddy, then."

"When I'm finished with you." I punch him, then raise my left hook and connect hard enough to stun him.

He raises his head, shakes it to clear it, and wipes blood from his nose. I catch my breath, satisfied I got some blood. At least I won't be the only one with an ice pack tonight.

He sees the blood on his arm and looks at me, impressed.

"TIME!" his coach yells out from the corner. "You two won't have shit for the fight if you keep up this nonsense."

Tate grins at him, then turns back and glowers at me. "You get enough?"

"Barely warming up here." I squint the blood out of one eye and raise my gloves. "Come get it, *Riptide*," I growl.

We go at it for three hours. His team is pissed with him. We end up bloodied and losing pounds of water from sweat. His team comes over with electrolyte drinks, and he tosses one my way with the crook of his arm.

"Same time, a day before the Atlanta fight. You have a lot to learn." He yanks off his gloves.

I say nothing. Out of pride, I shoot him a fuck-you look. But I know I'll be there.

I'M PROSTRATE ON the bed, ice packs wrapped all around my body. I don't get this guy. I don't get him at all. I'm being set up. I have to be. I wonder if Reese is in on it. If she's meant to be my distraction.

Fuck, she is.

I groan and take out my phone. I want to text her, but I don't have her number. I want to text somebody who gives a shit. My mom? No way. I text Oz.

You alive?

I am.

Where the fuck are you?

I want her to come over.

Can't get what you want, asshole, that mean little voice tells me.

I glance at the pail of ice water on the floor by the bed, toss my phone aside, and shove my knuckles back into the ice. Then I lift my eyes to my father's gloves, letting my anger fuel me.

TWENTY-ONE

THE AVENGER IS CLOSE

Reese

I haven't seen him since that night. I didn't go to the gym in Denver again, coward that I am. I've been stressing over the possibility of Remy finding out and deciding not to train with Maverick ever again. I've been battling the urge to seek out Maverick against feelings of betrayal to the Tates, to Miles, the logical but painstaking truth that our friendship is *more* than a friendship but probably won't go anywhere.

Now we're in Dallas, five days after I gave him my V card. I'm trying to focus on the fact that Miles texted to let me know he, Gabe, and Avery are coming to the semifinals. But the Avenger is causing a stir.

I heard the team discussing how he knocked out a few difficult opponents and ended up one away from fighting Remy again on the last fight. It's like he's a legend simply by trying to avenge the Scorpion alone. He's a contender. He's getting respect, admiration, and a lot of fear.

I couldn't bear to listen.

The thought of Maverick fighting Remy, who's part of my

family, is starting to be painful. So instead, as the team talked, I focused on Racer's trains, the perfect therapy if you ask me.

I'm at a Dallas gym. Today my conversation with myself has been focusing on how great it is that he's not here so I can actually feel calm as I exercise and also stay focused on supporting Team Remy. I'm *glad* when I head over to day care, ready to clear my mind with some good old Racer fun, when I get a text from Brooke.

Take the day 😊 R and I are taking Racer to the zoo

You sure?

Yes, picking him up right now

OK HAVE FUN!

Ending up standing in the middle of the sidewalk halfway to the day care, I suddenly don't know what to do with the rest of my day.

For some reason I find myself traveling the exact same path I came from. I push open the gym doors, greet the receptionist, and am aware of my heart starting to flip-flop in my chest as I slip inside. I pass the treadmills, bicycles, the weight section, heading toward the mats at the end and the boxing bags. I scan the area where I'd find him. There are several guys at the bags now. None of them are as big, or mysterious. Or hot.

He's gone from my life.

Maybe he doesn't want to see me ever again. I'm a Dumas, after all.

He's probably training somewhere with Oz.

I wait a couple minutes more before realizing I'm just acting stupid, holding out for him like this when he's clearly not showing.

I stride outside, then stare at the buildings across the street. The heat has been painful these past few days, but there's a breeze today, a partly cloudy sky.

Not ready to go back to the hotel yet, I wander to the park until I see a big shady patch of grass under one tree. In every park we go to, I find the perfect tree and this becomes my and Racer's perfect spot. I head there with my book and Racer's snacks and spread out my blanket, sit down, and pick up where I last stopped reading.

"Hey."

I hear his voice clearly, exquisitely clearly, and raise my gaze up dark torn jeans and a gray T-shirt straining at the shoulders with the lean muscles beneath.

Our eyes connect and my brain flashes to him holding me. *Am I hurting you . . ?*

His tattoo rippling . . .

His eyes flashing with passion . . .

He shoves his hands into his pockets and just looks at me. And those eyes are looking at me with caution and wariness now. *Maverick is gauging me.*

"How long do you have until you need to get back?" he asks, scanning my face as if for the answer.

I don't even know if my voice will work when I open my mouth. "A few hours. Mom and Dad took Racer to the zoo."

He unwinds and drops down beside me, lies on his back, and then stares at the tree branches and part of the sky. "I've been hitting a park every day. Didn't know which one I'd find you in."

"You have?"

He's staring at the sky, jaw tight. "Yeah. I didn't want to ask Tate."

"He wouldn't have told you if you'd asked. And I might have been hiding as I . . . processed."

"Processed what?"

I set my book aside, my eyes gobbling him up like breakfast, lunch, and dinner. Then I glance at the blanket. "How intense it was."

He shuts his eyes, exhaling and clenching his fingers.

"Do you want my number?"

He sits up and props his elbows on his knees. He nods. "I don't have my phone on me."

I search Racer's bag for one of my lipsticks and then I look at Maverick for permission.

He looks back at me, watching as I curl my hand around his wrist. It's thick and strong. I press the tip of the lipstick to his arm and write my number down. In coral lipstick, on his forearm. And it's the most erotic thing I've ever done.

He watches me tuck the lipstick back into the bag, then remains without touching me for a moment.

He stares down at his arm. Then he turns his face away, exhales, and turns back to me. "Reese," he whispers mournfully. "I lost control that night." He looks at my mouth, as if he wants it. And I want him to take it.

I shouldn't want him to but I do.

"I liked it," I say. *And I liked sleeping in your arms, if only for a second.*

I hold my breath, realizing what I just admitted—*no, Reese, take it back!*—and I don't move when he reaches out.

"Me too," he says.

And god, I want Maverick's lips again.

Hot and strong, waking me up from whatever sleep spell I've been in.

It won't go anywhere, Reese!

He slips his hand under my hair and his fingertips caress my scalp. "You totally bailed on me."

"You knew I had to leave."

"Yeah, I knew, but you have a blanking effect on my head. I'm sure you know this because you're smiling that crooked smile of yours right now."

"Crooked?!"

He smiles a little, cups the back of my neck, and draws me closer as he lies back on the blanket.

"Maverick . . . what happened . . ." I begin.

He pulls me a little closer. I put my hands on his chest to push myself back but end up just leaving them there, feeling the flat planes of his chest underneath as he murmurs, "What happened what?"

"What?"

"Are you going to tell me how mind-blowing it was or are you going to let me kiss you?"

One more kiss . . . oh god, I'm going to hell. I'm the worst person I know. The most reckless. The most intoxicated by Maverick Cage.

It's pure impulse. I'm burning and aching and I want to be close. Closer than close. I want to be his tattoo and the woman in his bed and the thing in his thoughts he can't quite force out and *this* girl, with him, kissing in the park.

"What happened . . ." I begin, *was wonderful and impulsive and frightening and reckless,* and I lean over, and I press my lips to his tentatively. He cups the back of my head, his tongue sliding into my mouth.

He groans softly and pulls me above him, grabs my ass. And I love his hands, squeezing, as our tongues start sparring, and I know I can't keep doing this, that this won't go anywhere, and it just makes me hungrier, my fingers fisting his shirt, my tongue pushing his, a moan leaving me.

His tongue, slow and leisurely, tastes me. There's a dog barking nearby, and people passing by the walkway, and when I make an effort to pull away, Maverick just holds my head and angles his, devouring me harder.

His hand slips under the back of my T-shirt. His fingers skim my skin, they're hot, calloused, and so perfect, I'm a whole shiver.

He rolls us around and sets me down on the grass, kissing me some more and slipping his hand down to encompass my waist, his thumb stroking my abdomen. "Reese." He breathes against my skin.

I blink up at the sky, then let my eyelids flutter shut as the feel of his lips trailing my neck overcomes reason.

"I don't take what you gave to me lightly. I don't want you to think that I did."

"I wanted to."

"And I want you." Maverick's voice is extremely thick right now. "The guy back home. He kiss you like that?"

"No."

And he just grins. He looks down at me.

"But . . ." I sit up then. *Reese, stop this.* "But we can't . . . you know. Do that again."

His eyes darken. "I think we should do it more often." He stares at me, waiting for me to say something, and I can only swallow nervously.

He signals to my book. "What are you reading?" He puts his arm around my shoulders. I stiffen them but somehow melt inside.

"A book."

"Really?" He lifts his brows, and I laugh and tentatively tuck a loose strand that came undone from my ponytail behind my ear.

"I've been hearing a lot about you," I say.

"All lies." He cracks a smile.

"You're kicking ass."

His expression loses its humor, and he stares straight ahead, thoughtful. "I'm going to kick Tate's ass, Reese."

I sit up, staring away. "I don't like to think about it."

"You root for him out of principle, I don't expect you to root for me."

I stay silent.

"I need to do this for me," he explains with a fierce and determined gleam in his eyes.

"Maverick . . ." I wrap my arms around myself. It's not easy for me to find someone I connect with. I haven't ever felt the kind of connection to a stranger that I felt when I started interacting with Maverick "the Avenger" Cage. "That night with you meant more to me than you'll ever know," I whisper. "I shouldn't have kissed you just now. I'm trying to find myself, and I can't do that if I'm lost in you."

He takes my chin and the touch triggers heat all over me. "I won't let you get lost," he promises.

"The Tates are my family. I don't think we should do what we did again. And Miles is coming to town next month."

"Miles, that's his name?"

I nod and glance helplessly at him.

The liquid look in his gaze starts to harden right before my eyes. "Yeah, I get it. He's not my father's son." He grits his jaw, his eyes dark, then we stare at each other. He starts to stand, but then, as if by impulse, his hand engulfs my cheek as he grabs my face and kisses me, almost punishing and hot. I stay there, melted, as he gets to his feet and walks away.

I exhale and shut my eyes and touch my lips.

It's over. We won't do it again. Right? Did he agree or not?

Yes, because he was angry.

I'm sure we will be civil but . . . apart. And I can't stand it. And suddenly I can't remember why we can't, why it's wrong.

Or why I wrote my phone number on his arm.

TWENTY-TWO

NO MORE

Maverick

I ran eight *MILES*, and it's midnight now.

Miles. Miles. Miles.

I stare at myself in the mirror in the hotel bathroom, looking deep into my eyes. And I smash my fist into the glass.

TWENTY-THREE

BROKEN KNUCKLES

Maverick

The next day we're training, Oz and I. We're training in a storage unit he got us for the day. The door's wide open, and he hung the bags from the iron beams in the ceiling. I'm using my left, over and over. Hitting. Listening to the sounds. *Smack, thud, thud, smack, poof.*

"Whoa, stop, stop. Where's your right?" Oz demands when he shakes himself out of a nap. The guy brought a fold-out chair and has just sat there for hours after we gobbled down two pizzas, one each. I might have had a few extra slices of his.

"I'm trying to strengthen my left," I lie.

He scowls at me. "You got a great left. Your left is almost as good as your right."

"Keyword 'almost,' " I point out. I aim for the bag.

"You hurt your right?" He comes over and grabs my right and I pull it free before he can pull off my glove.

"I fucked up, all right," I growl. "It'll be back to normal in no time."

"You fucked your right. During the season. When?"

"Doesn't matter."

"When?"

"Last night. I broke something."

"You broke YOUR KNUCKLES, THAT'S WHAT! You fuck your right on a temper tantrum? What the fuck? Am I gonna have another Scorpion on my hands? Huh?" He pushes me, and I let him, just stand there and let him have his tantrum. He gives up and stalks back to his chair.

"You might as well not go to the fight without your right," he growls.

"I'm not missing a fight."

"You should've thoughta that before busting your knuckles. This because of Tate? A girl?"

I hit the bag, then lower my arms and stare at the ground, inhaling deeply.

"Her name's Reese," I say, under my breath, frowning up at the heavy bag. "Reese Dumas."

He swears under his breath. Then he pulls out the flask. "Stay away, Maverick."

"How about you stay away from that flask, Oz?"

"I can't."

"So we understand each other." I get into position and start hitting. "I'm not quitting her." Then I test my right and jab the bag, and pain shoots up my arm. I yank my glove off.

I stare morosely at my hand, testing my fingers and curling them in.

"Members of the Tate team," Oz says, leaning forward in his seat, "even if they're not blood related, they're closer than if they were. She's not going to want to even look at you, Maverick."

I toss my right glove aside and keep hitting with my left. *I don't think we should do what we did again . . . the Tates are my family . . . Miles is coming . . .*

"I don't want to see you make a fool of yourself for a damn Wendy!"

I stop. Then slide my gaze to Oz and narrow my eyes. "She's no Wendy."

The frustration's building. I go back to hitting and I'm hitting the bag hard.

"Heard you trained with him," Oz says.

"Yeah. Would've told you if you'd been half-awake." I don't stop hitting.

"This means you won't need me now, huh."

"No. Just means I get more chances to find out how to beat him."

"He's getting the same chance to be sure how to beat *you*," he growls.

He swigs and stares mournfully out the storage unit door and I stare at the heavy bag and keep on hitting until my muscles burn out, and then I keep going.

TWENTY-FOUR
PATCHING UP MAVERICK

Reese

My mom's been calling, but I haven't picked up the phone. I'm afraid she'll hear my voice and she knows me too well, she will know there's something *haunting* my thoughts.

I finally cave in when Brooke knocks on my door. "Your mom called me. She's worried."

I was packing things into my suitcase, since we leave to the next location tomorrow—Atlanta. Racer is in a deep sleep in his room, all packed and ready, except for a little red train he likes to tuck under his pillow at night. "What did you tell her?"

"That everything's fine. Isn't it?"

I nod.

Brooke hesitates for a moment, then gives me a really warm smile. "Reese, I'm here if you want to talk."

All my life I've wanted to have someone to talk to other than my parents and now that I have her, I'm not sure that I can talk to her about what I most need to. "I'm good," I assure her.

She smiles again.

"I'll call her," I add.

"Great," she says, relieved, and gives me a thumbs-up before she leaves. I decide to call and soothe my mother's fears. "Mom, how are you?"

"Worried."

I sigh. "Don't be; I'm fine."

"You promise? Tell me you're making good choices, Reese. And that you're staying strong? We can come get you."

"NO! MOM!" I don't want to leave, I don't want to go back home, where I'm always the old Reese, where I can't grow and learn and discover and experience. "Mom, I'M GREAT HERE. I'm . . . just in a blossoming process and I need time solo, okay."

"Butterfly?" she asks hopefully.

"No," I say with a wan smile, "still a caterpillar."

"Tell me what you've been up to."

I tell her about Racer and my diet and the Tates, how great they are, and the team, and that Miles is coming over.

"Oh, this makes me happy! Don't forget to call every night or two, three at most. Okay, caterpillar?"

"Okay, Mom."

I know she cares, but when she doubts me, I feel hopeless, like I'll never be able to gain her trust again even though I have been slowly earning mine.

When I hang up, I make a note on my phone—CALL MOTHER.

Brooke peers into my room.

"Your mom's happy now? She was pretty worried."

I nod. "I guess it's her favorite thing to do."

"Well, you're her only daughter. This is why I absolutely want Racer to have a sibling. It's healthy to have a mother's obsession distributed."

I laugh, then stare wistfully at her. Wondering if I can ask her more about Maverick. I know Remy has been training with him. And every day it's torture not to ask.

"Is it the boy back home?" she asks me, as if reading my mind.

I open my mouth, wanting a friend, a female friend, but what do I say? Maverick Cage? I am obsessed. We had sex. I think of him, often. And I think of him as my friend even when I don't speak to him for days. I just don't understand it myself. I'm afraid to say it out loud. I'm afraid to make another big mistake, something that can hurt my family again.

So I just smile at Brooke and let her think that it is the boy back home. When in fact it's the son of the Black Scorpion.

❤ ❤ ❤

WE'RE IN ATLANTA, staying at a nice hotel in the heart of the city. Brooke and I are having dinner. I haven't seen Maverick since the park. Eight days plus a lot of long little minutes and seconds. He's been training with Remy, and Brooke hasn't really seen Remy either.

We've both brushed our teeth and slipped on our pajamas. Brooke wears T-shirts with little shorts to sleep, and I'm wearing my soft cotton lounge pants in light blue, like my eyes, and the matching top. We rejoin in the living room to read and talk when we hear low male voices—and what sounds a lot like cursing—outside.

The door swings open and the guys appear: Pete, Riley, Coach, and two tall, dark-haired fighters, banged-up and bloody, their T-shirts plastered to their chests. Brooke's mouth opens, then shuts, then opens again as she gazes at her husband. "Did you guys fight?"

"Yeah."

"Thought you were training?"

I'm staring breathlessly at Maverick.

Maverick in our hotel room.

Maverick in exercise clothes, sweaty, and . . . *Maverick.*

"Change of plans." Remy stalks across the room and says, "Help me patch him up."

"Let him bleed out, that'll take care of it," Coach says. Pete and Riley shuffle into the penthouse behind him.

"Patch him up so I can kick his ass again," Remy repeats.

He shoots Maverick a meaningful look and Maverick says, "Recess is over for you."

Brooke looks at me and I head to Maverick. "He can use my shower."

Brooke nods, and I don't know what possessed me to speak, because Maverick looks at me. And I'm sure that by the way we're both staring at each other, they all know we had sex, that we had sex and every day I remember it. "Come with me," I say, my voice odd.

He follows me to the bedroom. I shut the door, then go and open the shower and ask, "What happened?"

"Nothing big."

"Remington Tate never trains with anyone. Maverick . . . it's big."

He jerks off his damp T-shirt, and as he crosses the room toward the bathroom, he chucks my chin and looks at me with a half smile, his eyes absorbing me with quiet intensity. "No big deal," he assures me, and he steps into the bathroom and the door clicks shut.

I sigh and pick up his shirt. Maverick is the only guy I know not awed by the champion. The only *person* I know.

I'm pacing minutes later when Brooke comes into my room the very moment I spot the blood on his T-shirt.

"Are they crazy?" I ask Brooke, scowling when I show her the blood on the shirt Maverick discarded.

"Crazy," she confirms. "Here's a fresh pair of clothes. They might be a little loose on him." Maverick steps outside, his chest bare, his hips covered in a white towel, and Brooke's eyes widen. "Then again, maybe not." Brooke looks at him narrowly. "Yeah, not so much."

She sets the clothes aside, steps forward, and jabs him on the chest. "My husband's got it in his head to help you. He rarely trusts anyone and it's not easy to gain his respect." Maverick is quiet. "Whatever it is you have going on, he thinks you're an okay guy."

Maverick calmly speaks to Brooke but looks only at me. "Yeah, I'm an okay guy."

"Good." Brooke pauses until Maverick seems to force his gaze away from me and back to her. "If my husband brought you here, with his family, you're his friend," she says, and her voice softens when she adds, "so I guess it's nice to meet you, Maverick."

She hands me a few bottles of oils she had tucked under her arm. "Mustard oil, arnica, take your pick, all anti-inflammatory, get this on him. Racer, what are you doing up?" She plants her hands on her hips in a disappointed-mommy pose when we all spot him by the door.

"I want Weese!" he says defiantly, running inside.

"Reese is busy now. Let's get you back in bed."

She sweeps Racer up in her arms before he can reach me, and Racer says, "Mavewick, come see my twains!"

"Later, buddy," Maverick says, raising his arm to fist-bump with him.

Brooke eyes Maverick curiously, then shuts the door behind them.

"He's not the only one who wants Reese."

The dark-thunder voice that speaks rushes over my skin, and I find Maverick watching me with a wistful smile on his face.

My eyes widen.

And my brain leaps to picture me back in his arms, with his lips on mine, his hands on me. It takes every effort in me not to let my eyes trail over his chest, arms, every part of him.

"I want you too."

Did I say that?

Oh god, his face.

He looks ready to lunge at me. Grab me. Hold me. Fuck me.

"What are we going to do about that then?" he asks.

"I don't know. Maybe," I whisper, then shake my head. "I don't know. But I think of you."

"I think of you too, Reese."

I look at him as tingles race down my body, and we both smile. As if that's enough for now.

But is it really? I ache when I think of him. I don't like thinking that I *can't* be with him.

"So you and Remy are getting along, huh?" I ask.

He clenches his jaw and frowns. "We're competitors, not buds." He lowers himself down on the edge of my bed and leans forward, elbows to his knees, and the towel parts to reveal his thigh.

"But here you are," I say. "Remy brought you here and *you* let yourself be brought."

He turns to look at me with a new twinkle in his eye, and then looks down meaningfully at the bed we're, as of this second, now both sitting on. "Here I am."

In. My. Room.

"The boys say that Riptide wants his last fight to be worth it," I say, pretending to be busy now studying the massage oil labels.

He frowns thoughtfully, and I lift my eyebrows.

"You didn't know it's his last season?" I ask.

"No." He flexes his fingers, frowning. "All the more reason I'll be the challenger at the final this year."

I roll my eyes, but god, he's amusing sometimes. I love that he speaks without a hint of boastfulness, only fact. There's a slight frown on his face, and I can almost hear his brain working thoughtfully in the silence. "So pick one." I show him both oils.

"I don't need that."

"Yes, you do," I counter.

"I don't." He gets to his feet, keeps his back to me as he flips open the towel and lets it drop. My eyes widen at the glimpse of his perfectly muscled ass and long, muscled legs as he jumps into a pair of jeans. Then he grabs the T-shirt and slips his arms inside and jerks it over his head, his tattoo rippling with the move. The gray T-shirt falls to cover his abs as he turns.

And I lift my eyes to his.

"You don't want me to touch you," I murmur, heartbroken. "That's why you don't want these. Isn't it?"

"I only want your touch if I can touch you back."

We stare at each other, his eyes challenging me.

I inhale deeply, then blurt out, "If you give me one minute to get this on your shoulders and torso, I'll give you a minute too, if you keep it G rated."

He laughs softly. "G rated is not half of what you'll be doing to me; you'll be touching my chest."

"So?"

He raises his brows.

"I'll even let you go first. Come on, let me patch you up," I continue.

He suddenly nods. "I go first?"

I clutch the oils convulsively in my fists as my world starts to spin.

Maverick approaches.

Oh god.

I'm holding my breath when Maverick raises his hand to my hair.

It's just hair, I tell myself, but the way he rubs a few strands of my hair between two fingertips, looking at them as if they're gold threads, makes my knees weak.

And I realize I always wear it back, except for rare occasions. Or bedtime. Like now.

He strokes the strands, from the roots to the tips, sliding his two fingers downward, and I feel the touch in the marrow of my bones. His eyes flick upward, and he looks into my eyes, penetratingly so, as he raises his hand to stroke his fingers gently down my face. As his three longest fingers feather down my cheek, his curled pinky finger traces the shell of my ear.

My body becomes lava.

He cups my cheeks gently in his palms, and his thumbs brush my cheekbones and eyelids.

Raw need. That's what I see in his eyes.

That's what I feel.

And I see something tender and warm. In those platinum eyes. For me?

"You have the world's prettiest face," he says. "On the prettiest body. With the prettiest smile. And a voice I think of when it's all quiet."

He flexes his jaw and eases back, then he rips off his T-shirt and sits down on the edge of the bed, inhaling deeply. When Maverick whispers, like he just did, that dark-thunder voice of his *ripples* through me as if he speaks from somewhere deep inside me.

God. I'm patching him up, and he's wrecking me.

Trembling, I uncurl my fingers from around the oil bottles. Which I'd seemed to be grasping like my life depended on it. I try to keep things businesslike as I pour a little mustard oil into my palm and then I set my fingers on his shoulders.

His tattoo stares back at me.

The phoenix is so close I can almost breathe it in. I am breathing it in. Because the phoenix is him. And he smells like the shampoo in my bathroom and the very soap on my skin, but warmer and earthier.

I stroke my fingertip over the phoenix head. I want to kiss it.

I do kiss it.

I lean over, my lips brushing over the head so lovingly I hardly touch his skin.

He hisses out a breath, turns around, grabs my head as if to bring me close for a kiss, then lets go and stands, exhaling. "You're playing with me."

"No! No. I'm sorry." I'm so embarrassed, I clutch my stomach and get oil on my shirt, then I pull my arms away and curl my fingers into my palms, struggling not to bury my face in my hands. "I don't know why I feel the way I do when I'm with you."

He narrows his eyes. "You have no idea what you do to me."

The silence is everywhere.

He exhales and comes back to sit again, his broad back to me. He curls his hands over his knees and turns to look at me, shoulders tense.

I look at him and although my brain understands why, my body can't seem to grasp why he's not closer to me.

Maverick, kiss me.

Tell me not to be afraid and just kiss me.

But I *am* afraid. And if he kisses me, I have to push him away because this can't be.

Exhaling, I pour more oil and I force myself to smooth it all over his back. His flesh ripples and tightens beneath my fingers, and I can feel him in every pore of my body. I'm still eyeing the tattoo of the phoenix and the scorpion.

"This tattoo . . ." I trail off, dragging my hands over his back.

"I got it the day I turned twenty-one."

His neck is thick; he's staring down at the carpet now, resting on his elbows as I rub.

"When I stopped waiting for him to come get me. To say he fucked up, that he chooses my mother and me. When I found out what people saw him as, I made a new me. Not with his help, but despite him. Rising now. He's a part of me I won't deny, but there are other parts of me too. Better ones."

He looks at me with half-closed lids, and his voice drops. "I'm not him, Reese."

He stares back at the wall, then he reaches to stop my hand, and an electric little singe runs up my arm as he turns to look at me again. "You're trembling. Are you afraid of me?"

I shake my head. "I'm afraid of myself. When I'm with you."

His eyes shine a little, and his smile comes out. "I like the way you are when you're with me."

"Because it's the only Reese you know, I'm usually calmer and less impulsive."

His eyes sparkle in pleasure over my confession, and he leans forward as if to take my lips. I set a hand on his torso, shake my head. "Maverick . . . you make me too reckless."

"I know," he says, and then he dives his head and presses his lips to my neck.

I put my hands on his shoulders to stop him, but when his hand roams intimately over my back as he draws me close to him so gently, I moan softly and sink my nails into his skin.

He moves his mouth up my throat, testing me first, and when I open my lips recklessly, he starts devouring their softness. His kiss sends spirals of heat through me.

It's a quick kiss. A stolen kiss. Nowhere near what I want. Nowhere as deep as I want. Or as endless as I need.

And it still shakes me to my core.

I'm unhappy and empty and lonely when he eases back. He looks into my eyes for a long minute. "I like your pajamas."

My ears get hot.

His smile starts to fade. He cups the back of my head. My heart leaps again and pounds like mad.

He's going to kiss me.

And I'm going to let him.

My usual Maverick palpitations are overboard right now. I set my hands on his shoulders, and this time, start to pull him a little closer.

I stiffen when there's a knock on the door and start to ease backward on the bed. But Maverick calmly uses his hand to pull me back to where he wants me as he ducks his head, crushes my mouth with his hot, hungry, strong lips, and his tongue flashes inside, stealing my soul when he takes this one more stolen kiss. . . .

Then he stands, shoving his hands into his pockets as he faces the door. Blocking me from view as it cracks open.

Brooke peers inside. "Food's on the table."

She's gone as quickly as she peered in.

Maverick drags his hand over the back of his head in restlessness, then he cuts me a look that's dark and frustrated, as if he's sorry for the interruption.

I shouldn't be, even though I also *am*.

My mouth. My mouth feels *tingly.*

Keeping a healthy distance between us, I follow him out to the living room and dining area. Brooke and I have already had dinner, but the guys are obviously ravenous and I notice there's a place set for Maverick too.

Maverick waits for me to sit, then he drops down across from Remy and they quietly eat their meal.

"They're like a married couple. Can't believe how serious they are," Pete says.

Riley looks at me and grins. "No wonder they like each other. They communicate by not communicating at all."

And while the men enjoy their dinner, I look at everyone at the table except Maverick. Even though I can feel Maverick looking just at me.

TWENTY-FIVE

CLEANING UP OZ

Maverick

After last evening with the Tates, with good food and good company, I couldn't sleep. To see what Reese is accustomed to. How big fighters do it. Today I hit the grocery store, and once I've set the bags on Oz's and my small kitchenette, I stalk to the couch with a trash bag. Oz is watching TV, bottles littered everywhere, bags of open chips scattered on the coffee table before him.

I swipe an arm over the table and send everything crashing into the trash bag.

"What are you doing?" He lowers the bottle he was about to take a sip from.

I go and pluck it from his fingers and toss it into the trash, cutting him with a look. "It's over, Oz."

"What's over?"

"Your fucking pity party. It's over. We want to be pros? We act like them." I take out water bottles from the bag of groceries I brought in.

"You're pulling my leg."

He laughs, stomps to the minibar, and pulls out a small bottle. He takes a rebellious swig and plops before the TV again.

"We're going to AA."

"I'm not going anywhere."

He takes another rebellious swig. I dial the hotel staff and, minutes later, they're retrieving the minibar keys.

"You little asshole! You're just a kid! You think you can come here . . . just because you're buds with Tate now, you think you're the shit?"

"I know I'm better than what you've been giving me. And you're better than what you're giving yourself. Hell, I'm better than what I've been giving myself. It's changing, Oz. We're not going to be the underdogs for long. We're eating like champions and we're acting like them."

"You won't last three minutes in the ring with Tate in the final. Nobody does."

"I'm not nobody." I toss his new bottle into the bag too. "Go clean up, get in the shower, sober up. We're going to AA or I'll carry you there. This has gone on long enough."

WE ARRIVE LATE to the meeting. Rows of occupied chairs face a little podium where a guy is telling his story to the rest of those attending. I stop to pick up a booklet titled *12 STEPS* and settle with Oz in the back row.

When the guy leaves the podium, I say, "Go up, Oz. Take a page from his book and go up there, make a promise to yourself."

Oz is already restless without the booze. "You're a fucking asshole, Maverick."

"But I'm all you've got. Here." I pass him the booklet, and he grabs it and looks ready to combust. And that's when I hear a familiar voice through the speakers, and I lift my head.

"I'm Reese and I've been sober for a year."

Everyone nods in respect.

And I sit here, like a moron, staring at her like I've never seen her in my life.

"I'm shy in nature. Not very verbose and—" She stops talking when she spots me, her eyes flaring wide in a mix of surprise and concern and relief.

And I sit here, still a moron, ready to hang on to every word that comes out of that mouth while something like the scorpion on my back pricks me in the heart.

"I . . ." she struggles to continue, tearing her eyes free, ". . . didn't have a lot of friends. My father taught in army school, so we traveled a lot. New schools every four years. It made lasting relationships difficult; impossible for me, really." She pauses and swallows.

Reese Dumas.

Untouchable no matter how many times I've touched her.

A perfect body that makes my hands itch with the urge to run them over that figure, an old soda-bottle figure, tiny waist, perfect breasts, perfect ass.

I can't fucking take my eyes off her.

"When I arrived at my last home at fifteen, I felt like I didn't have anyone on the planet. I was too shy to reach out, even to those who were nice to me. I heard about the school parties, but I spent my nights at home. One New Year's Eve, I had a glass of champagne and felt a little woozy. I ended up going to my first party, and I was invited to the next. I liked how free I felt, how fearless. It gave me courage to go out. Make friends. I got drunk the next weekend too. I talked more; I was fun; I wanted to be accepted, to connect. I was too closed off on my own. With alcohol, I made new friends, was invited to go out. I thought I was accepted, but when I was sober, I could see I was a diversion. And thinking my friends didn't really like or know me made me want to drink more to make that go away." She exhales.

"My parents realized what was going on about two years in. They might have suspected for a while, but I think they chalked it up to me being young. Two years my addiction was permanent, and they finally got me help. It was difficult at first. I started eating a little more in the beginning, to help curb my anxiety. I gained some weight, which I've been slowly losing at last. I have," she looks at me, "a few friends now. But I am my own friend now too. I want what's best for me. I want to be known for who I am, who I consciously choose to be, work hard to be. I've been sober for one year, and every day I beat this is a win for me. Thank you." She nods, and before she leaves the podium, she's looking at me. Just me. Eyes hopeful and bright, and a little apologetic too.

She ducks her head and leaves the stand, and then she takes her chair.

Too far away from me.

Too fucking far away from me, a world away, when I want to crush her in my arms and tell her she's amazing.

All this time. Reese quietly fighting her fight.

I sit here, still a moron, staring at the back of her head, reeling and knowing for a damn fact that I'm in love with this girl.

I want to set up house.

Pop out a couple of babies with this girl.

I want to protect her from a bottle or a man or a word or a fucking raindrop or from fucking me.

That's how much I care about this girl.

Guess I'm not emotionally stunted after all.

Guess it just takes a second to realize what stares you in the face, slamming you like a punch in the gut.

She wanted a friend in me. I'll be her friend, but I want so much more.

"You see her," I whisper to Oz, and he frowns and nods. "That's her. That's my girl."

TWENTY-SIX

UNVEILED

Reese

The room starts emptying when the session ends, and I find myself on my feet, unmoving, as the wall of lean muscle at my eye level starts coming toward me. I know this chest. I've touched it. I scratched it in orgasm. I know its owner, and for some reason I still can't find the courage to look into his eyes.

Until Maverick stops before me.

Tall, that chest broad and big and begging me to get close to it if only to borrow its strength.

I inhale, and force my eyes upward.

Something happens when our eyes meet. The air shifts and whirls between us. Everything falls away until it's just me, raw and bare and naked and without any real secrets left, and him.

I don't expect what he does next. He wraps his arms around me and gives me this huge hug, pressing me to him until we're like one big entwined tree, the kind of hug my father or mother would give me when I was "brave," and when he kisses my forehead with such passion I feel his hot, wet mouth on my skin, I want to kiss him so bad I ache inside. "You're incredible," he whispers in my ear.

Oh god.

For some reason, I want to know why I hadn't told him. Why I don't ever tell anyone. Even the Tates only know because my mother wanted to be sure I made at least one AA meeting per city, and I resented that they had to know. If only because I didn't want to look weak in the eyes of people who are strong and nearly perfect to me.

But they didn't judge. They didn't look at me with pity. They welcomed me into their team, their home, their lives, and let me get close to the most precious thing they have: Racer.

"I didn't want . . . to be someone who was recovering to you. I wanted to be me. The new-and-improved me that I'm working on."

"You *are* you," he says fiercely.

The way he says this pushes an emotional button, and I swallow. "I wanted to be special on my own, without a bottle or a story about me, just me. This trip . . . was about that for me."

Until it became all about you.

"I was sixteen. When I started, and then I . . . stopped completely at nineteen. I'm not even at a legal drinking age and I've already vowed not to do it again," I say, smiling wanly into his face. "I'm not even tempted. I want what it gives me, maybe, to feel free and . . . But I don't want it."

I glance at the door where Oz left. "He didn't want to talk?"

"Not yet."

"Does he need a sponsor?"

"Maybe."

"If he takes those twelve steps, they'll be the first steps to a new him."

Maverick won't take his eyes off me. His arm is possessive around my waist. And then, Maverick slips his hand under my hair, his eyes dark and quietly loving. "I'm on fire when I look at you," he says, his voice reverent and his gaze electric on me. "You decimated me just now."

I exhale and blink back the emotion in my eyes. Not everybody sees this, when they see someone recovering. They see someone who could fall again. Who could be weak again. Who already fell. They don't see the strength it took to overcome it and push through, sometimes they don't see the humanity, and sometimes they don't know that to someone who's recovering it's hard to stay in a world and a reality where the reflections of themselves they see mirrored in others' eyes are so lacking.

"Do you need to get back?"

I nod, regretfully. "I said I'd just come to the meeting."

"I'll take you."

I smile, and duck my head. "I'm glad you brought Oz." And I add, "I'm glad you know."

There is something about telling someone a secret that binds and locks you together. And there is something about somebody knowing everything about you that makes you aware of how much work you still have to become a better you.

WE RIDE IN the back of the cab in this order: me, Maverick, Oz.

I'm feeling raw.

Too attracted to him.

More than ever.

Maverick sits beside me. Quiet. And I sit here. Quiet too. He watches me in the darkness and when our eyes meet, he smiles.

He reaches out and takes my hand.

His hand is rough and warm, dry, and my hand fits just right in his.

My mind and my heart and my soul seem to flutter.

I wonder what it would be like to spend all night with him, not just an hour, nothing between us. Set my lips on every inch of his skin. Rest my head on his chest. And just be there, talking. Or silent. Or kissing.

I set my head on his shoulder.

He inhales slowly.

I need to be closer, I can't control this. It's like a need to breathe, an impulse toward him, the body reacting strongly to what it needs to survive.

We can't get our hands off each other. I pry my hand free to touch his thigh, and he sets his hand on my thigh, rubbing slowly up and down. There are other people here. So really, our hands probably need to stay where they are. There's the cabdriver, and Oz. But I am only aware of *ONE*. One Maverick riding beside me. His shoulder hard against mine. His legs skewed open so one touches against mine.

I press closer and turn my head just as he seizes my chin, ducks, and our lips meet. His tongue, wet, slips inside my mouth. Impulsively, I slip my hand under his T-shirt. Just because I need to feel his skin. He's hot as a furnace, his skin smooth under my fingers. I push my hand higher, to catch his heartbeat in my palm. I rub a little as he sucks hungrily on my tongue, shifting his shoulders as if to cover me.

I open my mouth wider and let his tongue lead mine.

Oz clears his throat.

Maverick tears his lips free. He glances in his direction and groans in exasperation. "Come on, Oz, you were young once."

"Nope," Oz says.

Maverick digs into his pocket and pulls out his phone, and then his earbuds. "Put those in and put on some music, and look away until we get there," he tells Oz.

He looks back at me as Oz grumbles and does what he's told.

"How do you fucking work this?" Oz demands.

Maverick turns back to him, grabs the phone, and presses Play on the music. Then Oz slips the earbuds in and looks out the window with a grin.

Maverick looks at me again, then he curls his fingers around my skull, and my eyes are heavy-lidded, his eyes slits as he lowers his head and takes my mouth. I slip both my hands under his shirt and kiss him with all I've got. I rub his muscles with my fingertips, realizing I've missed the feel of this chest though I've felt it beneath my fingers only once before. . . . *You're turning me into a nymphomaniac, Maverick.* . . .

And Maverick is kissing me like he has all the time in the world and like he's never going to let my mouth go.

I feel so reckless, I want to do more, I want to feel him everywhere, touch him everywhere, be touched everywhere. . . .

Impulsively, I let my fingers wander down the planes of his chest and over his stomach, but Maverick seizes my face with one hand and as he forces me to look at him, he slips a hand into the hair at my nape.

"Look at me."

Oh god, he's so beautiful. I've never felt as naked before him as I do now.

"How do you do it?" he asks quietly. "How do you have me hanging on every word you say? Every expression on your face?" He looks intently down at me and then runs his tongue over my bottom lip. "Every look you give me," he says.

He holds me closer against him and shifts his shoulders to keep me from being seen, and softly, tenderly, he kisses me again, running his hand down the back of my head in the most tender caress.

When I slip my hands around his neck, I nearly claw my nails into his flesh. I want him so much I'm in actual physical pain.

His lips keep tasting, hot, exploring, friendly, and also intimate. He trails his lips downward to my neck, and tugs down my shirt a bit, to kiss the top crest of one of my breasts.

He then kisses his way to my earlobe, and when I turn my head to bite on his earlobe, he groans into my ear—he sounds *tormented*—and he eases back to just smile at me. Smile at me as if he's happy just to be kissing me tonight.

I can't even smile back. What is wrong with me?

He's turned my body into a firestorm.

I grab him, and my hands go up his back, over the exact spot where I know he has his phoenix tattoo. Then I take the back of his head and draw him back to me.

Our kisses get wilder, my control dangerously close to nonexistent.

We're burning and fevered and then there's no more talking. No more playing. No more training. No more anything but heat and Maverick Cage's mouth.

Fitting perfectly on mine.

His hands rubbing up and down my back, restless. I want them to go other places. I want those big calloused hands on my breasts, between my legs, on my bare skin.

And this mouth, this mouth—I want it on every inch.

My body is on fire for Maverick.

I hurt so much I want to cry. I want his every secret, his every dream, and I want to be in one of those dreams; I want to be one of those secrets.

Soon I'm going to be in my room, alone. Alone and Maverickless.

All the nights I've been remembering what it was like in his bed . . . all the nights trying to do the right thing—the thing that's right for my head and feels so wrong for the rest of me—are coming to a near boil.

He stops kissing me and stares down into my face. Maverick's eyes have a new, possessive glimmer. Still shielding me with his body, he gives me a firm peck on the lips again. My tongue flashes out greedily, and he smiles down at me, his eyes burning with hunger and happiness.

"It's as hard to keep my hands off you as it is to keep from looking at you," he whispers.

Touch me, see me. . . . I want to beg, but I'm so out of control that it takes every ounce of me to be quiet. Instead I wrap both my arms around his neck and I breathe in the scent of his warm skin.

I want you, Maverick Cage. . . .

I bury my lips against his throat, and as I peer past his shoulder, I recognize the passing scenery and I realize we're almost a block away from my hotel.

He groans as he forces his mouth away from roaming over my temple.

God.

I think about the fact that our kisses nearly pushed him over the edge.

When will we be alone again?

Will we *ever* be alone again?

"Maverick . . ."

He laughs softly to himself and rests his head against mine, his intimate stare only confirming that he *knows* that I recklessly wanted to do more. I feel my ears start to get red.

I glance at Oz, and thank god he's facing the window, snoozing as he listens to the music.

Maverick watches me run my fingers down my hair.

I look back at him. His eyes are absolute flames and I want to tear his clothes off and memorize every hot, hard inch of him.

He makes me so reckless, I don't know this girl. I like it, but I'm afraid of it too. "I want to spend the whole night with you. I want to know what it's like to lie on your chest. And talk about things."

God. I don't know why I said that, but I blurted it out. I force myself not to take it back. To own it.

We stare at each other as the cab slides to a stop in the hotel driveway.

Maverick helps me out, then leans toward the cabbie. "I'm walking her up, stay put."

"Keeping the meter running," the cabbie says.

Maverick nods and shuts the door behind us. His fingers press into the small of my back as he leads me across the lobby, pushes the Up button, and we wait for an elevator. When it tings and a couple shuffles out, he steps inside with me. And then we ride, all alone, to the penthouse.

He takes my hand in silence, dipping his thumb into my palm and staring down at me in smoldering male satisfaction.

"I should be embarrassed. I'm never this reckless," I admit.

"Good. But I want you to be reckless with me."

I laugh and duck my head, really embarrassed now. There are lights above us, and they feel brighter than usual after the shadows of the cab, and I'm utterly mortified.

"You know who I am. And I know who you are, Reese. And none of it has to do with what you said just now, or with who our fathers are."

He pulls me so close that I can feel what our make-out in the cab has done to him, and his lips cover mine again, softer now, achingly soft.

A feather of pleasure ripples down my back as he shifts me and we end up flat against the wall. I'm sandwiched between the elevator wall and tons of Maverick.

We're so hungry for each other that we can't get our mouths off the other.

"You make me drunk, Maverick," I say worriedly, as we kiss.

"I take it"—he frowns—"that's a bad thing?"

I search his face. "I don't know."

"You make me want to go all out, Reese. Do everything."

We kiss a little hotly again.

"You bring out a different me," I confess, gripping his chest as I try to catch my breath. "I wanted to be her. But I don't know this new me. I'm a stranger to this new me."

He eases back with this slow, adorable smile. "I can see her perfectly."

When the elevator arrives, he follows me out to the big doors of the three-bedroom suite. As I fish out my key, he says, "Hey. Find out where you'll be staying next location."

"Why?"

"I want to stay at the same hotel."

I stare.

He nods soberly. "I want to find out what it's like to have you lie on my chest. Spend the whole night with me. Talk about things." He smiles as he quotes me.

I think I fell just a little bit deeper.

I inhale.

For two people who don't talk a lot, this is huge.

To want to spend a night together. And talk.

"Hey," he says quietly, lifting my gaze to his, "I want you in bed with me."

I laugh.

"I've never spent a complete night with a woman, not in my life."

I stop laughing.

Oh god. He's emotionally a virgin too.

What are we doing?

His expression intensifies, and he takes my hand and kisses

my knuckles. Knuckles, which are the way he makes a living, probably one of his most prized body parts after the obvious one. "I liked what just happened in the back of that cab, Reese."

"I liked it too."

"Then don't regret it," he whispers in my ear.

He heads to the elevator.

"Maverick." I stop him.

I want to kiss him for luck.

I want to kiss him for me.

"I wish I could be at the next fight," I say instead.

He stops by the elevator, hot and delectable, laughing softly as he rakes his hand through his hair. "I'm glad you're not."

"Why?"

He shakes his head woefully. "I need my head with my opponents." He sends me a meaningful look, as if I fuck with his head.

"Riptide is undefeated, Maverick. He's . . . unstoppable. I don't want either of you to get hurt."

He comes back and tells me gently, "One of us will." He chucks my chin. "Don't worry about me. I can take a beatdown. I learn best when I'm on the ground 'cause I fucking hate it there."

He goes back to the elevator, and I lean on the door as he disappears inside. I open the hotel room door, dine on cereal, and head to my bed. I lie there, still breathless, squeezing my eyes to relive what just happened in the back of the cab with him.

I have never been so scared.

Reese, is this really you? Are you ready to be bold and brave?

TWENTY-SEVEN

HER

Maverick

When we reach the hotel, I take a shower, drop into bed, and I'm restless. I replay the cab. I replay her kisses. I replay her words. I replay what she said about herself.

You make me drunk, Maverick. . . .

Fuck, I shouldn't have taken her to her hotel. I should've brought her with me. To lie here, on my chest. Like she wanted. And talk all night, either with words or with silence.

And I'll kiss her, for hours, her tongue coming out to play with mine, and I'll have her breasts in my hands. She's going to moan into my mouth. And I'm going to draw out those moans, because when I'm with her, I'm intoxicated and I'm crazed and out of control.

Reese in bed, looking nice and sweet, wrapping her arms softly around me as I spread out on her. Her saying my name in a way I know she wants me, needs me like I need her. "Maverick."

I can't talk, I'm groaning against her mouth, then squeezing her ass in my hands as I taste her nipple. I turn her around and kiss the mounds of her ass too. Slip my fingers between her legs, and she's all wet and juiced up. I'm memorizing her. It'll take me forever, but I'm dedicated and I want to memorize every tiny inch and pore with my eyes and my fingers and my tongue.

Her breaths jerk and she rolls around and grabs me to her and takes me inside. She's hot. Wet. I can't get enough. She accepts me inside her. She welcomes me inside her. She rubs her hands all along my back, over my tattoo. And she knows what it means. She's the only one who knows what it means. It's not about my father, it's about me.

And I know who she is. I know she's strong and sweet, I know she fights to balance what others need and what she needs. I know she's finding Reese, and I know that I'm the lucky guy who's gotten the privilege of watching her find herself.

TWENTY-EIGHT

STRONGER

Maverick

One . . . two . . . three . . .

Fifty-seven . . . fifty-eight . . . fifty-nine . . .

A hundred . . . a hundred and one . . . a hundred and two . . .

I'm doing sit-ups. Training in an empty hotel room Oz and I wrangled for the day.

I'm thinking of finals six weeks ahead. And of her. Always of *her*.

I know losing can get to your head. I know losing can ruin a fighter's life. I also know you'll never win if you don't believe you deserve it. Because when your body's about to give up, and you're on your last push, you won't ever go that extra mile if only a fraction of you didn't believe you could nail this.

Maybe it's my rebel inside. I've always believed I could; mainly, because I don't think anybody else did. I believe I can. So I will.

And she is mine. I'm claiming her as mine. Slow and easy. That's how we'll do this.

But in the ring, I'm not going easy. I'm getting stronger, I'm getting faster, and I'm getting shit done.

I'm pumped up after yesterday.

I'm pumped up thinking of Reese, in the back of a cab, putting my hand between her legs. In my mind, the better I become, the more deserving I will be of Reese formally dating me.

"Oz, you need to watch Tate when we're fighting. Tell me if you see an opening."

"Maverick, *I* tell you what to do, not the other way around. Get yourself to semifinals first."

I stop with the sit-ups and ease to my feet, jumping rope now. "Still mad I took you to AA?"

He glares, takes out a water bottle, and guzzles it down.

I toss the rope aside and go slap his back. "Hey. You can do this." I toss him the tape so he can tape up my hands. "Oz, I can't be everywhere in the ring. You need to tell me if you see weakness 'cause his coach is sure as hell telling him mine."

"Not his coach, YOU ARE. All those times training with him? That guy's been studying you like an encyclopedia." He scowls bleakly.

"Good," I murmur, letting him tape my hands. "I'll know my own weaknesses before finals when he comes at me. I've been studying him too."

"Get yourself to fucking finals first. Twister's all up on standings, climbing the ranks. There's talk that he's cheating the system, pumped to the balls in steroids."

"His balls have nothing but air." Hell, I'm insulted he thinks I'm losing to Twister. I already beat him once. I glare. "I can take him."

Oz guzzles more water. I narrow my eyes. "You dehydrated?"

"What?"

My eyes widen when he closes his bottle like it's holy water and slips it into the inside of his jacket. I reach out and wiggle my fingers. "Give me that water."

"No."

"Oz."

He tosses me a new bottle of water from a small cooler. I catch it, set it aside, and take a step. "You put vodka in your water bottle, Oz?" I ask quietly.

He stands up and puffs out his chest as he looks up at me, trying to intimidate me. "Drop it, Cage."

"Give me your water, Oz."

"I said it's water," he growls.

"Are you drinking?" I ask.

He glares, stomps away, and slams the door shut.

I grit my teeth and stare down at my untaped hands, curling my fingers into my palms. Then I run after him before he catches an elevator.

"Oz, come on. Let's talk about it."

The elevator arrives, and he boards defiantly. "There's nothing to talk about. You're gonna be on my back, then I quit."

"Oz."

"You either lay off me, or I'm not going to be spending time here to be lectured. I got enough of that before with Wendy."

"I'm not Wendy, all right? Just chill and we'll figure this out. Get back on this fucking floor, Oz," I growl.

He glares but steps off. "I'm *chill*. Just back the fuck off." He storms back into the room, and says, "Heavy bag."

I follow him inside, simmering in frustration as I spread my hands out in helplessness. "I don't know how to help you, Oz."

"I can take care of myself. You worry about you. Heavy bag."

I grind my molars. Then I go hit the bag, bare-knuckled. And get the perfect sound. And I keep going. And going and going. Getting it all out of my system. Getting ready for a fight.

❤ ❤ ❤

THE CROWD ROARS outside, and then there's silence and the announcer speaks. "For the first time in Chicago, ladies and gentlemen, we give you the man causing waves . . . the man causing whispers . . . the man you all fear . . . the first rookie ever to get this far in an Underground championship . . . We give you, Maverick 'the Avenger' Cage!"

I turn to Oz. "If we win tonight, promise you'll try again tomorrow."

He smirks. "I'll promise tomorrow." Then he sobers and opens the door, where the crowd starts with a combination of name-calling and booing. "Let's do this, son. One match at a time."

I nod and I step outside and head to the ring.

TWENTY-NINE

RUN WITH ME

Reese

He won. I heard it from the team. Depending on the rankings of the fighters, they get to fight on separate nights in each location now that we're heading to semifinals. Even numbers fight on one night, odd numbers on the next.

Maverick didn't get to fight Remy in Chicago. But he beat every single man put in his path.

We're in Chicago now, and he's shot up in rankings from 148th (where he started, with no record) to thirty-ninth (after his first five match nights) to seventh now. Everybody is talking about the way Cage "cages" his opponents against the ropes, then knocks them out with what they're calling the Maverick Jab because of his long arms and incredible reach.

The question on everyone's mind is if he has it in him to stay there and make semifinals and win against the experienced fighters he'll be facing.

But the main question is if he has it in him to beat Riptide.

"I'm telling you, he does. You need to stop training with him," Coach said that night after the fight.

"The more you tell him not to, the more he's going to do it," Pete advised Coach Lupe when Remy stayed mum.

"Why, Rem?" Coach demanded.

"Because he's unstoppable, and I'm challenged to see if he'll stop . . . or not. I'm hoping not." He lifted his fist and looked at his bruised knuckles that reminded me exactly of Maverick's bruised knuckles.

"So you help Scorpion leave a legacy rather than protect yours?"

"He's less the son of that bastard than he thinks he is," Remy answered. "All he has of his father is the scorpion on his back. Scorpion was never this good this early on. Hell, ever. And he was never this clean."

"I still don't agree with you mentoring him," Lupe growled.

"You don't have to agree, Coach."

"FUCK, RIPTIDE, LISTEN TO ME! That kid IS POISON! He's a SCORPION IN THE MAKING."

"Coach." Remy's voice turned threatening.

Coach quieted down. And Remy just sent him a look that said to drop it.

"I like Cage. He's got fire burning in that soul," Riley said.

"Saying he was on fire in the ring tonight is an understatement," Pete said.

Coach Lupe shook his head. "Talent like that, untamed, can go wrong in so many ways. Like it did with the father. One trigger, and it snaps, and he'll be the worst nightmare you've ever encountered up there. *Anyone* has ever encountered up there," Coach warned.

I was so sick of spying on the men to hear about the Underground that I headed over to Brooke's bedroom, where she was lying on her stomach on the bed reviewing the flight schedule.

"Brooke, is there somewhere online where I can watch the fights?"

She sat up and reached for the pad and pen on the hotel nightstand. "Oh, of course. Sometimes, not always, depending on the location. Here, I'll list a few sites." She tore off a page and scribbled down half a dozen web links. "Try those," she said, handing over the page.

I headed to my room and did a search on my phone, trying to see if the latest match was being replayed. I found an image of Maverick's broad, muscled back with his phoenix tattoo, and there were hundreds of comments on it. *This guy fucking scares me but I can't get enough of watching!*

I kept scanning for the fight when he texted me. For the first time *ever.*

> Hey Reese Where are you training tomorrow?

And let me just say that those elusive little butterflies, the ones I'd always overheard girls talk about but I had personally never met until Maverick, they have found a new home in me.

I can't tame them when I think of him. Hear his name mentioned. They've become a part of every thought of him. Of remembering him in my room, of bending down to kiss the beak of his phoenix. Wanting more. So much more.

Trying unsuccessfully to tame them, I text him the gym I planned to be at, and he replied, I'll look for you.

I spent all night watching the matches, wincing when he caught a few hits. Most of the time, I winced for the others.

Maverick is an intimidating force, slowly and surely overtaking the Underground.

❤ ❤ ❤

NOW I'M STARING at the doors of the gym as I push myself hard on the stationary bicycle.

Chicago is windy, but Brooke tells me to enjoy it because Miami—our next stop—should be blistering. I'm blistering now in the crowded gym. I've grown addicted to exercise, the endorphins, the way my body reacts to the stimuli. Sweat beads on my forehead. My body's hot and my muscles burn. I've never felt stronger. My muscles are getting so firm and lovely. Even breathing is easier now: my lungs becoming more efficient these past few weeks. Same goes for my heart. It takes more to agitate it, much more.

I keep pushing, breathing in and out, in and out, and then I breathe in and hold it and my heart definitely gets the kick it needs when Maverick "the Avenger" Cage steps inside.

The gym quiets.

Really, the more people hear about him, the more scared they become.

I'm scared of him too, but in a wholly different way.

I'm scared of the power he has. Not in his fists. But over *me*.

I stop pedaling, the wheels keep turning on momentum, and I feel as if my whole world is spinning too. *Lungs and heart, here's your favorite workout now . . . approaching soundlessly like a panther. . . .*

And his lips are forming the sexiest male smile ever smiled on this earth. "Look at you," he says in that deep-thunder voice.

Oh god.

I can't look sexy right now, not like Maverick looks sexy now. He's freshly showered, his lean, muscled, tanned body covered in a pair of sweatpants and a clean T-shirt, a little sexy cut on the corner of his lips.

I'm concerned about the cut.

And oddly attracted to it, for it is right on that lovely smiling mouth of his.

"Did you get hurt last night?" I ask.

He shakes his head like that cut is nothing. He notices that I'm panting, I guess. He lifts up my water when I try to reach for it and cracks it open for me. He watches me take a long swig. I down it all, then gasp for air, smiling. "Sorry."

He steps before me and straddles the bicycle wheel, then he folds his arms over my bike handles as he looks directly at me. The shirt is straining over his muscles. His voice low and barely audible through the gym's background music. "Hey. Want to go for a late-night run with me tonight?"

I lift my finger and absently touch the cut on his lip. Then I realize what I'm doing and pull my finger away. "What?"

His eyes twinkle happily. So . . . he likes me touching him? "Come run with me, Reese."

I hesitate. But somewhere between meeting him and giving him my V card, I've come to feel things for him that I've never felt for anyone in my life. He's also my friend and I miss him. "I'd love to."

"I'll pick you up at your hotel. Ten p.m.?"

He steps closer, and I roll my eyes pointedly at the people in the gym, staring covertly at us. He's the Avenger. People have been talking about him nonstop.

He glances at them in silence, then they all scatter or turn away, and he looks at me. "Is someone bothering you?"

"No."

He nods and heads to the vending machines, brings me a new water, sets it down, then we look at each other.

He stares at my face as if he misses the look of it.

And I stare at his face, missing the look of his.

I find myself staring at his retreating back, at the black T-shirt that ironically reads I DON'T KNOW WHAT I'M DOING in white letters.

I exhale, aware of all the looks coming my way. I pull out my music, turn on "Geronimo" by Sheppard, think of us as if I've been oddly finding a little bit of us in every song I hear, and pedal like I want to burn off the arousal Maverick left lingering in me.

IT'S 10:02 P.M. when I step off the elevator, dressed top to bottom in exercise gear, the laces of my sneakers double knotted, and from the blazing lights in the hotel lobby, I walk out into the cool streets. I see his hooded figure, waiting against a wall at the start of the hotel driveway.

I start to walk over and then trot, and he quietly starts trotting next to me. Silently. I follow him toward the park.

Yellow lights dot the walkway, but the deeper we head in, the darker it is. I can smell freshly cut grass. And fresh air. And guy.

Guy who makes me happy inside. And tremble.

And ache.

And *yearn*.

"It looks different at night. Almost mystical," I say when we've been running for fifteen minutes. The sound of our feet smoothly hitting the pavement eases up as he slows his pace, and I slow mine.

We end up stopping to look at each other.

Or rather, Maverick seemed to want to look at me.

I laugh. "I'm silly."

But when he tips my face up to the moonlight, I don't laugh.

It's not silly.

This is serious.

Him. And me.

I gave him my V card.

And he's the Avenger.

And I want him.

I don't know if being brave is stopping now or going all the way. I only know what feels good right now. I edge into the shadows, backing away from him. Maverick follows me.

We silently drop down on the grass, on our backs, and we stare above.

"Makes me sad when I stare up at the sky and can't see any stars. It's like all the noise in the city and the lights keep you from seeing what's right in front of you," I admit.

He takes my hand. "I don't want that to happen to us."

I turn my head.

"All the noise," he specifies, studying me. "Keep you from seeing me. And me from seeing you."

We're kissing.

Completely.

I tip my head upward, and he props himself up on one elbow and leans down, grabbing the back of my head to pull me up higher so his lips—his glorious lips—can settle on mine. Firmly, without hesitation, like his mouth was made for me and mine for him.

We pause for breath, and I find myself lifting his hand in mine and stroking my fingers across his knuckles.

"Did Tate know you were coming with me?" He runs the back of one finger down my face as he asks. The touch is achingly tender, very unlike the violent passionate need in his eyes.

"No, but I think they suspect."

His eyebrows furrow thoughtfully, and a muscle starts to flex in the back of his jaw. "Tate won't let you spend time with me?"

"I don't know, Maverick, but they're not judgmental. And Remy seems to like training with you."

"We respect each other professionally," he says.

Once again, I stare at the scars on his knuckles. I raise my brows. "And you don't like him at all?"

"It's not whether I like him or not. It's that he's standing in my way."

He plops down to his back and uses his arm to pull me to his side, inhaling my hair for a long, delicious second while I also discreetly inhale the soap on his shirt. "Are you close? You and the Tates?" he asks me.

"We've grown very close these days." I hesitate for a second. I want to ask him about his dad. I peer up at him: "You and your dad?"

Shadows cross his face. "Not yet."

"And you and me? Are we close?"

He looks at me with frustration. "I keep thinking of how it was being inside you. I want you that close again. All the time. I get frustrated that we can't spend time together out in the open."

"Is that why you asked me out for a night run?"

"Would you say yes to one by day?" He looks at me, his face in shadows.

"No, but because Racer's awake, not because I don't want to be seen with you."

"It raises questions. You're with the Tates."

"What happened between Remy and your father? Do you know?"

"They've been at odds for years. Supposedly my father did anything to stop Tate. He was obsessed with beating him." He scrapes a hand down his face, his eyebrows low over his eyes. "I have to believe there's more to him than what I've heard. I have to believe that. For me."

I'm feeling so much for him, I can't find words.

He eyes the sky, deep in thought. "He was in an accident recently. He was driving a stolen car. Went down a cliff . . ." He shakes his head against the ground, lips pursed as if he's struggling to be at peace with it. "He was up to his eyeballs in drugs. Had nothing on him, no ID, nothing but a picture of Tate with a target mark on him." He exhales roughly through his nostrils, and shifts onto his shoulder. Then he softens his expression. Softens his *voice*. "What about you, Reese? Tell me about yourself."

"You heard my story." I sit up and wrap my arms around my folded legs.

He sits up and wraps his arms around his, eyeing me. "Yeah, I heard."

I rest my chin on my knee and look at him. "I wanted you to know."

"I'm glad I know."

"My V card," I say, smiling wanly when I slide my eyes shyly away and then peer sideways at him. "It was all I had left that I didn't give to the alcohol. It was something nobody could take from me unless I chose it."

His jaw tightens visibly, his whole face tightens visibly. He holds my gaze as he reaches out and gently runs his knuckles down my cheek. "I wanted it to be me."

Oh god. This guy.

This. *Guy*.

My soft voice returns. "I wanted it to be you too. You turn on all my lights, Maverick."

His smile flashes and proceeds to do exactly that, warming me in every shadow of my heart and mind and body, in every cloud in my soul. How does he *do* that?

Even Racer adores "Mavewick!"

"Racer will get jealous I got to see you and he didn't," I blurt out happily.

He laughs. "That little guy? He gets the most time with you. I'm jealous of him every day."

"Ahh! But he doesn't get my kisses."

My eyes widen when I realize what I said, but Maverick's eyes start to smolder so bright that I don't regret saying that one bit.

He plants a hand on the grass between us as he starts leaning over, and I slowly start to lie down on my back. My heart pounds. The night envelops us. And he's so close, his eyes are all I see.

I want him inside me. Us alone, in privacy. I want that again so bad.

No.

I want more than that. I want every tiny layer of his personality for me to see, every ambition, every thought, every memory . . . and I want, I desperately want, to be seen by him. All of me.

Lying here with my hormones all crazed, I'm telling myself that I'm not going to do anything sexy until *he* does it to me when he exhales.

He shifts, his hands curling a little at his sides as he looks at me for a long time.

I look at him for even longer.

I'm looking at the Avenger right now.

His eyes. They feel like hot, sheet-clawing sex on my skin.

I brush my hips against his. He groans. "Reese."

I open my legs to fit him against the part of me that aches and I slant my head, sliding my hands into his hair.

We kiss for a long, long while, and I can feel how much he wants me in every kiss, in the tension coming off his body. He's holding back, and knowing he's doing it for me makes me weak inside.

"I feel like I'm on top of a mountain with you," I whisper, as he kisses my neck. "Let's never come down."

Looking at me, he spreads my arms up over my head. "I want to make you feel like you're on another level, and I'm going to do everything I can to put you there." Determination shines in his eyes as he smiles down at me. "I want to show you how I see you. Everything about you drives me crazy. You're irresistible on every level, Reese. The way you talk, move, the way you taste." He presses his face to mine, tasting my lips briefly, then he melts me with his metal eyes again. "You're incredible, Reese." He wraps his arms around my torso and lifts me up for his kiss.

And our mouths mesh again, and I *feel* incredible.

Incredible.

❤ ❤ ❤

WE MAKE OUT in the dark, on the grass. No more talking. Only whispering. Only knowing each other. Touching each other. Kissing each other.

❤ ❤ ❤

WE'RE HEADING BACK two hours later. I'm fixing my clothes and he's zipping up his hoodie as we walk to the hotel.

He takes my hand on our way there, and we walk instead of run. Prolonging the moment we leave each other.

"I fight tomorrow, Reese," he says when we reach the corner of the hotel driveway.

"I know."

"My kiss," he demands.

I grab his hand and open it, then meet his smoldering silver gaze as I kiss his palm. He curls his hand again, and he grins.

"Reese. Tell me how to help Oz," he says softly.

My eyes widen, and my heart starts aching for him and Oz. "Does he want to get better?" I ask.

"I don't know." He shakes his head, drags his hand over it, his expression tightening with frustration.

"Do you want me to talk to him?"

"No," he says with sudden protectiveness, but a flash of

determination crosses his face. "You're done with that. But I'll do everything I can to help him."

"You won't be able to if he doesn't help himself though. Oz needs to believe he's better off without it. He needs to believe he can overcome it."

He nods, smiles one of his slow thank-you smiles, and heads away.

"Maverick."

He turns.

"The fight is tomorrow night, right?"

He nods. I walk up to him, raise on my toes, and quickly kiss his lips. "The other kiss was for fun. This is for luck."

Then he grabs my hips and pulls me to him and kisses me a little harder. Deep, possessive, and wet. And he says, "I'm in love with you, Reese."

And he walks away, pulling his hoodie over his head.

THIRTY

UNSENT

Reese

Miles: So we've got our plane tickets to the Boston semis. Gabe, Avery and moi

Me: That's great.

Miles: That's all? Hmm. I'm gonna need to wrangle some more words out of you when we get there.

Miles: Were you able to get us tickets to the fight?

Me: Pete has you three in second row

Miles: Who's Pete?

Me: Remy's PA.

Miles: Cool. Can't wait. Wait, you're not coming to the fight w/us?

Me: No. But see you all in Boston

Unsent text message to Maverick Cage, 3:02 a.m.: I'm in love with you too

THIRTY-ONE
FASTER

Maverick

I'm getting faster.

Getting better at predicting my opponent's moves. I got to fight Tate again in the ring, and I lasted double the rounds. He knocked me out but hardly cut me this time around. He went to the body and wore me down.

We're training too.

He's a fucking beast, but I'm determined to put him to the ground.

I get a call from his people during our stay in Miami. "Maverick, Riley here. You up for training with Rem this afternoon?"

"I'm up. I've got some steam to burn off." I glance at the chair where Oz is snoozing again. I've tagged on to Oz for the past three days, trying to keep him from drinking. He still finds a way to drink behind my back: in the bathroom, when he says he's taking a nap or is fixing us a meal.

I shove my gloves into my duffel bag, change into a new T-shirt, and head off to the gym.

Tate likes to work out alone. It keeps his opponents from studying him too much and it also keeps him focused. Most fighters don't like to allow the competition a glimpse into their training routine. But training with a worthy opponent makes you better, and both Tate and I know it. One day, I'm not only going to train with my worthiest opponents. I'm going to train on my own with an entire gym surrounding me. Just me, the bags, the rings, my coach, and the few sparring partners they toss my way.

Tate's warming up with the rope. "Avenger," he says, dropping the rope at his feet.

"Tate."

Pete picks the rope back up and hangs it on the wall.

"Where's Oz?" Tate demands, frowning.

I drop my duffel bag on a bench and then nod at Riley so he can tape up my hands. "Helping plan your funeral. Thought your team could use the help since you keep them so absorbed."

He cuts me a look as his coach laughs under his breath and tapes up Tate's hands. "Your coach is your second pair of eyes," Tate tells me, shooting me a meaningful look. As if I should know better. "It's a team sport. Your coach is your team. Your extra eyes. If your coach isn't helping, then you're up there alone. Do you want to be alone?"

I curl my fingers, testing the tapes, and nod at Riley again before I look back at Tate. "As far as I'm concerned, it's just me and you up there."

"Wrong. It's you up there, plus me and Lupe here." He slaps his coach's back. "We're two against one on you."

"Oz is fine," I grumble as we both shove our hands into our gloves.

We get ready and go for it. I can tell he likes sparring with me. We don't spar—we fight. No headgear; it's a match. Over and over. The adrenaline is sky-high when we're both in the ring. We're both competitive, strong, smart.

We dance, dodge, counterpunch, punch. We duck, swing,

hit, miss, and end up bloody and sweaty as usual. We take a lunch break and his coach sets up some power shakes for him on his side of the cafeteria table. I grab something from the vending machines and drop onto the seat across from his, straddling the chair.

"That's what you're eating?" He signals to the granola bars and my Coke.

I look at my food. Carbs. Energy. That's all I see.

He sees something else. "Listen. It's fine to break down your body, but you need to build it up, and not as fast as it can—FASTER. Don't eat junk." He grabs it and dunks it in a trash can a few feet away, opening a Muscle Milk bottle for me.

"I can fight anyway. My body doesn't need your fancy food to run."

He slides the power drink across the table to me. "They're all just fighters out there. Don't be just a fighter, be an athlete foremost. Your body needs to be in prime working condition—you hear me? Without your body in prime form, with prime ingredients for energy, no fight."

"I'll tell my chef." I lift my Muscle Milk in mock toast and guzzle it down.

He laughs at that, then looks at me a moment. "Take glutamine. And eat protein like you breathe oxygen."

We head back to the ring and spar again. We discuss power, tactics, speed, precision.

I can't see any weakness in him. Even after all our sessions.

Until his wife enters the gym.

He stops punching and looks at her. Hell, he grins at her. I swing out and crush his jaw. Then I laugh.

He smacks the laugh right off me.

I clean the blood off the side of my lip, then shake my head as Tate walks to the ropes to talk to his wife.

And that's when I see Reese through the gym window.

The glass is tinted. I can see her, but she can't see me.

I walk forward and lean on the ropes, enchanted.

She's walking in place with Racer in her arms, and she's playfully poking a finger into Racer's dimple. She's smiling. She's happy. She's vibrant. She's young. And she's mine.

I watch her walk up and down the length of the window, nodding her head to something Racer says. I grab the rope with my glove, bracing myself as my heart picks up a whole new rhythm. The Reese rhythm that gets the blood going everywhere except my head. I'm starved for her; nothing sates me anymore. Not food, not winning, not fighting. My eyes are gobbling up the curve of her hips. The curve of her ass. The curve of her breasts. The curve of her bottom lip. The curve of her lashes.

I want to take her out to dinner. I want to know if she'll lick her fingers, if she'll lick *my* fingers if I feed her something. I want to know what she'll order, salad, or steak and potatoes, or pasta. I want to know what she'll drink.

I want to know if she stretches in the mornings. If she wakes up with tangled hair, and I *want* it to be tangled, and I want it to be tangled because of *me.*

Brooke meets her outside and they start heading off. My gut coils with the need to run after her and ask her to give me a kiss. Not for luck. Not for anything but because I get high on it.

But instead I'm in this ring . . . exhaling while I watch Reese walk away, my body coiled tight as a bowstring. She's this mouthwatering, sweet, nice, strong, feminine little thing and I am fucking crazy about her. I want to know where she's going. I want to know when she'll be back in my arms. I want to know why she let me make love to her that night. Why she let me make out with her in the park. Why she wants me but doesn't want to want me. I want to know how fucking drunk I make her. And I want to know if the guy from back home ever made her feel the things I do.

"You fucking done staring at my wife?" The snarl comes from behind me.

I turn and look at Tate's murderous gaze. I raise my brows. "I was beginning to think you didn't have a weakness."

"Oh, I'm mortal, all right." He watches them leave. "Every time I'm fighting, I'm tempted to look at my wife. See if she's looking at me."

"Is she?"

"Every time." He grins.

"Why look at all?"

"Can't master that impulse."

"I'm going to use this against you, you realize?"

"Good. That'll teach me to stop looking. At least during a fight."

Speaking of fights, I push away from the ropes and tap my gloves together.

"Gotta hand it, Maverick, you're the best sparring partner I've ever had." We head to center, and he narrows his eyes. "You remind me of someone."

"My father."

The most loathed fighter in history.

He raises his brows, shakes his head, and says, "Me."

I exhale.

I'm . . . relieved.

Then I frown. "I don't want to be like you. I want to be better than you."

"Go for it. Every day *I* want to be better than me too."

And we go for it.

Back to dancing, dodging, counterpunching, punching. Back to discussing power, tactics, speed, precision. We duck, swing, hit, miss, and sweat and bleed as usual.

Except this time my game's off.

It's so off, I don't last three rounds before I'm bleeding out of my mouth and from that same cut on my eye that keeps opening.

"Where's your head?" he snaps, mad.

Never been this fucked-up before.

I glance at the window just as I've been glancing back to see if she's walking by again.

"Ah, I see. You like her?"

"Aren't you going to tell me to stay away?" I shut my eye as I get the cut temporarily fixed.

When I turn, scowling and braced to fight for her, he's got his brows up, and he says, "I'm not her father. Nor yours."

We hit.

"Don't go after her if you don't think you can deserve her."

He hits me again and I block, then jab him. He eases back and prowls around. So do I. "Deserve her first. Then go after her."

"I'm trying."

"Every day I try to deserve my wife. Reese is her cousin. One of mine. You take care of her, or I'm going to need to take care of you, and you'll have nothing more to avenge." He hooks and I deflect. I see an opening and take it.

I pummel his side, three times, fast, then ease back. "Understood."

We prowl again.

"You're the one who gave her that penny? The one she's always looking at?" he asks, amused.

I cut him a warning look. "Fuck you. It was all I had."

He nods, some new respect visible in his eyes. "Keep fighting like you do and soon you'll be able to give her the world."

I grit my teeth in determination and simply nod, because if I win, I'll have respect. I'll prove I'm better than my father. Tate won't think I don't deserve her, nobody will.

And I don't tell Tate that in more ways than one, Reese is

already mine. That I'm still trying to deserve her and I'll die trying to deserve her. But she's already mine. I know it, and for her to know it too, I just need time.

We fight for another three minutes, then we take our corners to catch our breath.

"Who's my toughest fight? In semis?" I ask him.

He leans forward in his chair. "Yourself. It's always yourself. Can't win if you don't think you deserve it. Other than that?" He thinks some more on the question. "Taz is wicked fast. Toro is a fucking meatball. You get a fist on your face and you're done for the night. I always dance around the fucker until he's dizzy, then go for the head. Least fleshy part of the asshole." He shrugs. "You can go for the body too, but it takes more swings and if you wear down before he does . . ."

I nod and think about it, then I start asking him about everyone else. Twister, Spidermann, Hot Shot, and Libertine. And for the first time, I willingly listen to what Tate has to say.

THIRTY-TWO

COME WITH ME

Reese

"He was training with Maverick," Brooke says offhandedly as we head three blocks down to the inflatable kiddie party place.

My heart does a double dip and a pirouette and other stuff *I don't even know the names of.*

I almost stop walking.

"Oh" is all I say though. So cool, I sound.

But wow. That's all you can say, Reese?

Because I want to say so much more. Ask so much more.

"Mavewick is my fwend," Racer says, puffing out his little chest.

"How do you know Maverick? You've seen him twice," Brooke taunts Racer, rumpling his hair.

"Uh-uh," Racer denies, shaking his head.

"We'd bumped into him at the park before," I hurriedly say.

Please, please, Racer, don't say anything about Maverick kissing Reese on the cheek in the park.

Please don't mention Reese sleeping in Maverick's arms while he looked after you. . . .

I will be your slave storyteller FOREVER!

And push you hard in the stroller no matter how much my butt bounces and EVEN if Maverick is watching.

Racer is thankfully too busy keeping his eye out for our destination to say anything else.

"At the park? Really?" Brooke asks him. Then she eyes me and I feel a telling heat inside that climbs all the way up to my ears, which are thankfully covered by my hair today. "He is absolutely as gorgeous as they come," she says with a female sigh.

And I think the small, painful little groan I just heard was mine. "God, I *know*."

Her brows shoot up to her hairline in alarm. And cautiously, she adds, "He's also dangerous. We don't really know much about him. His intentions."

"I know, but . . ." I try to find words. "Sometimes you just know. Someone. Don't you think?"

"True." She nods and purses her lips thoughtfully. "I do sometimes wish Remington would just finish this season in peace. Why does he want to . . ." She shakes her head, pursing her lips even tighter and then sighing. "Coach Lupe says he's helping Scorpion's legacy. But the truth is, Reese"—she drops her voice—"Remington *believes* in Maverick. Remy wants to make sure that *his* legacy is Maverick."

I'm burning inside. I'm burning with hope for Maverick. For me. For us.

I want to tell Brooke that I have never felt like this before.

I want to tell her that I feel like a light when I'm with him.

That I don't feel shy.

Or judged.

That I feel alive and bursting and free and accepted and understood.

And so female.

And so good.

And so pretty just because of the ways Maverick Cage looks at me.

And . . . I think it's love.

They say love is a chemical thing, a brain thing, a hormone thing.

Call it whatever you want to call it.

I'm buzzing and obsessed, without sleep, without appetite, without want of anything but to be with him, talk to him, think of him.

I'm really, for the first time in my life, in love.

Not calm love, like with Miles, where it made sense to try to be in love.

This love makes no sense. It's complicated and confusing and scary and I still have it bad for him and I still feel it. And I know it's rushed and I know it's dangerous and I know it's maybe a little bit doomed, but I also know it's true.

I want to say all that, but I'm afraid of her not understanding. This. Me. Us. I'm afraid nobody understands but Maverick.

I stay quiet as we head into the inflatable indoor playground.

And instead I ask, "How long will they train for?"

"All day for sure." She stops to get us tickets inside. "Though Remington promised to run early with me today. He should be home by seven. The gym is booked for the day though. Do you want to use it?" She leads Racer inside, looking at me over her shoulder as I follow. "I can take Racer in the stroller with us."

"Are you sure?"

"I'm sure. Make use of it."

So I do.

❤ ❤ ❤

IT'S 7:11 P.M. when I get there. The gym lights are low, and there's no background music. Instead, I'm greeted by the rhythmic sounds of the speed bag being hit at lightning speed far away. A part of me wonders if Remy decided to stay, but when I peer past the weights and the ring, to the far corner, it's not Remy killing the speed bag. Oh, he's dark-haired and tall, all right, and muscled like there's no tomorrow, but the guy at the speed bag is Maverick.

He's bare-chested, wearing nothing but his low-slung sweat-pants. His tattoo is alive, rippling in all its winged glory as he hits. Biceps flexing. Shoulders clenching. Abs gripping.

Am I hurting you . . ?

Flashes of him mounting me swim in my head. Flashes of his hands all over me. My nipple disappearing into his mouth. Me, being filled. Being taken. Being reckless. Being free.

I watch Maverick for a moment in silence. In awe. All that male power, perfectly controlled as he measures his punches. Each landing on the spot where he wants it to land, hitting precisely, expertly, one arm rolling after the other.

I don't get many opportunities to look at him—not really, because when I do, I'm usually seized by the fact that Maverick is looking at *me*.

But now he's concentrating on the speed bag, the same guy in the hoodie I met weeks ago who piggybacked on me at that gym.

His muscles have grown a little. He looks a little tanner, maybe he's been running outside? He looks corded. More male. More adult. More dangerous than any fighter I've ever seen— because there's no one who has as much to prove to all his haters as he does.

And I lean on the wall and watch the look of concentration on his profile. So lethal, so quiet. Every second that I watch, I feel this excruciatingly painful sensation of want mingled with happiness squeeze my chest.

He stops hitting.

Exhales.

And slowly frowns, as if deep in thought.

Did he sense me?

He's starting to turn.

He *sensed* me.

Because as he turns, his gaze slides, without stopping, and pins me in place. His eyes smolder the instant they connect with mine. And I smolder inside.

"I'm on my way back to the hotel, I just wanted to say hi," I nervously say. Even my voice sounds soft when I talk to him. All of me goes soft.

I wait a beat, and while I wait, this gorgeous smile starts to pull at the sides of his lips.

"So hi," I finish, awkwardly lifting my hand.

He pulls off his gloves with the opposite arms, never taking his eyes off me, and I slowly lower my hand.

He starts approaching.

"Hi," he says. He walks with that swagger and that look in his eyes that says, without apology or hesitation or remorse . . . *I remember you in my arms last night, Reese.*

Inhaling sharply at the memory, I need to cant my head back to meet his gaze, and when I do, he's still smiling that powerhouse smile at me.

I thought I wanted to be loved. But now I realize, I don't just want to be loved. I want to be loved by one man. This man.

He doesn't look anxious or worried at all. He looks pleased, like a guy who's just worked out as if he was born to sweat, and punch, and kick other men's asses. Like a guy who knows he's getting the girl at the end of the day—or like a guy who knows he already has her. Even if she hasn't said "I love you" yet. Even if she's with the Tates. And Miles is still out in the world somewhere.

"When are you leaving for Boston?" he asks me, taking my chin—just like that—and kissing me on the lips—just like that.

I gulp. "Tomorrow."

My knees.

My poor tingling *toes*.

"Would you come with me?" he asks.

"What do you mean?"

"Come with me to Boston, Reese. For semifinals."

"Like . . . travel with you?"

He nods.

My eyes widen. "I . . . YES."

"Text me your traveling info when you get to the hotel. I'll get us both on the noon flight."

Me and him, together.

I don't even know how I'm going to make this happen. I just know I'm *making* this happen. Brooke is always so understanding, and Racer always sticks by his dad when they're on the plane. I can't even fathom the Tates denying me.

He strokes the back of my head, then fists my hair in one hand as he draws me an inch closer. "I'll take you to dinner, someplace nice. And I'll drop you off at your hotel after."

I find myself nodding. "Okay."

"I'll send you the confirmation."

"I'll send you my info."

I should really probably stay away, but instead I lean forward and he steps closer, lifts me in his arms so that my mouth is leveled to his. And he kisses me, a toe-curling kiss that twists up my panties.

He sets me down and pats my butt. "Go then. Text me."

"I will."

I head to the doors. And I steal one last glance at him over my shoulder. Maverick is standing in the same spot, and when I catch him staring possessively at my ass, it makes me start to love the Himalayas like never before.

When I get to the hotel, I wait in the living room for the Tates to come back from their run. I hear Racer chattering outside and swing the door open.

"Hey, guys," I say with a broad smile.

"Reese." Remy brushes past me, carrying Racer up over his shoulders. Brooke pushes in the stroller and I help her fold it.

"Hey, is it okay if I go to Boston on my own? I'm meeting up with a friend," I tell her.

She carries the stroller to lean it against a corner wall. "When do you get there?"

"To the hotel? By ten p.m. Maybe we'll grab early dinner too."

"It's fine with us. Just tell your mother and it's absolutely fine."

"No," Racer decrees from the kitchen where he and Remy are scouring for food.

"Racer, come on, let Reese enjoy her friend," Brooke says, then she smiles and eyes me speculatively. "A boyfriend?"

"I . . . no. Just a friend."

She smiles knowingly. "The guy back home?"

"Wee comes with me on Wemy's plane," Racer keeps protesting.

"Dad," Brooke specifies. She groans and sends me a what-will-I-do-with-this-kid? look. "He hears us all call him Remy and he's determined to call him that too. I'm going to have to start to call my own husband Daddy to see if it sticks."

I laugh.

"Right, Daddy?" she calls as Remy lifts his head.

"That's right," he says as he fishes out a gallon of milk and pours Racer a small cup and himself a big glass.

I smile when Brooke joins them, then take out my penny and head to my room, kissing my lucky penny like a dope before I pull out my cell phone and text Maverick my info.

THIRTY-THREE

FIRST CLASS

Maverick

I'm wired today. Couldn't sleep. Spent all night making our reservations, then picking the perfect restaurant in Boston to take Reese out.

I texted her the confirmation number and flight times, and she replied, I'll see you there

My cock's on fire today. My whole body is on fire today. My brain is on fire, my whole body buzzing in anticipation of fucking holding her, fucking looking at her, fucking making her mine again.

I read the text again while I wait at the airport and wonder if she got held up at the security checkpoint. "You masturbate daily, Mav?" Oz asks to my right.

"Yeah."

I'm hard. So what. She does that to me.

"Do it more often."

I clench my hands at my sides and exhale, trying to get it to come down. We're at the boarding terminal, Oz and I.

I want to be alone with Reese, but I'm keeping a close eye on him too. Him and his "water." I know it sure as heck isn't water.

But at least he's cut it down some, now that I'm watching him so closely.

I want him to be well. I want him to *want* to be well.

"You won't be able to take your hands off her. You need to woo a woman with your head, not with your cock."

"I'm bringing my best game, Oz. Really. I'm taking you both out to dinner. Someplace nice."

"So." He pats the water bottle he mysteriously brought back from the men's restroom a while ago, as if to make sure it's in his jacket pocket. "Does Tate know she's coming with you?"

I remain silent.

Tate is a touchy subject now. Oz hates that I train with him. He can go on for hours on what a bad idea it is to get in bed with the enemy, yada yada.

"Yeah, you're right," he answers himself. "Tate can go fuck himself. Or his hot wife."

"Oz . . ." I shoot him a warning look. "We respect Tate. And his wife. Right?"

"Me?" Oz asks.

"Come on, Oz; we're professionals."

He frowns. "Tate's gonna bust your face when he knows you've got it hard for his wife's cousin."

"Tate fucking knows, all right? And he's not stopping me." I rub my palms on my jeans and I glance at the clock.

The speakers flare up again for the second time: "Now boarding flight . . ."

The line is diminishing by the second.

I want to text her.

I'm too proud to text her.

I'm aware of Oz staring at me with an I-told-you-so look.

I get up and pace, then lean against a pillar, hands inside my jeans as I scan the walkers heading in our direction. I wait a little longer.

I text her.

You ok?

I call her. Voice mail picks up. "Reese? You all right? Call me."

I check my phone for messages, nothing. I check my ticket and I stare out at the plane window.

Oz looks at me, the last man boarding.

I shake my head.

He sighs and heads inside.

And I watch the plane taxi out. Watch it head to the line, and then watch it take off.

The plane disappears on the horizon. I wait for two more hours. Dragging my hand through my hair, over and over. Then three hours.

Four hours later, I head to the ticket counter and change my ticket to coach.

Flying first class on my own just isn't on my agenda.

THIRTY-FOUR

RACER

Reese

I've cried so much that now I'm hiccupping, curled in a blue chair in the hospital waiting room. Hiccupping and then, softly, to myself, crying again. There are a couple others in the waiting room. All much more composed than me, reading magazines and pretending they can't hear me.

I've been waiting here for an hour, or maybe two. I don't know. All I know is that it's been Groundhog Day for me for the past few hours. Except I'm reliving the same ten minutes over and over in my head.

Racer.

Us, playing with the trains while Brooke finished packing and came to relieve me and I could leave for the airport.

More trains. Me, getting restless, looking at the time, the penny in my pocket.

Racer, getting mad that one of the trains kept charging off the track.

Me . . . fixing the track.

Racer . . . very quiet behind me.

Too quiet behind me.

Not breathing behind me.

"Hey."

I hear Remy's voice and I jerk upright, wipe my tears, and set my feet down on the floor.

He comes over. "He's all right," he says, low and even.

He looks down at the penny in my palm, the penny that I had been staring at like some lost soul staring at a door that leads back home.

I jam my penny into my jeans pocket—still haunted by the sight of the train with three wheels that had been sitting next to Racer as he choked on the fourth wheel.

My hand trembles as I let go of my penny and pull out my hand, feeling my eyes start to water again. "I'm so sorry, Remy." I force myself not to cry, but the stupid tears are slipping.

When I yelled for help, Remy had turned Racer over but the train wheel seemed stuck in his windpipe. The ER was three blocks away, and I don't think I breathed until we got here.

"He's all right. Okay?" He pats my shoulder in a fatherly way and heads back to check on Racer and Brooke.

They come out soon, the three of them, and Racer sees me, then he turns away and buries his face in his dad's neck. As if I'm some Judas. As if I failed him. Because I did.

I can hardly look Brooke in the eye.

"Brooke, I'm sorry."

She nods, her face red from all the tears she cried too.

I wipe my tears and follow them outside, where Pete is pulling the SUV into the driveway. When they bring him into the car, I notice Racer's not purple anymore, but his face is all red like Brooke's and probably mine are.

I want to squeeze Racer to me, but he still curls against his father's chest and avoids my eyes. I think of Maverick's chest for some odd reason, at a moment like this, and I would give his penny—the one he gave me that I never wanted to let go of—to have that chest right now for me to curl up against too.

"I'm sorry you missed your flight," Brooke says softly after a moment.

I nod quietly.

"Call Miles and meet him later," she says.

I realize at this moment that Brooke thinks I was traveling with Miles.

"I don't think . . ." I shake my head. "I just don't know." I don't know about me and Miles.

But what about me and Maverick?

I'm disappointing the Tates, who've been nothing but good to me, over and over.

I've been lying all this time, hiding behind their backs, because I'm so scared of anyone or anything taking Maverick away from me.

Suddenly it all feels so dreary, suddenly I feel hopeless, and undeserving, and foolish to hope there could be something amazing and unexpected for me.

"Did he take the flight to Boston?" she asks.

"I . . . I don't know. I left my phone at the hotel when we rushed to the hospital." I look at my phone, now that Pete and Riley fetched our belongings from the hotel, and I really need to see him in person to say what I want to say.

But I see his texts and my heart hurts. I text him:

I'm sorry I couldn't make it

"If he didn't make his flight," Brooke adds, "I'll get you two a pair of plane tickets. You can invite him when we head to finals in New York."

"No," I say, my voice raw. "It's all right. Thank you."

"Reese, I know you're scared. I was scared too; I lost my shit. I was yelling for help but not at you. It's okay."

"Thank you. I think I yelled too."

I want to yell right now. Inside, I'm screaming right now.

Maverick hasn't answered my text when we reach the airport, climb into the enormous private jet, and take the flight to Boston. I sit in my usual seat at the back of the plane with the family, while the team sits in the front club seats. Except Racer doesn't want to tag on my lap now. I feel desolate as I stare out the window. All I want is Maverick's chest to lay my head on. I don't want alcohol, and I don't want another plane ticket. I don't want anything but that chest right now.

I want to be sitting in an airliner right next to him right now. I want to tell him *I am in love with you too*, because, who knows?

One second you're playing, and the next, life tosses you around and threatens to take everything from you.

I can tell that the Tate team is worried about how this will sit with me. I feel their glances, and I bet they're worried I'm going to go and guzzle a bottle of Johnnie Walker or anything in sight. And I won't. I'm going to breathe and breathe and breathe until I can breathe without consciously doing so.

I'm having trouble believing I'm good at anything now, but I'll still be something.

I was thinking of becoming a teacher, because I enjoy my time with Racer so much. Now I wonder if I'm even capable of watching over one kid, much less a roomful. But I want to be capable, very much. I want to believe that I'm capable.

I glance at Remy and I want to tell him Maverick is not Scorpion.

Maverick is driven and no bullshit and unique—he's a guy who can say thank you both with words and with a priceless little IOU of a penny simply because you helped him out.

But as always, I don't speak because I don't think I'll be heard.

I'm mute during the flight. Midway to our destination, Remy kicks me playfully on the ankle to draw my attention. I lift my head, and he hands me his iPod.

I smile shakily and take it, and start playing on shuffle, closing my eyes as the music starts. I exhale and listen to a few songs, some new to me, others familiar. But when "Fight Song" by Rachel Platten starts playing, I'm suddenly back with Maverick. And Maverick is with me.

He's just . . . with me.

And I'm not alone anymore.

❤ ❤ ❤

WE REACH THE hotel and settle into our rooms. I'm determined to make it up to the Tates. To Racer. To Maverick. And to myself.

Racer is staying away from me, but when I knock on his door and ask him if he wants to play, he comes over and hugs my leg. My heart trembles as I drop to my knees and I squeeze him. "I'm sorry. I love you, Racer. I love you so *so* much, you have no idea. You're like my favorite train in the world." I tighten my hold, and he soon gets bored and squirms.

He smiles devilishly and looks down at my penny. He's intrigued by the object and reaches out to take it.

I hesitate to let him have it, but I do. I watch him study it.

"It's a penny, for good luck," I quietly explain. "But you don't eat it, you just hold it. And . . . make a wish."

"Okay," he says.

He holds it for a little while and squeezes his eyes shut, as if he's wishing, then he takes it to his train box as he takes out the trains to play. I keep an eye on the penny as he sets it aside and starts trying to build his track.

"What a nice picture." I glance at the door, and Brooke is grinning at us. "Reese, you haven't had time to have any fun here," she says, kneeling. "Go out with the boys, Riley and Pete are going out on the town."

I shake my head. "Oh, no, I have a blast with Racer."

"Come on, go out with the adults tonight. There's another circuit party. Diane's staying in and she offered to sleep over with the little guy." She smiles to convince me and settles down to play with Racer, and, reluctantly, I sit back on my heels.

"I'll meet you guys there."

She nods.

Quickly, I fish up my penny and tuck it back into my pocket, and I'm relieved to spot Pete with his mega-sized leather-bound agenda in the kitchen. "Pete, can I ask you something personal?" I say.

"Shoot." He's scanning something in the agenda—the fight schedules, I think.

"You usually know . . . where all the fighters are staying. Right?"

He nods absently.

"Can I see the list of fighters and their hotels?"

He narrows his eyes as he scrutinizes me with brotherly concern, then, reluctantly, he flips the pages and shows me the list and I scan for Maverick. I slide the agenda back to him.

"Thank you."

"Reese, I don't need to say it," he warns.

I know that it's wrong, that it won't come to anything, that he's the Avenger, that I'm in over my head. But I need to see him. I need to talk to him. I need to explain why I didn't make it and I need to tell him what I've decided to do. I can only pray he'll hear me. And that I'll have the words to explain.

"There's something I need to do."

THIRTY-FIVE

BOSTON

Maverick

On my flight to Boston I google him. My dad. Every rumor. Every bit of news.

Drugs. Doping. Abuse of coaches. Lawsuits. Girls claiming he raped them.

He and his thugs assaulted them.

I turn off my phone and toss it into my duffel.

This is your father, Maverick.

The man you want to make proud.

My mother said he used to be good. He used to want things, good things. But he went into fighting. He didn't like losing. He became bitter, obsessed, and rather than get things the right way, he chose to get them any way.

This is why I'm poison to everyone.

This is why Reese should stay away. *Is* staying away.

I've got poison in my blood. But growing up without him gave me more will than any father's pampering or spoiling could've given me.

I AM Scorpion's son.

I AM the Avenger.

I AM a fighter.

I AM after Reese.

She's more under my skin than my father is. Than Tate is. Than anyone's ever been. She's under my skin, in my fucking veins, in my lungs, in my heart, and in my brain.

I will buy a hundred tickets if I have to. One day she's flying first class with me. Having a nice dinner with me. Sleeping in a nice hotel bed, with slippery sheets and cloud pillows with me. One day she'll be in love with me.

❤ ❤ ❤

I FIND OZ waiting at the terminal. I cashed one of my six-figure checks, so I set up Oz and me in a nice hotel. Oz is blown away as we wander inside. Two bedrooms, huge living room, a bar, and views of the harbor.

"This is great. Now where's the girl?"

I drop his suitcase in his room. "Go change. We're going to the circuit party."

"Says who? Don't think so."

"I say so, Oz."

"I don't mingle."

"Don't mingle. Sit there, for all I care."

"Why the fuck will I do that?"

"'Cause there's a chance Reese will be there."

He looks at me like I've lost it. And yeah, I've lost it. I'm fucked-up over her and I'm not denying it. I need a Reese-aholics Anonymous but I'm not ready to sober up, as far as I'm concerned. I'm ready to keep drowning in her.

"If she wanted you, she'd have made it," Oz says. "I had a fucking SUNDAE on the plane. You totally missed out."

"Just get dressed," I snarl, then I wait and cross my arms,

staring out the window. I know what she feels for me. I know she wants me. I know it's not easy, but nothing worthwhile ever is.

Oz comes out in boxers and a white T-shirt. "Won't mind hanging around here while you go. Have fun."

I shake my head at him, then I hit the shower. In two days, semifinals begin. Two nights. Multiple fights. I need to end up second or I'm over.

I need to train harder than ever. Concentrate more than my brain can possibly even accomplish.

But tonight Reese is haunting me.

THIRTY-SIX

MY FIRST BIG CHOICE

Reese

He's staying at our hotel. At our same hotel. It made it easier to get the room number, since the Tates are known by the hotel staff. But it made me all the more nervous when I rode the elevators to the seventeenth floor, keeping my head down.

Ting.

I step out, my nervousness and anticipation reaching new levels when I start scanning room numbers. Down the hall, I check the number and I knock on the door. Oz opens the door, squinting.

I exhale. "Is Maverick here?"

He focuses on me. "A little late, aren't you, little lady?"

God, I can't get into a battle with Oz right now. "So he's not in?"

"He's not."

Fuck. "Well, do you know where I could find him? Is he training?"

"Look, girl, I'm not a guy who gets up into someone's business but he's *my* champ, and I won't stand for him being played. So maybe leave a guy with a mission time to *focus* on it . . ."

"*Oz.*" I hear an angry voice speak behind him. *His* fucking voice. So near and so excruciatingly real, I'm trembling as my heart turns over in my chest.

Oz sighs and opens the door, and there's my Maverick. My rebel. All alone, except for Oz.

And now me.

He's wearing jeans and a black button-down shirt, and he looks like death by sex, and I feel like dying tonight about a dozen times over.

I stay outside, peering into where he is. The suite is huge, and seeing Maverick among such luxury makes him look like a dark prince of the underworld.

"I came looking for you," I lamely say.

"And I waited for you."

His deep, resonating voice sounds lower and more thunderous than ever, and my stomach grips in reply. I wait for him to say something else—to tell me how much I *suck*.

"I'm sorry, Maverick."

He comes to the door, and then lowers his voice, one hand on the doorframe as he leans forward. "Did they keep you from me?"

He's gauging me and I'm gauging him back, not knowing what to do to be let in.

"No."

"You're here to tell me we're a mistake." He's searching my expression with a new rawness in his eyes.

"No."

We stare at each other.

I'm about to ask, beg, "Can I come in?" when he takes my hand in his and starts backing in as he leads me inside. And as he does, he watches me with bare, thirsty, impaling eyes, and my knees feel like rubber as I follow him, ready to tell him what I came here to say.

Maverick stops to look at Oz. A look that says he wants to be alone. With me. And Oz shuffles into one of the bedrooms. He steps out a minute later, clothed, shoes on.

"You don't have to leave," Maverick says. "Just give us some privacy."

"Nah, nah, you two need it," Oz says, and says he has something to do. And then he leaves, looking at Maverick as he shuts the door.

He cares about him.

And so does Maverick for Oz.

My heart can't take the heaviness I feel.

I realize Maverick is looking down at me now, waiting, expectant. His hand is still gripping mine. Lightly, almost as if he expects me to draw away. And then, his other hand lifts to my cheek and he cups my face and runs his thumb beneath my eye.

"You've been crying."

Just like that, with his tenderness—so unexpected for such a tough guy—he makes my eyes sting a little again.

"How do you know?" I whisper.

"I just know." He dries the other corner of my eye, looking sad. "You okay?" he asks.

"I am now," I croak, and I look at his chest, and up at him, and swallow. "You look very handsome in black. Are you going out?"

His lips pull a little, and his eyes are still full of questions—and tenderness. So much tenderness I feel flooded with it. He shakes his head. "Not anymore."

I like how silent he is, how every look of his says something. We're both silent now. And I think he knows why I'm here.

Or does he?

He's studying me too deeply. Almost tortured. And I realize maybe he doesn't.

I take his hand and open it, and then I set the penny inside.

His eyes raise to me, questioning.

"I want you to make love to me."

He inhales sharply and closes his fingers around the penny, his voice rougher. "Only that?"

"No." My voice is low and very soft, but on fire with meaning. "I want you to love me very hard. Because I'm pretty sure I've never loved someone as hard as I love you, Maverick."

His every muscle tightens when I say it, his shoulders, his jaw, his arms, his legs, and I can see a flash ripple in his eyes as if he can barely keep himself in check.

He's known rejection, and I almost feel as if acceptance is new to him.

As if he doesn't know what to do with it.

"I know that we still have a lot to learn about each other. But I also know there will never be another Maverick in my life," I keep going. "I came here to find myself. And I think I did. And I also found . . . you."

"And I found you," he counters gruffly, standing suddenly closer, his eyes devouring me.

"So." I clear my throat and go on, "I want to be with you. For as long as we have. An hour, a week, or just for the summer. I feel things for you that I don't understand and I want to. You're not your father, and I'm not my family. And for some reason, Maverick, I think that you're quiet enough that you can hear me. And with you, I don't need to wonder what you mean. Because you say what you mean."

"I fucking want you, Reese," he growls, impatient.

"Have me then. Right now. And tomorrow."

"Both of those. And after." He grabs my waist and lifts me, and I curl my arms around his neck. I see his jaw tighten as he looks at me, studies me. Memorizes me.

His eyes drop to my breasts. His hands shift lower, to my ass. And he raises his eyes to mine.

"You're priceless. Gold. Not gold, you're the whole fucking mine to me. Do you know that?"

God, those eyes. So stormy right now.

"Maverick, Racer swallowed and choked on a little train wheel," I blurt out. "He wasn't breathing right, he was purple—"

"He all right?" He sounds harsh and angry, his hands clenching my hips convulsively. And I know it's because he cares.

"Yes. He's okay. I just . . ." He sets me down. "I was distracted. Thinking of . . . our trip together. And the next thing I saw was him choking. I didn't even know it was the train wheel until I realized the train he'd been playing with had only three wheels. Remy twisted him upside down and then tried to pull it out, but it seemed caught. . . . We rushed him to the hospital." I wipe my tears. "That's why I couldn't make it to the airport. I wanted to come. I ended up at the hospital, but I clung to your penny and to thoughts of you. And so I came here."

His eyes cloud with a mix of sad tenderness. "Reese, what you're asking me to do—I don't need you to give me back the penny. It was all I had to give you. But now I have more. And I'll have even more still."

"But I want you to have the penny for a while. For luck."

He tucks it into his jeans pocket and then raises his hand and lays his fingers on my hair, runs them through the strands as he uses his free hand and gently pulls me into his arms.

I'm knotted up, waiting for his lips, waiting for his skin to touch mine. But he's running his fingers down my hair as if it's lovely. As if it's made of streaks of honey or rays of sunlight or yellow diamonds. When I tip my head up, I feel him place his lips on the bridge of my nose, five times. On my . . . five freckles?

I tip my head up higher, and Maverick finally yields to the impulse and tastes my mouth. I taste him too, soft, hungry. Gripping his shirt in my fists. A shirt I want to take off so badly.

The things this man does have no precedent, will have no predecessors; they couldn't.

I boost myself up with my fists and curl my legs around his hips, and his muscles ripple beneath me as he starts walking us to the room. My fingers trace the tattoo on his back, over his shirt. He stops walking. Closes his eyes. He holds me tighter, close.

"Reese," he whispers in my ear.

He tips my head back and clenches his teeth, his eyes raw and violent.

"What?" I pant, pressing closer. My breasts ache, my sex aches, my whole body aches.

"When you do that . . ." he begins, dark and hot.

I run my fingers over his tattoo again, and he presses me against the nearest wall, and crushes my mouth with his in a kiss that curls my toes and makes me clench my legs around his hips tighter as he grinds himself to me.

I touch his face. "You're the first big decision I've made on my own. The first good decision."

He looks hazy with desire as he gazes hotly at my smile, then frowns at me. "How do you know I'm a good decision?" he asks, his voice rasping in his throat.

"Because I know you."

His expression flashes darkly with emotion.

"Spend the night," he says. Nuzzling me.

I nod. "But I need to be back by the time Racer wakes up."

"Okay," he concedes, stroking a hand down my bare arm, savoring me. "How long do we have?"

"I'd say it's long." I giggle.

God.

Maverick is so hard against me.

His eyes dance playfully. "Dirty girl."

"I'd say five a.m. would work?"

He cups my face tenderly and kisses me again. "You want to lie down with me now?"

"My head on your chest? Like that?"

He scoops me up from the wall with both arms. "Just like that."

I'm floating and everything is a blur as he carries me to the bedroom, kicks the door shut, and sets me down on the oversize bed. He opens the buttons of his shirt and I hear it land softly on the carpet, and I scoot back and watch him crawl over the bed, muscles rippling, like a panther, lying next to me and pulling me to his side.

I swear Maverick is wearing his heart in his eyes as he looks down at me and holds me against his chest.

I set my cheek on his bare pec.

"Oh," I say.

He frowns down at me. "Oh what? Not comfy?"

"VERY."

Hard. So warm. I can smell his aftershave, his soap and his deodorant and his *skin*. I slip my arm around his waist and scoot over closer, and he tightens his arm around my shoulders and stares up at the ceiling, exhaling slowly, as if he's at last relaxed.

I'm quivering with the feel of his arms around me. And I feel him tense at the feel of me. Smelling my hair, his body taut as my fingers absently trek the dents of his abs. I can almost hear him tell himself, *Easy, Maverick. . . .*

But his hand is on the move already. His fingers—long, tan— slip under my shirt and cover my breast through my bra. He squeezes a little, brushes his thumb over my nipple. It's already hard. I gasp when he caresses, and he takes the gasp into his mouth.

I fall to my back as he leans over me, sliding his other hand under my shirt to cup my other breast as he kisses my mouth, slow and easy, but with his tongue. His marvelous tongue.

The noises I make, soft, fluttery, make him groan in his chest.

"You like that, Reese? God, I like my hands on you." He tugs my shirt over my head and reaches behind me to open my bra.

He leans over to memorize the shape of my breasts, the weight, the form, the taste, the look of my nipples, the texture. He sucks me gently, murmurs, "I want you wet. I want you wet when I dip my fingers here." He drags his hand between my legs. I arch my hips on impulse, craving the touch.

"I *am* wet," I gasp.

He unbuttons and unzips my jeans and slips his fingers inside, into my panties, and then he groans when he brushes his fingers between my folds. And I'm soaked. My panties are soaked, my folds are soaked, soaked for him, and he says, "I could drink you, Reese, and never get thirsty."

I brush my hand against his cock and he groans.

"It hurts?"

"Best kind of pain, the one you give me." His tongue flashes out to rub across my nipple again and I let my fingers wander his shoulders, his flexing arms, and his perfect back.

"I love touching you, Maverick," I whisper as I arch again and lick my tongue into his mouth. This is only my second time, and I'm curious. I'm alert to the way his breath changes. The way my body softens and weakens and wets for him. The feel of my nipples grazing against the flat wall of his chest. The way my hips seem to lift, wantonly and on their own, upward. Asking for it.

I'm already high and I keep rising and rising as he eases his finger inside me. I bury my nose in his neck, and Maverick presses me closer to him. I'm panting, and he's breathing deeper than usual.

I bite his throat exploratively and drag my fingers over his tattoo, tracing it in my mind.

"Reese," he rasps. "When you do that . . ."

"What?"

He looks at me with eyes that look heavy and hazy with desire.

Desire for *me*.

And I think . . . maybe. Love.

"You're the only person in the world who gets this tattoo," he rasps thickly, and then he crushes my mouth and kisses me, ravenous and deep.

We've been waiting for this and we're both so wired, we can hardly speak. Maverick tugs my jeans down my body, gets rid of every scrap on me. And then he gets rid of his perfectly sexy clothes and he is so . . .

Freaking.

Perfect.

Naked.

Hot.

And in fucking bed. With me.

I don't even have time to be self-aware. Or time to feel a little too voluptuous. I'm a little firmer and sleeker now, though still curved. But the way Maverick's silver-metal eyes eye-fuck me as he comes over to lie on top of me tells me that this man, *this* man, thinks I'm gorgeous and perfect and amazing and female. The proof of that is, though I have never seen another erection in my life, I'm sure there could not be one as big and hard and greedy-looking as Maverick's.

He shifts above me so that our bodies are at maximum contact. So I can feel his cock between my legs, and I like the maximum contact so much. Too much. I shiver and fist his hair and breathe rapidly in and out, anxiously, through my mouth. "Oh god, Maverick, I've wanted this too much."

"I still want this too much, Reese," he says as he goes to his knees, and I watch him, and I know that he can see me watching him—his chest, his arms, his abs, his erection.

Just as he's watching me. My chest, my abdomen, my hips . . . my pussy.

We're impatient.

I start grabbing him to me and he's high on me, I can feel it in the strength of his kiss, his arms as he grabs my hips and drags me down the bed toward his erection, hard and Maverick's, and he watches me as he plunges. I gasp, my cheeks hot, my hair getting tangled behind me as I toss my head to one side and then to the other. The pleasure of this man inside me is absolute.

He's all I want.

He takes my knees and drags my legs around his hips, driving in deeper. So deep my vision goes blurry, and his eyes go dark, almost engulfed by his pupils.

I raise my head and kiss the scar above his eye, where I stitched him up once. He groans, undone, and sets his forehead on mine. He slides a hand between us, rubbing my clit with his thumb.

"Are you letting go for me?" he murmurs.

He buries himself deeper, grabs my hips and holds me down so I have no choice but to take him, deeper and deeper, as far as he wants to go. As far as I want him.

Hands on my hip bones, he moves in me, and I move with him. Like a dance. We go faster and faster. And I never want to stop. I never want to stop moving, watching, tasting, getting fucked by Maverick Cage in Maverick Cage's bed.

I always wanted to be loved, and I think he loves me because I'm ready to be loved, and he's ready too, and here we are.

We're having hot sex but we're making love, him and I, and I want to say it. I want to say the *I love you* because who knows if there's tomorrow, if I'll ever get to say it again, if I'll see him after the season; who knows what happens tomorrow and yet *I know now that I have to say it.*

I'm coming and I want to bring my heart to an emotional climax too, and when I can only gasp and see colors and stars and Maverick's gorgeous male face before me, I hear him.

"That's right, Reese," he says, kissing my lips until my chest is ready to explode along with the rest of me. "You're with me now."

❤ ❤ ❤

IT'S EARLY IN the morning. Three, maybe, or four. And I'm the Sexpot in Maverick Cage's Bed. The Lucky Sexpot.

I'm enjoying watching his muscles as he shifts and moves above me.

The clench of his jaw when he's moving inside me.

The chameleonic shifts in his eyes as we start making love . . . and finish making love.

I'm addicted and drunk with all the ways his lips know how to move and pleasure, torture and reward. He's fucked me, he's made love to me, he's . . . well, he's gone down on me.

"How many, tell me?" I coax now as I wonder what he's going to do to me next. I told him that I was a virgin, and I now want to know how many girls he's been with besides me.

"No." He's not looking at my face; he's too busy with my body. "They don't count. Nobody counts until now."

I'm sweaty, glorying in the hurricane intensity that he's brought to bed with him. The sight of his cock, full and stiff for me, has me panting. You cannot believe someone so powerful could hold all of that energy under control, but Maverick does it so well, it's exhilarating to be under the attention of such force and be receiving one controlled, delicious, calculated dose at a time.

He gives me only what he measures I can take.

"Mav, I want to kiss you here," I say, trailing my hand over his erection.

"When I'm done with you first, maybe." His thumb circles my belly button, then he teases his tongue inside a little bit. "Only one of us can be properly undone in this bed, you do it so much better. You like that?" His lashes lift as he speaks huskily and watches me, dipping his tongue into my belly button again.

He moves his mouth lower, toward my sex, and I'm tensing in preparation of what's to come. I try to sit up when he nudges my thighs apart, but he presses me back down, caressing my breasts. Then he urges my thighs open, my sex drenched before his eyes. He looks at me, rubs a finger over the folds, checking that I'm wet and ready.

"Maverick," I protest weakly, utterly embarrassed.

I can never stop feeling vulnerable when we have sex, and I feel so raw and needy.

"You're as beautiful here as you are everywhere else." He leans up and his mouth slides across mine, then he's kissing me between my legs again, gently, and wetly thrusting his tongue with gentle rhythm, driving inward, pulling out, making me complain when I'm empty. I'm overloaded with Maverick, his scent, the feel of his kiss where I'm hottest and wettest and in a place where I can't even see.

I'm panting hard while he works his lips up my sex, up my flat abdomen, between my breasts. When he kisses my mouth again, I'm ready, I was made to receive him, and his body was made to take mine, and we fit just right and I'm empty without him. I'm a huge, trembling nerve, quivering in need.

When I'm begging, he rises to his knees, braces up on one arm to keep from squishing me.

He looks extraordinary. This absolutely mystical creature, he's so beautiful, his body in its prime, his face harsh with lust and his eyes shimmering in all those metallic-silver hues that make me want to stare at them for hours at a time.

I stare now. And they stare back at me. Memorizing me and visually fucking me before he physically does the same.

I love the way my body tenses in anticipation. And how my

abdomen feels firm and so do my thighs as I curl my legs around his hips.

Curving his hand on my hip, he holds me as his thick, throbbing flesh fills me to the hilt. The sensation of him entering arches my body, so delicious my thighs skew open wider so he knows he's more than welcome here. He's *needed*.

I mew softly in pleasure, and he groans and stays there, inside me, like he did the time I gave him my V card. Letting me adjust to him.

"Reese . . . give yourself to me, Reese," he coaxes. He crushes his mouth to mine, slides one arm upward, and holds my wrist in one hand as he pulls out and thrusts in. The headboard slams.

I groan. His body ripples against mine. Muscles flexing powerfully with each move. I'm locked beneath him, drowning in the power of him. All this time with him is just making me care.

I don't want to care this much. . . .

I'm scared to care this much. . . .

When the summer is over, I need to leave. Back to school. And the saying "fight or die" applies to this guy to a T. Maverick would die if he's not fighting.

And I feel like the light in my lamp is going to flicker off when I go back to where I used to live. And maybe, who I used to be. . . .

No, I am not her anymore. Not after this trip, this summer. Not after this man.

He moves his arms, and with our hands linked above my head, he keeps driving inside me, his skill delicious and smooth, but strong. Eyes on mine, he teases me with his lips, and he eases back to keep watching me as he takes me to the heights of pleasure, before teasing his lips across mine again.

"God, to have you like this every night . . . soft and wet and undone for me, Reese . . ."

His pace quickens, slamming harder, our hands clenched tight; I moan, arching and writhing, feeling him inside me, every stroke, every plunge maddening me. My nerve endings crackling. Hungrier than ever. Needing him more than ever. Closer and closer to my climax, his harsh groan running over my skin. Then we tense, together. My head tosses aside, the pleasure going on forever. He lets out a growl, then he slams his lips to mine as we're both coming.

❤ ❤ ❤

I'M IN HIS arms, needing to go. I'm buzzing. My body and I content with each other.

"So why didn't you cash your penny in before?" He smirks at me and lifts his brows as he smooths his thumbs down the bridge of my nose, one after the other. "You could've asked for anything. Didn't I say you could?"

"I don't know. I couldn't let it go. I had you with me." I see it in his palm and try to snatch it back up, and he squeezes his palm shut.

"Uh-uh." He shakes his head. "Earn it."

"Come on. Be gentlemanly."

"Earn it."

I laugh and playfully slap his shoulder, and his eyes dance; I can tell he loves my teasing slaps and that it doesn't hurt him one bit.

He falls sober the next moment.

"Sorry about Racer. You love the little guy," he says then, setting the penny aside.

"Very much. He was mad at me after a while and didn't want to be with me. I felt like shit. So rejected."

He kisses me. "You lose some, you win some."

I grab his head and kiss him. "I need to go."

He glances at the clock. "Yeah, I need to train." He flops to his back and exhales happily.

I do the same. "People in love mimic each other, did you know? I read that somewhere. One grabs their hair and the other unconsciously does that."

"When you grab your hair, makes me want to grab your hair too, not grab mine."

I laugh and cuddle a little. "You're funny."

"No." He sounds grumpy now.

"You have a sense of humor."

"I'm just happy right now."

"Really?" I ask, raising my brows.

He raises his pointedly. "Really."

"See! You just lifted your brows like me."

He groans and shakes his head. "Don't even, Reese. I'm not a couple-y kind of guy. I don't do costumes and I definitely don't do matching costumes and I don't do anything other people do."

"That's fine. Just do me."

He smacks my butt as I get out of bed and squeezes it and pulls me down and kisses me. "You're out of control, girl. Someone needs to keep an eye on you twenty-four/seven. I volunteer."

I kiss him again, then I slap his chest playfully. "I'm going now," I warn.

He sits up too and strokes my hair, then lowers me to his knee and looks down at my nipples and plays with them. "I'm going for a run with Tate today. I'm going to tell him about us. I want this out in the open."

Butterflies wake up vigorously in my stomach. "Okay."

He looks up at me meaningfully. "I want to take you to dinner tomorrow, after the semifinals."

"Ummm." Shit. I twist my mouth to the side as I think about how to phrase it. "Maverick, I wanted to talk to you about that.

You see . . . tomorrow Miles is in town, and my other friends. I'm supposed to meet up with them once Brooke gets back from the fight."

His eyebrows shoot up, then he narrows his eyes. "You want me to hang back while you go frolicking with Miles?"

I slap his thigh playfully. "Yes, because he's just a friend. He's always been just a friend. I thought . . ." I shake my head. "Maverick, I didn't know the real thing."

He narrows his eyes even more.

But, I admit, the possessive look I see there thrills me a little. No, a lot.

Maverick not only looks possessive, but he sounds possessive too. "You'll go out with them after the fight, but you won't come to watch my fight? Reese?" he says, frowning and cupping my breast again, as if to remind me who makes me moan.

I drop on the bed, tug the sheet up, and playfully hide my breasts from him. "You said you didn't want me there because I'd fuck with your head."

He tugs the sheet back down to look at me, then he rubs my breast tips with the pads of his thumbs. "I said that before. Before I wanted you so badly on my side."

My eyes close.

"What? No slap?" he teases.

I slap his shoulder, then set my hand there, possessively too. I squeeze his hard arm, with meaning, though it hardly budges at all.

"I'll meet my friends tomorrow. And I'll find a way to make it to the championship match. To see you." I get up then and wait for his answer.

He nods at that, slowly, his gaze a little threatening. "Just remember." He cups my butt as he stands and gently bites the top of my ear. "This ass is mine."

THIRTY-SEVEN

SEMIFINALS

Maverick

I'm ready.

I'm tapping my foot restlessly on the concrete floor of the Boston warehouse. It's the second night of semifinals in Boston. Tate fought yesterday and won. Still undefeated, still ranked at first. I'm currently third.

I've been training like a beast and eating like a caveman, and I feel primitive now. Ready to take my place in the Underground tonight.

Oz says the place is packed. He's told me a dozen times that I need to take out every single fighter out there. Some bigger, some faster, all of them more experienced, but not a single fucking one of them is as determined as I.

Most of the fighters out there do it for the money. Yeah. Boatloads of green are fine, but green is the least of my driving forces.

I watch Oz finish strapping on my gloves and think of the run I had with Tate yesterday. We didn't say a word for seven miles. The conversation with him began and ended when we finished and guzzled down our electrolyte drinks. The conversation went like this:

Me: Reese and I are dating. And it's serious.

Tate: Good. I'm serious about what I said too.

Me: Good.

Tate: You love her?

Me: Adore her.

Tate: Then there's nothing more to say except don't cheat, don't hurt her, and don't make her regret choosing you.

And I won't. I fucking won't. Even if tonight, I'm simmering in frustration over the fact that my girl will be all around town with *Miles*.

I want her here. With me. Or anywhere safe. Anywhere but with *Miles*.

"That fucker won't have a thing for you."

"Hmm?"

"Toro," Oz assures me.

I know I'm glaring, but I'm too mad to do anything else. "I thought you meant Miles."

"Oh, dammit, Maverick, you think *Miles* holds a candle to you?" Oz scowls protectively. "Nobody does!"

"Oz." I laugh at last, then run my hand through my hair. "Never felt this way before. You know? I don't like not knowing what I'm up against. What he's like. What she saw in him."

"Give me that damn hand, I'm not finished." He takes my wrist and starts wrapping my hand in black tape. I watch him closely, beads of sweat across his brow. I feel for Oz. I know that every hour he spends without his flask is costing him his soul.

"You kind of grow on a guy, you know," I say.

"Yeah?"

I nod. "Yeah."

"Does your girlfriend hate my guts? I don't want either of you to think I was a dick to her the other day. I was irked. For good reason. My champ stood up at the airport after going through all the effort of first class . . ."

"She had good reason and she doesn't hate you. Reese offered to be your sponsor, Oz. She's anti-Wendy, like you and me. She's one of us."

Oz exhales as if I just lifted the whole city off his shoulders.

I test out my hand before shoving my fingers into the black boxing glove he extends. "You haven't drank today. Right?"

"Not for a few hours," he admits, opening the other glove for me. "But I'm craving it, son. I'm going to need a fix soon."

"If you're even tempted, tell me and we'll find something funner to do."

"Yeah. Go break a few noses for me." He signals to the door and steps back to make room for me.

I get to my feet and stretch my neck; the crowd is getting noisier.

The announcer calls out my opponent as I shove my arms into the black robe Oz holds up. I jerk the sash closed, then I loosen my shoulders, keep eyeing the door. My muscles are already heating. Adrenaline pumps in my veins. I'm sky-high on testosterone and I not only have tonight's important match to thank for that, but *Miles* too.

"Toro! Toro! Toro!" the crowd outside cheers.

I hop in place, loosen my wrists, my arms. I'm impatient. I'm hardwired to fight the moment I put my gloves on. I'm ready.

Come on, motherfucker, call me up already. . . .

"And now, ladies and gentlemen. He's reckless! He's determined! He's got eyes of steel that will cut you to the quick, and fists with unparalleled reach. Maverick. 'The Avenger.' Caaaaage!"

I head with Oz down the walkway, lights shining down on us as the crowd shuffles restlessly and even gasps. Oz takes my corner, and I climb the ring.

I'm fucking primed to fight. My eyes land on Toro as Oz pulls off my black robe, and suddenly I can hear the silence, as always, when my tattoo is revealed.

Nobody sees the phoenix really. All they see is the scorpion that marks me.

I purposely do not get rid of that scorpion.

I am who I am.

I come from where I come from.

That doesn't mean I'm shit.

In the far back, I hear a few females scream, "GO MAVERICK!"

"Well, look at that! I like them!" Oz happily cries.

He squints into the lights and raises his hand to shield his eyes as he tries to locate my fans as I head to center and focus on the guy before me.

Joel "Toro" Waltzinger.

Bull in size, height, and he even breathes like one too. Sweat glistens all over his body, as if the guy already wore himself out climbing the ring. Hell, I hope he's ready to get his guts smashed.

Ting.

We go toe-to-toe, tap gloves, and he tries a couple of jabs.

I block and duck, easy.

He throws his arms out again, and as I duck, I hit. I go for the body first, *poom, poom, poooom.*

He grunts.

I smile and prowl around him. "Not too bad for a rookie, huh?" I try baiting him.

He swings out again, I block and hold his arm up there with mine, opening his side. And I hit again, crushing his ribs.

He's winded. And that's when I drive my hook upward, straight to the head. First the left hook. Then the right hook. And then I shoot my arm out straight and bust his face, his nose crunching beneath my knuckles. He falls to the ground.

Next up is Hot Shot.

I keep my guard up, brace my legs apart, and hold my balance. Everything I learned from Tate.

We go toe-to-toe. I double punch, hit, stunning him.

I protect, then attack. Protect, attack. Stay away from the ropes, prowl back, then prowl forward until I've got him caged.

And then I pummel him. Gut. Ribs. Gut. Temple. Jaw.

He's on the ground.

The adrenaline is rushing inside me. I'm bloodthirsty and I'm eager for it. I'm taking this ring tonight no matter who they put before me.

With Taz, we dance a lot. Hop, duck, leap around. He's fast but I'm just as fast, and I'm stronger. I catch a few hits. They hardly graze. Mine don't graze *him*. They land and crunch bone beneath my knuckles, knock him to his knees.

He tries to come up and his leg quivers, and he falls.

I take Libertine out within two minutes of taking the ring.

Spidermann avoids the ropes. He's been studying me?

I play it different. I let him get in a few hits to the body, let him bring me to the ropes, and then I flip us around, cage him in, and fucking finish him.

Twister is last.

Oh, I'm going to have fun with him. Flirting with Reese? Busting his nose last time was not enough for me.

I prolong it this time. I raise my fist and crunch his nose under my knuckles—in case he doesn't remember who fucking busted it before.

He yells, and when his hand flies instinctively to the source of the pain, I go straight for his liver.

He chokes on a breath and gets blood all over my chest as he tries to lean on me for balance.

I shove him back (I'm not his hugging post), then let him recover before readying to hit again.

"You motherfucker," he hisses, charging.

I smash my hook into his mouth, then hold his head between my folded arm and hit him three times with my fist. Then I drop him splat on the ground.

There's a wave of shocked gasps across the crowd. I look around the arena as it falls silent, clenching my jaw, narrowing my eyes, and then I raise my arms and let my fist punch the air, saying, *This is who I am!*

"Absolutely ruthless! No mercy from Maverick Cage, NO FUCKING MERCY TONIGHT! Ladies and gentleman, we give you . . . Maverick 'the Avenger' Cage!"

I'm catching my breath as my arm is raised, and then I pull free and leap out of the ring to where Oz waits to lead me down the walkway, to the back room.

"You just got into the fucking final, Mav. YOU'RE IN THE FUCKING FINAL!"

"Yeah." I pull my gloves free inside the back room and then grin up at him in wonder, disbelief, and a high you couldn't believe.

"Come here, you little fucker." He squeezes me and I squeeze back, both of us laughing, then I shove my hands out. "Help me take these off. I want to tell Reese."

Oz works one hand free and I use my teeth to pull my tapes off the other as fast as I can. Suddenly I'm on fire to tell her. I can't wait another second to tell her.

There's only one thing I want right now. One thing that will make this real. Telling Reese she'll be watching me fight at the final.

THIRTY-EIGHT

MILES

Reese

I'm stepping out of the shower when Miles texts me the club address where they're waiting for me. I answer his text:

I'll meet you there.

And quickly change, let Brooke know I'm leaving and Racer is asleep, and I head off, assuring her I'll be safe and home before Racer wakes.

The club is packed, bustling with dancing bodies and thrumming with music. Inside the club, I spot Miles, Avery, and Gabe. I head over. Avery is pressed to Gabe's side. They've been on and off together for ages.

Miles is wearing his contacts, his hair slicked back, wearing a polo and tan slacks. Gabe is in jeans and a pastel polo. Avery is dressed to slay in a sequined top.

"Well, well, well!" Gabe says when I ease into the booth in the only space left, next to Miles. "Our worldly little lady is here."

"Thanks, Gabe."

"Won't you say hello to me, Reesey?" Miles asks, waiting.

"Hi, Miles," I say.

I used to leap at the opportunity to kiss his cheek, but it's too clean-shaven and white, and I hesitate. I lean over and briefly brush my lips to his jaw.

Miles leans back with a frown. "You look different." He eyes me.

"She looks radiant! You look so . . . fit!" Avery says, disgruntled.

"I can see that," Miles says, studying me in appraisal.

I would've killed for this look before. But it's such a lukewarm look after the smoldering ones I've gotten lately. I'm amazed how unaffected I am. I'm amazed by how much distance puts things in perspective.

The three of them look different to me.

Miles sits there, the computer wizard that he is. Preppy and confident and just a tad too smug.

Gabe is outspoken and chill, but half the things he says are bullshit.

And Avery . . .

I never really knew Avery. She's always with Gabe and Gabe is always with Miles, and Miles, for some reason, liked to hover around me.

I wonder why I liked to hover around him too, and then wonder if maybe I'd truly felt so lonely, I'd rather have them than no one at all?

I'm not real with them, and I guess, neither are they with me.

I realize now that they always seem careful and distrustful around me. As if they believe I'm falling off the wagon any second now.

They order drinks. "She'll have water." Miles signals at me.

I smile. I used to be grateful that he looked out for me. Now I'm annoyed that he feels the need to make the decision for me, the request of water for me.

"I'll have a sparkling water with lime," I say. "Thanks."

"Spill the beans, Reese. What does it feel like to travel the country and be part of all the excitement?" Avery asks.

"I spend more time with Racer than anyone else, and he's very exciting. ER visits included."

"Ohmigod, poor you. Why even work during the summer?" Avery asks, pulling Gabe's arm tighter around her shoulders. "You should've come to the fight with us," she says. "The eye candy was ridiculous!"

"Reese is immune to all that, she likes brains rather than brawn, right, Reese?" Miles says.

"I like both, actually," I say.

Miles lifts his brows. And I lift mine back.

"Riptide is scrumptious. Avenger is absolutely wicked! He's scary though," Avery continues.

"Dude, I'd piss my pants faced with that," Gabe says, laughing.

"Speaking of." Miles stretches his arm out on the seat behind me. "So the one-on-one with Riptide? You think that's possible?" he asks.

"It would be incredibly cool," Gabe seconds.

I shift forward. Not liking Miles's arm near me. It's new for me, and it makes him shift a little closer.

Our drinks arrive, and I'm reaching for my sparkling water when the waiter sets a penny right on the corner of my napkin.

I blink and look at it, and my stomach starts whirling. I lift my head and anxiously scan the crowd. I don't notice Miles, Avery, and Gabe are looking behind my shoulder, in shock. I don't notice how my body is starting to crackle. I don't notice how my heart is speeding. I don't notice anything but the fact that I'm scanning the crowded club for a glimpse of dark hair, gorgeous metal eyes, and my rebel maverick.

And with the achingly delicious make-out song of "Madness" by Muse in the background, I start when I see a flash of dark hair in my peripherals.

Lips against my ear whispering, "Dance with me. . . . "

He takes my hand without waiting for my reply, the hand clutching the penny. He takes it from my fingers and, when he wraps his arm around me, slips the penny into the little pocket at the hip of my dress.

We're in the center of the dance floor.

We stand there, among the shimmering dresses, the bustling bodies, the noise. At the booth, my friends are gaping. Avery is doing Maverick with her eyes and I don't want her to look at him. I don't want anyone to look at him. He's *mine*.

He's looking down at me, jaw clenched a little in frustration, eyes smoldering with desire.

I check him out in his worn jeans and the soft T-shirt he's wearing. He looks freshly showered and shaven. There's a light shade of purple, high on one cheekbone, and it only accentuates his hotness.

I can't breathe or concentrate or think when Maverick slides his arm around my waist.

I feel drunk. I'm a puddle in his arms.

His lips curl a little when I can't move, and he takes my wrists to wrap them around his neck. "You don't dance, Reese?" he teases me huskily. "You put one hand here"—he settles it on the back of his neck—"the other one here"—he settles that one on the back of his neck too. "You let me pull you close." He does. Until our bodies are flush and I can feel him and I'm alive. And he whispers in my ear, "And you move with me."

His hands open on my hips and splay outward, to encompass my ass.

This ass is mine. . . .

I lift my head, and he looks wicked. Smiling wickedly. I'm drunk with the sight of him.

His gaze flicks to my mouth, and I can feel him kiss me.

I suddenly press a little closer, then he whispers in my ear, "That's right, Reese, *dance with me*," and he reaches up to slide his hands down my bare arms, over my shoulders, down my curves as we start dancing.

He just fought. He just got into the finals, and I know this because I was clinging to news from the team like a junkie. Testosterone pulses through Maverick's body in the usual fighter's high, and I grab his jaw and press my lips to his, then quickly embrace him and keep moving with him as I whisper, "You're going to the finals."

He whispers back to me through the music, "That's right. And I want you there with me."

We're still moving, but he eases back to put a few inches between us and study my face. His face is raw. His eyes are hungry.

There's something more than desire in his eyes. There's something primal.

And I think Maverick wants me for Christmas.

And for Thanksgiving. And Easter.

And I think Maverick wants me right now.

On the dance floor.

I wrap my arms around his shoulders, the square muscles that are straining his shirt. "Miles was my sponsor in AA," I say, close to his ear so he can hear me through "Rollercoaster" by Bleachers. "AA prefers for heterosexual men and women not to sponsor each other, but I thought he genuinely wanted to help. He kept telling me that he saved me. And I thought I was in love with him because he gave me a chance to try to find myself. But a real man would've told me the truth. That I saved myself."

"That just makes me want to pull out his testicles and feed them to the asshole."

He pulls me a little closer, looking down at me in frustration, rawer and rawer as the music hums and beats around us. Bodies move, but the fire inside this building is alive as Maverick presses my body to his.

He lifts his head and scans the second-story balcony of the club, then stops dancing. Lacing my fingers in his, he leads me up the stairs and stalks purposely down the hall, peering into some curtained private rooms. He spots an open blue velvet curtain and he pulls it wider for me, tugging me inside, and I wait. Anticipation and nerves and need and love swirl around me as I stare at his back as he closes the velvet to the tiny private room with its cushioned bench a few feet away.

"Hey." He comes over and takes one of my hips in his hand, pressing me back against the wall, eyes on my face. "I don't like the way he looks at you. I don't like him looking at you at all."

"I hadn't noticed he was looking at me, only sensed that *you* were close—"

He cuts me off, saying, *Not close enough.*

Lips taking mine. Tongue flashing into my mouth, his hands gripping my ass, squeezing my ass, lifting me by the ass and pressing me to his erection. "He's looking at you like you're his. And you're not. You're *not* his, Reese." He sucks my tongue, commanding and without restraint as his fingers fly down the front buttons of my demure black wavy-skirt club dress.

"Did you wear this for him?" He touches the skirt of my dress, lifting it a bit before dropping it.

"No, I wore it for me," I lie. "Because it's soft and comfortable and it didn't take up too much space in my suitcase."

He grits his teeth as if he wanted me to say I wore this dress for *him*—my rebel maverick—and I breathlessly admit, "I bought it today thinking of you."

"Fuck, I wanted you to say that." He sets his forehead on

mine as he runs his hand up the side of my dress. "You're right, it's soft, but your skin is softer and I want to take it off." He dips his head lower and bites the top edge of my bra. He pulls it down roughly with his teeth, exposing me. Then his mouth is at the peak, drawing it in. Sucking and suctioning, licking and tasting me.

I'm seeing stars.

I reach out to grip his shirt—touch him.

His body is humming from the fight, and he still wants to fight Miles and I know it. He's gritting his teeth in frustration as he lifts me and all his muscles are around me. I gasp against his throat and drag my mouth over any part of him I can kiss, taste, bite. "Are you jealous?" I whisper.

He looks at me with a bleak frown. "Of course I'm jealous; you wanted a future with Miles."

But now I want one with you, I want to say.

Now I only want you.

I can't talk, I'm so turned on. "Not"—I start to bite—"anymore," I strain out. I hungrily bite his jaw, his chin. I can feel his breath, coming out fast with arousal. I bite his lip and he nips me back and suckles my lower lip, then he shoves his fingers into my panties. "Oh!" I say.

He uses his teeth and tongue to unhook the front of my bra. "It's just me now, Reese."

"Yes."

Ohmyfuckinggod. His teeth. His fingers.

Pure heat blazes in his eyes. He's gritting those teeth, feral as he looks at me. I snake my hands up to his shoulders, sinking in my nails. I claw them down his backside, then shove my hands into the back pockets of his jeans and sink my nails into his ass to pull him closer. He grinds himself to me, fingering me and pinning one of my arms to the wall and lacing his fingers through mine. He squeezes my hand and gives me a soul-crushing kiss that squeezes around my heart.

I wanted to see him fight. I wanted to be at his corner. I wanted to see him tonight and here he is. Not only letting me look at him in his most testosterone-filled moments after a fight, but having him see *me*. As he holds me here. Pinned. Helpless. A horny mess. In love. In want. Fingered and kissed and reckless and palpitating for my jealous Maverick.

I'm starting to shudder and bubble out incoherencies. He says, "Hold my neck and don't let go of me."

He takes out his finger, pulls my panties off, and when I grab his neck to frantically climb him, he quickly unzips and thrusts and takes me. We groan. His hands squeeze my flesh as he moves. Pounding into me. So *hard,* like he needs me to live. Catching my moans with his mouth. Squeezing my ass as he drives into me. It's pure raw, pure need, him needing to be inside me and me needing him there. Here. Here. Frustrated. Desperate. Faster. Deeper. Our mouths fusing and moving and out of control until my body convulses, and he comes and holds me tighter to him.

"You're spending the night with me." He fastens my bra, then lifts his gaze. "All night?"

"I'll see what I can do," I say flippantly.

He frowns, but his lips quirk as he grabs my hand and takes me out. I can't breathe or concentrate or think when Maverick leads me back to the table.

A new song starts just as we sit down in the booth.

He sits beside me, and my friends all go mute as he stares at them. No, not them. He stares at Miles, singling him out immediately.

I struggle to find a way to introduce him. "Guys," I say, and put my hand on his thigh as he stretches his arm behind me and curls his hand on the back of my neck. "Miles, Avery, Gabe, this is . . . Maverick."

"I think I just shit my pants," Gabe says.

Miles purses his lips in displeasure.

Avery is about to burst with excitement. "You . . . you two . . . know each other, Reese?" she declares, eyes wide.

Maverick waits for me to speak.

I don't know how to explain him to them.

How to explain my avenger to anyone?

"Hey, Reese. Can I talk to you?"

Maverick is just staring at Miles. Especially after he said that.

His orgasm tamed him . . . somewhat. But he's still putting out dangerous airs and watching Miles like he's the next man to hit the canvas—and soon. "Is something wrong?" I ask Miles.

Miles looks tortured. "I wanted to talk to you . . . alone. About . . ." He looks at Maverick, then at me. "I've been thinking about you . . ." he begins.

"Hey, dude." Maverick leans forward, his face as harsh and violent as I've ever seen it. "She's with me." He takes the back of my neck and pulls me back into his arm, keeping it around me and silently looking at Miles after that.

Miles scoffs. "A guy like you? For how long? Huh?"

Maverick cuts him a cocky smile. And he keeps it simple as always. "Forever."

❤ ❤ ❤

WE'VE BEEN IN the club for a half hour—Maverick and I stealing heated looks and touches of each other—when Maverick's gaze trains on two guys coming in our direction. One looks Native American, beautiful and olive-skinned, with dreads tied into a ponytail that hangs down his back. The other has closely cropped hair and a big diamond earring and a thousand rings on his hands and bracelets on his arm. They're both wearing T-shirts that read WE'RE HERE FOR THE FIGHT.

"*Fuck*, man, the flight delays just pissed us off. Heard you took over," the one with the jewelry says as Maverick stands to slap his back.

The one with the dreads leans over to pop an olive from Gabe's drink into his mouth. "Hey, people, I'm starved," he says, and then he straightens and looks at Maverick. "You fucking lethal cunt, you're an asshole, you know that? You wiped it clean tonight and didn't wait for us?"

Maverick reaches for my hand and draws me to my feet, looks at me with pride. "Reese, these are my guys from back home, Ward and Seneca."

Ward is the one with the jewelry. "Ah, the girl who walks on water," he says drolly.

I smile as he kisses my knuckles in mock gallantness. "I can swim too."

Seneca grabs my other hand and kisses the back. "At last we meet the lucky charm." He looks at Maverick. "That face can cure cancer, man," he says, then he turns to my friends, who look as entertained/shocked/disbelieving as if they were watching a thriller. "May we?" Seneca signals to the table and the food there.

Avery drops Gabe's arm and scoots over. "Please," she purrs, lifting the little plate of olives for Seneca to devour.

"You look a little pale, man. Can I get you a drink?" Ward asks Miles.

Maverick is smiling smugly as he takes a seat and, since we're all so crowded, draws me onto his lap. His friends are clearly both rebels at heart, like Maverick. And a whole lot of trouble compared to my friends. But we end up all having a good time, even

Miles, who's soon overcome by the fact that he's clubbing with the Avenger and his buds.

"Hey," Ward tells me, jerking his scowl in Maverick's direction as Seneca tells him about the waves the rumors of his fights are making back home. "This fucker left without a word. Without a goodbye. Obsessed with proving himself. Don't let him forget he's not alone, huh? His mother misses him. *We* miss him. He's not fucking alone."

"I know," I say.

"You're with the Tates, aren't you?"

"But I'm with Maverick too."

He's still scowling. "But whose side are you on at the final?" He raises his brows, then lifts a beer to his lips. "You can't be on both."

I nod and stare morosely at my mineral water, with its little lime at the top. And I remind myself the strength and resolve I need right now won't come from anywhere but me.

THIRTY-NINE

INTIMATE

Reese

Love is a funny thing. I don't even know if you can call it a "thing," precisely. It's a force. An energy. A feeling. A moment. A look, a kiss, a smile. All of those things in one.

It sneaks up on you; you never see it coming. And when it does finally hit you, it isn't a small little poke. It's like a rhinoceros rammed itself against your chest. Or you just got run over by a car. It knocks the wind out of you. Slams you against the wall. Kick-starts your heart.

You lose your appetite. You can't sleep.

Some can call love a sickness.

Seriously, you're sick over another human being. You belong to them. They control your feelings with a look in their eye. They change the way you see yourself, feel about yourself. You feel like your world shifted, and everything's the same, but you aren't.

I say it's funny because it seems to bend and twist every concept of reality you have.

You can survive off nothing. The only thing sustaining you is this feeling, energy, force. You can go days without decent sleep.

You're not hungry for anything except that one person who seems to occupy your every thought.

Time slows down when you're without them. Seconds feel like hours, minutes like days. And when you're together, time moves at the speed of light. It's all a blur, and when it's over, you don't remember half the things you were doing but you just remember this feeling. This bliss. And it is all over in a flash. And you're back to counting the long, eternal minutes until you see him again.

I miss Maverick.

We have just arrived in New York.

Ward and Seneca have gone back to Pensacola. They "got shit to do" but they "leave our Mav with you, Lucky Charm and Water Walker, so don't fail us."

They told me at the club about fearless Maverick, who broke every single bone in his body before he turned sixteen.

They told me about stubborn Maverick, who would do everything he was told he couldn't do.

They told me about Maverick's mom, who is a teacher—exactly what I've decided I want to be, I'm now sure—and who used a gentle hand when raising a rebel like Maverick.

"She'd cook us the best meals just to keep us getting together at her place, just so she could keep an eye on our mischief," Ward added. "Can't believe he hasn't told you all this, but then again, I can. Seneca and I are glad to have been witnesses to his mischief, or the rebel acts would have gone unrecorded."

Maverick accompanied them to the airport and then dove straight into training, since those two consumed him for forty-eight hours.

For forty-eight hours I haven't seen him.

I miss his face, his smile, his voice. His hands. My heart feels like it's being blown up into this big balloon; I'm not sure it can fit inside my chest anymore. I crave him. I feel like I'm on this high.

I find myself tucking Racer into bed and then walking down the block, to his hotel. With the key that he sent me. It's midnight, and I can feel streetlights whispering across my face as I head toward him.

I can't think straight but all I know is that it's six days to the final and I need to be with him right now. My stomach is in knots; my heart is pumping blood, adrenaline, and a million kinds of drugs.

My mind is focused on one thing and one thing only: him.

Time slows down, and every step closer to him it slows down even more. I'm trying to temper my pulse but I can't, because I know what's waiting for me when I get there.

I enter his hotel and I text him that I'm in the elevator.

One minute and ten eternal seconds pass before I see a door crack open and he's in my space. Before me. His smell is intoxicating. He's just gotten out of the shower.

He's in jeans and a navy V-neck shirt. I force myself to look at him, and he gives me this look. This fucking look. A cocky smile, and he asks, "Where are we going?"

I don't say anything. I just look down at the basket I have and grin.

The whole way to the elevator, and down the blocks to Central Park, he is driving me nuts. I'm surprised we don't crash against a tree or something. He takes my hand while I walk and slowly traces his fingers along the veins at my wrist. He rubs my palm softly with his thumb. Then he raises my knuckles to his lips and gives each one of them a quick, soft kiss. By then I am walking on automatic. Like I said, I'm surprised we don't ram into a tree or stumble on a rock.

Then he has his hand on my hip. And the longer I walk, the higher his hand goes, up my rib cage. I don't say anything, but I can feel my face stuck in a huge, excited, childish grin. His hand is large, warm, his calloused fingers rubbing against the bit of skin revealed under my top.

I can feel him looking at me the whole walk, but I can't look at him. I just feel him. His intoxicating, addicting presence only a few inches from mine.

"We're here," I say, showing him my perfect spot.

Right in front of one of the park's shimmering lakes.

The moon is out. The air is warm. I had to bring him here from the moment I discovered this spot when I pushed Racer up the bridge this morning, and now I stand here dumbly until Maverick takes my hand and leads me to a small clearing where the grass is cut short and the edge of the water is only a few feet away.

I sit on the grass, and he takes a seat behind me.

"I missed you," he says. He leans over and traces his lips along my shoulder. I stay completely still. He pushes my hair to the side and starts kissing along my neck.

His chest isn't touching me, but I can feel the heat of his body completely envelop mine. My heart is squeezing and I want to cry from how exquisite this feels.

I barely hear myself whisper "Kiss me" to Maverick.

He stills on my neck and takes me in his hands and turns me to face him. He cradles my cheeks in his palms, his steel eyes drilling into my soul.

He slowly kisses my chin. And then my nose, then rubs his lips along mine. I can feel my self-control slowly melting away and I know in this moment, I am completely at his mercy. Maverick Cage owns me. Every part of me.

I can hear myself breathe, feel it. In every pore of my body. Every part of me wanted him, longed for him. He is so close but I need him closer. His hands belong on me. His lips were made to kiss me. I was made for him. Never in my life has something felt so right.

And just then, he kisses me. Soft, long, hot, wet. Exquisite. Painful. Hot. Completely, totally right.

"You were made to be mine," he says against my lips, kissing me between breaths.

"You know that?" he asks. "You're mine. My hands were made to touch you; my lips were made to love you," he says as he sucks along my neck, his tongue trailing down my throat.

He goes lower and bites my shirt, pulling it down with his teeth, kissing my chest.

"My eyes were meant to see you," he whispers in his voice of thunder as he slowly unbuttons my shirt.

"My tongue was made to taste you," he moans against my breasts. His kisses sucking, licking, branding me.

Then I feel him leave me, and I see him fall back until he's lying on the ground. I find myself following him. He takes my leg in his hand and hooks it on his hip so I'm straddling him. The wind brushes my hair against my back, and he's lying beneath me, his arm behind his head, his other hand brushing the outside of my thigh, rubbing me just how I need him to. But his eyes. Fuck, his eyes. They are drilling into me. Looking at me. Looking *for* me.

They are steel-gray, practically glowing in the dark. The moonlight casts shadows on his face and he looks like a wolf waiting on his prey. He looks like he wants to devour me. He looks like he's challenging me. Daring me to lose myself in him, *with* him.

Daring me to let him have me, every part of me.

I bend down and kiss him with everything I've got. I pour all I have into him. Everything I want to say, every fear and anxiety ripping me apart because I've found out that a part of me *does* belong to him. A very big part of me belongs to him. A part that I cannot bear to live without.

He kisses me back, his hands rubbing my back, sliding lower

to my ass. His hands completely encompass it, and I groan because his erection is pressed against the one part of me I need him to touch.

He kisses my collarbone, his hands on my hips coaxing me into a delicious, grinding, maddening rhythm. A rhythm that makes me want to come apart for him. He takes my lips and groans, "Give me your tongue," against my mouth.

I slip my tongue tentatively into his mouth and he starts sucking on it gently.

I feel my body go weak. He holds on to me like I'm his anchor, and he kisses the life out of me.

We're both panting, moaning, grinding, dying with every second that goes by and we're apart.

"What do you want?" I ask him.

"What do I want?" His eyes flare open and his hand grips my hip. His eyes search mine, pure, lovely, flowing gray. "You know what I want, Reese. I want you now. And I want you in my arms tonight."

"Whatever you want, take it," I groan.

He studies me, devours me.

"Please," I whisper.

I don't need to say anything else because he flips us over until I'm on my back, and he's on his side, looking down on me.

I caress his face, run my fingers down the scruff on his jaw. Rub my thumbs on his cheeks.

Trace his lips.

"You drive me crazy," I whisper.

And we kiss and kiss by the lake in the park, my picnic basket forgotten because there's no other hunger for me than him—and I can tell, his lips tell me, that there's no other hunger for him greater than me.

❤ ❤ ❤

LATE AT NIGHT, he leads me into his room and I strip and slide naked into his bed. And as soon as he strips and joins me, it's warm beneath the sheets, his body steel-hard and smooth and muscled and hot. And I link my legs to his and rest my cheek on his chest.

I trace his nipple with my finger. His breathing changes when I slip my other hand down his waist to stroke his abs. "It's not that your chest is muscled and beautiful and tan and perfect," I whisper, almost to myself. "It's that it's warm and wide and strong and all your male strength just surrounds me when I'm on it."

His breath catches, and then he lets out the most delicious groan. He flips me to my side, and he spoons me and tongue-fucks my ear as he starts to fuck me slowly in the dark, sliding his hand down my abs to caress me between my legs as he drives inside me, over and over, and then he rasps in my ear, "I love you hard."

"Mmm. How hard?"

"This. Hard." Driving deeper. Faster.

A low moan leaves me. I turn my head to him and we start kissing, and after we fuck as hard as we love each other, we settle down to fall asleep, spooning for the rest of the night.

FORTY

THE PHOENIX AND THE SCORPION

Maverick

It's pitch-black when my cell wakes me. Reese stirs beside me, and I blink to focus. I smile when I see her curled up to me, warm and soft, her hair tangled up somehow around my arm. I ease it from beneath her, hearing her mumble, "No," and I smile.

The Tates' hotel was fully booked, but I'm staying just down the block.

I want her close.

I ease off the bed, snap on some boxers, and head out to the living room to take the call.

"Maverick Cage?" a female voice asks.

"Yeah."

Fuck, it's 3:00 a.m.

I pull the phone away to scan the number. I'm frowning as I put the phone back to my ear and peer out the massive window at the blinking lights of New York and the long, shadowed rectangle of the park. "It's about your father."

I hear the word "father" and I'm immediately transported to the moment I first saw him; the broken man I last saw in the hospital bed.

My body engages like it does before a fight. "He's awake?"

There's hope, stupid hope, in my guts when I ask that.

Hope that for the first time in my life, my father will look at my face.

For the first time in my life I can stare at his eyes and say, *I'm fighting, Dad.*

"Unfortunately, he didn't make it. They tried to ease him out of the induced coma and . . ." She trails off when I inhale sharply. "The doctors want to speak with you about what's next."

Disbelief.

Denial.

Anger.

I grit my teeth as I lift my free hand and stare at my bruised knuckles in the dark.

"Sir?"

I turn my hand and glare at my palm.

Is it bigger than his? Wider than his? Does he have all the calluses I have? Does my strength come from him or from his *denial* of me?

"Sir?"

I glance at Reese as she stands at the bedroom door with the crisp bedsheet wrapped around her shoulders, so fucking lovely my eyes hurt, and I gruff into the speaker, "I'll take the next flight out."

"Maverick? What's wrong?"

I scrape my hand down my face and end the call, then I toss my phone aside, go and scoop her up, and take her back to bed. I set her down, look at her face, and just want to bury myself inside her again, all night. The rest of my life.

"My dad's dead. I'm taking a flight out. Get some rest." I reach for my jeans and a clean T-shirt.

"I want to go with you, Maverick." She reaches for her clothes.

"No. I don't want you near him."

"Why?" She halts, then drops her clothes and stares at me in question.

I shove my legs into my jeans, zip up and snap them, and then stare at her for a moment, and slowly shake my head. "I just don't."

I'm ashamed for Reese to know my father. I'm ashamed for her to see where I come from. *You're the good in my life, all of it. My lucky charm. I don't want you near the bad.*

Not even my own mother wanted to be near him again, a woman who once loved him. I don't want my girl near him either.

"I'll be back for the fight," I say, shoving into my T-shirt and quickly grabbing my stuff.

Reese clutches the sheet to her chest, her eyes loving and tender and full as she comes to me.

Comes to me and lovingly kisses my lips.

I'm slayed by her.

Everything she does touches me.

Everything she does pleases me.

Everything she does cuts me.

"For luck?" I ask thickly, probing into her eyes, desperately searching for the measure of peace I crave to find.

She calms me; but there's no calm for me now.

She shakes her head, smiling with more liquid emotion in her eyes. "For love."

THEY NEEDED SOMEONE to claim the body—and nobody had. He died alone. In a fucking hospital bed. Never knowing his son. Leaving . . . nothing but his old fucking gloves.

Next was a burial, a service, and no one seemed to want one. Not him, and to be honest, not me.

I still buried him. Just me, standing there among thousands of other headstones, with a priest I'm sure he would've cussed at.

My eyes are dry. I've got cuts and scrapes from the fight, and my ribs still hurt like a bitch when I move to open my backpack.

I shift and grit my teeth, forcing my body to take the pain as I pull out the old gloves my dad sent me and toss them into the grave.

All my hopes follow those worn, torn black gloves.

I will never look into his eyes. Will never know if what they said about him was true. Will never know if there was something good in him or if all I'm spawned from is pure, undiluted asshole.

I feel no pain. Only frustration. Frustration and anger.

When the priest leaves, I speak to him for only the second but last time in my life.

I say, harsh, low, angry, "Goodbye, Dad."

FORTY-ONE

LEGEND

Maverick

I feel poisoned just from looking at my dad in a casket. Just being near him and reliving all the years of waiting for him, waiting to prove myself to him.

I've run until my lungs are on fire, quads, calves, abs burning like firestones, my brain flaming with flashes of him in a coffin.

Flashes of Tate in the ring.

Flashes of me putting on my boxing gloves.

Flashes of Reese, saying, *Love me hard.*

Flashes of Oz, drinking.

Flashes of my mom, getting a check from me.

I hit the hotel and spend an hour under the shower spray, shutting my eyes. My phone has been buzzing, but I don't pay attention to it.

Oz has been calling.

The final is in three days. I get back to New York tomorrow.

That's all I know. I fight my fight in three days.

And I fight Tate—more father than I've ever had. It won't feel good to beat him. It won't feel good to lose, either.

While my real father died, I was training with Tate.

His greatest enemy. Who took me under his wing.

I got close to them. I got weak, thinking I was getting stronger. I've got more muscles but less walls around me. I can't be weak, I can't laugh with them, talk with them.

Fuck, I can't believe I was so careless.

I dropped my guard. Like they'll accept me? Fucking nobody does. They're watching me, guarding what I learn. Like the saying "Keep your enemies closer. . . ."

And I fell like a love-starved puppy begging for a damn bone.

Because of Reese.

And *He's with me.*

And blue eyes and six freckles now.

And smiles that fire me up.

Fingers that feel soft.

A cheek on my chest.

And secrets about her dark days and her new ones.

And my favorite ass in the world.

I don't want to have anyone.

I don't want to need anyone.

I don't want to feel anything.

I don't want to feel like *this.*

I want to be alone.

Me, Tate, the ring.

But even with Reese miles away, she's with me more than ever. When I fight the fight, she'll be in my head more than ever.

And chances are, I won't be the guy she's rooting for to win.

I turn off the water and towel off, pull on a pair of sweatpants, grab a jump rope, and take it on with a vengeance.

❤ ❤ ❤

IT'S PAST MIDNIGHT and I crave her voice like I crave nothing else. I dial her phone, get the voice mail. And listen to it like a junkie, *Hi, this is Reese. I can't come to the phone but leave a message. . . .*

I leave no message. But I text:

He's gone.

I toss my phone aside and shove my rope back into my duffel and drop on the bed, then punch my pillow and plop to my stomach, hating that all that's left of him is in me.

FORTY-TWO

THE DARK AVENGER

Maverick

New York is rainy today. I've been back since noon, and I've spent the afternoon tossing the stupid tennis ball against the bathroom wall of my room until I catch it, crush it until it's flat, then toss it away. I head to my phone, go online, and spend a half hour on the airline sites. Then I text my mom a message. The only woman I'm sure roots for me, since I'm not sure whose side the woman I love is on.

> Fighting the champion tomorrow
> I just emailed you an airline reservation
> If I win, I'll always regret you not being there to see it
> And I'm going to win, Mom
> Come to my fight

I look up Reese's number, and my finger pauses. The thought of her takes pieces of my brain. I'm simmering inside. I sigh and drag a hand down my face. I won't back down. I can't lose.

I won't lose.

I have one chance to see if I've got it. One chance to bring it to this one fight.

But what if winning means hurting her?

Who's my girl rooting for?

The Tates are her family. They treat her well—give her love, support, and acceptance.

My dad did none of that, and I was still with him. How can I expect less of her and the Tates?

I'm still going to prove that I deserved the Black Scorpion's time, his attention, his respect.

I'm still going to prove to myself that I am good fucking *enough.*

I'm going to be accepted by the whole goddamned world even if I wasn't accepted by my own dad.

I'm going to be a legend.

And a legend will never be gone, even when six feet under.

And a legend gets the girl.

A legend *wins* the girl.

I'm a fighter and I'm fighting tomorrow night.

But fuck my life, I don't feel like fighting when I think of my girl not backing me up.

I grab the tennis ball again and try to give it shape, frustrated that I can't, when there's a knock on the door.

I set it down and open, and Riptide stands out in the hall.

I stalk back in the room and leave the door open behind me, then watch him from across the room as he shuts the door and follows me inside.

"I'm sorry about your father."

I shrug. "Yeah, me too."

He seems to feel the need to specify: "I'm sorry for *you.*"

I lean on the wall and cross my arms. "I've been alone my whole life. I don't need anyone to win."

"Yes you do, and you have her. Reese let us know the day you left whose side she's on. And it sure as fuck ain't mine. She'll be in her seat on the front fucking row on your left. Right next to the woman I love, who will be cheering for me."

I clench my jaw, my chest expanding painfully as I process this. "She said that?"

"Crystal clear. And I respect that." He nods, then shoots me a warning look. "I won't make it easy for you tomorrow, Maverick. I'm bringing my A game."

My fighter instinct engages, and I push away from the wall and brace my feet apart. "I'm bringing all the game I've got."

He grins then, and we're back—our competitive juices flowing. He raises his fist, and I instinctively take a step forward and raise mine. We bump knuckles. And it's on.

It's. Fucking. On.

"I'm still bringing it home, Tate," I warn.

"Bring it home, Maverick. I'm still gonna lay it harder on you than anyone." He steps closer and raises his brows warningly. "And just so you know, whatever it is you think you're fighting for— Avenger is *my* legacy. Not your father's. Mine." He grabs me by the back of the neck and looks me in the eye, squeezing in some sort of combined threat and encouragement. "You're a good kid, Maverick. If you're going to take the ring, you're going to need to fight to the teeth for it. And if you best me tomorrow, fair and square like your father never did, I'm going to be proud. I'm going to give something back to this ring before I go. I'm going to leave them you."

He walks to the door, and I growl, "I'm game."

He grabs the doorknob but waits a moment. "You're in an identity crisis. Who you think you are and where you come from versus who you can be and where you're going. I can relate."

I laugh. "How can *you* ever relate to that?"

"I'm bipolar." He looks me in the eye, unflinching. "So yeah,

I can relate with the monsters inside. Mine's in my head. Yours is in your blood. Don't let it win."

He jerks the door open, and adds, "That's our real fight. The one that lasts a lifetime. The hardest to win. You win that, a fight like tomorrow's is a piece of cake."

❤ ❤ ❤

I HAD TO call her. I had to see her face. I had to know that what Tate said was true.

As soon as she says she can come over, I open the door of my suite and wait for her. I hear the elevator *ting*, and see her step out. She stops when she sees me, and I watch her come to me, every step just a little faster, until she throws herself into my arms.

"You've been in New York for a while and you didn't call me?" she asks, hurt, clutching me closer as she whispers against my neck.

I breathe in her hair and speak against the top of her head, stroking a hand down the back of her head. "I'm sorry, I needed to be alone. I'm so used to being alone."

"But I'm on your side," she protests, chiding me with a scowl.

I nod and scoop her up, bring her in, and shut the door. She's in my corner. And all I want to do is hold her to my chest tonight.

FORTY-THREE

THAT MORNING

Reese

I peel my eyes open early, at around 4:30 a.m., when I hear the shower running.

I open the bathroom door a little bit and peer into the stall. He's soaping himself up in all the glory of glory itself. I am so very addicted to this man.

My mouth waters as I take in his wet, golden muscles. "Are you going to let me soap you up?" I hear myself ask, sex vixen that I woke up being today. "Because I have never, ever done that in my life and I just added it to my bucket list of things to do before I die."

His eyes go dark and look a little possessive as he reaches out and takes my hand, urging me inside. "What else is on that list?"

"I just made it up." I smile as I take a few steps toward him and the water spray. He's so beautiful. One touch of my fingers on his wet skin and the cock that started hardening when I peered inside fills up completely.

I start to blush when he looks at me naked. Have I ever stood naked before him for so long, completely naked, with this much light? "What is this? Are you blushing?" He lifts my face by the chin. "I appreciate looking at you like this," he assures me tenderly, running his wet hands over my body.

"I'm realizing." I laugh a little.

I'm hot with embarrassment and trembling in excitement as he reaches out and runs a bar of soap down my arm. He soaps me up, every spot possible except between my legs until, point blank, weak with anticipation, I hold on to his shoulders and bite down on his wet tendon as I part my legs a little.

He laughs softly in my ear. "Did I miss here?" he teases me, running the bar over my sex.

I blush and nod, wrapping my arm tighter around his broad shoulders. "I'm so reckless with you," I whisper in his ear.

"I thought you didn't like it," he says, lifting an eyebrow as he turns me to the spray.

"I kind of do." I reach out to stroke him as I kiss his neck and soap him up next.

We end up transferring the soap between each other until we're both lathered, until I don't know who's soaping who, where my hands are, where his hands are, but the sensations are coming from all over the place as we fool around in the shower.

When he finally brings us out of the shower, he grabs a towel and wraps it around my shoulders, then he grabs me by the hips and lifts me.

He stands in the middle of the bathroom, lowering me down on him as he kisses me. I catch the reflection of us in the mirror on the side—unexpectedly. His every muscle cut and flexing. His powerful legs, his abs and ass as he thrusts, his arms and chest and shoulders as he lifts me and lowers me. And me, so pale, my blonde hair wet and streaking down my back, the towel sliding down my body—his cock submerging into the pink, shiny, swollen lips between my legs.

I'm eroticized by the sight of us together because I've seen movies, I've seen porn, I've seen pictures and art, but I have never responded to the sight of a couple making love the way I respond to seeing Maverick spreading me open as he lowers me down on him.

I see myself, and I don't look like the girl I saw in the mirror several months ago. I'm not self-conscious. I'm sexy. I'm woman. I'm wanted. I'm made perfectly for him.

Gasping his name, aware of the intensity of my feelings, I'm the first to come, but he comes as hard as always, buttocks flexing, body pumping as he nibbles my neck.

I'm shy when I notice he catches my gaze in the mirror, and I whisper, smiling, "Aside from being for my purely selfish purposes . . . that was for luck."

He mock-frowns at me, as if terribly disappointed. "And for love?"

I nod, grinning happily.

He still holds me aloft with one arm and cups the back of my head with the other, looking at me as if I'm the eighth wonder of the world. "You're a shot of pure fucking heaven in my veins."

FORTY-FOUR

IT'S TIME

Maverick

It's a half hour to the match and Oz won't open the door to his room. "Oz!" I bang the door. I jerk on the doorknob and bang harder, resisting the urge to crash through with my shoulder.

Three minutes later, I come back with a member of the hotel staff, who unlocks the door.

He's in the small sitting area of his room, bottles all over the place.

"Oz, Jesus." I grab the bottles and start tossing them away, then I go and stand before him. He won't even look me in the eye, his bloodshot eyes staring past my shoulder.

"Oz, we have a shot tonight." I grab a glass of water and bring it over. He won't take it. Sighing, I set it aside, drop to my haunches, and level my nose with his. "I'm fighting tonight, and I need you in my corner."

"What do you need me for?" he scoffs.

"I need you in my corner, Oz."

"Get out."

"We have a shot, Oz."

"We?"

"*We.* Look, you want to prove something? Here's your chance."

Oz doesn't get up. He shifts forward and stares at the floor. "Men like us, Maverick, we don't get the good stuff."

"How do you know if you don't make a grab for it?"

"Because I've lived longer, that's why. I tried shooting for it plenty of times."

"Oz. Look—"

"Don't sermon me, Maverick! You and the Tates. You and your girl. You're not an unwanted anymore. Like me," he growls, frowning.

"Oz. Fuck, man. I found this girl. And she's lovely. And she gets me. And I get her. And I want to be with her. I'm crazy about her in a way I never thought I'd be. I've been training like mad for tonight. Just one night, Oz."

"You've been taking me for granted, Maverick."

I stand and curl my fists at my sides. I lower my voice. "I don't take anything for granted. I know better."

"You don't need me anymore. You got me because no one good enough would take you on. Now you got something better. You got Tate as a mentor."

"Except I'll never forget you were the one on my team when nobody else wanted in."

"Your best buddy Tate's got an in now," he says resentfully. "You can get anyone you want at this point."

"Then fucking realize it's me who's standing right here asking *you* to be in my corner."

He shakes his head and wipes his face, then folds his arms, and he starts crying.

I groan and drop back to my haunches. "Don't do this to me, Oz."

"Just fucking go."

"Not without you."

He grabs the nearest bottle and tries to drink.

I stop it midair, yanking it away from him and setting it aside, my voice low. "So that's how this goes. You want to sabotage us, Oz? Do you?" I'm mad now. I'm so fucking mad I can't see straight.

I plant my hand on the back of his seat and lean forward. "Be fucking man enough to fight the fight we set out to fight."

His eyes shoot daggers at me. "*Go*, Cage. This isn't my fight anymore," he says, glaring at me.

I curl my hands into fists, go slam my palm into the wall, then I come back and drop down before him.

"Why are you still here?"

"'Cause you're still here."

He glowers.

I glower back. Then I lean in my seat and stare at the room. "Good rooms compared to where we started, huh."

"Pretty damn fine," he grumbles.

I sigh and drag my hand down my face. "Oz. Talk to me."

He glances down at his empty hands. "I try leaving it but I can't. . . ." He exhales and looks away. "Seventy-eight fighters I've trained in the past decade as coach. Fighters I'd nurse to health. Fighters I'd wake up at three a.m. to get them ready by four to train. Fighters I helped cook for, helped dress, hell, I even helped some stay sober. They all leave. Every rung up the ladder of success, every match I helped win, was just one more rung to the top where they'd say goodbye to me. I gave everything up for so many of them. Didn't have kids—my champs were my kids. Gave up time with the wife. They all leave. And so will you, Maverick."

I lean forward, looking at him. "Whether this is the end of something great or the beginning . . . win or lose tonight . . . I want you in my corner always, Oz. Always."

He frowns and clamps his lips tight, his eyes red. "Even like this?!" he cries, disbelieving.

"Hey." I lean forward even more, nodding somberly. "I'm going to support you. You can get through this and you don't need to do it alone. Just because you've lost this fight before doesn't mean you'll lose it forever. I won't let you. I'm going to support you to win yours like you've been supporting me to win mine. If you need me right now, I'm here."

He exhales through his nostrils, then sets the bottle aside. "Fine. I'll take the damn twelve steps."

"Good. I'm proud."

He glowers. "You really want to fight tonight or are you turning into a pussy?"

"My dick's just fine tonight, Oz, and so are my fists, but I want you to be there."

"Well. Guess I will just take *one* step first. 'Cause if my champ needs me and *it's not out of pity*, then he's got me."

"Good. 'Cause if my coach wants me, he's got me." We share a look of understanding as we both stand, and I glance at the clock. The seconds have never ticked faster.

We have seven minutes to get to the Underground.

Once outside, it's five minutes and counting. I take a look at the hotel cab line and swear.

Half a dozen people in line and no cabs pulling in.

"All right, Oz. Let's get you a much-needed workout." I trot to the sidewalk and check to make sure that he follows, and he groans and tries to catch up as I start running like hell to the Underground.

FORTY-FIVE

RINGSIDE SEATS

Reese

"Reese?" Brooke calls my name from the bedroom door. "You ready?"

I leap out of the bathroom, where I was tying my hair back in a braid, and nod. "I'm so nervous."

She laughs and hugs me, happily so.

"*You* don't look nervous," I tell her as she goes to give some last-minute instructions to Racer and kisses him good night.

She grins privately. "Whatever happens, Remington will be celebrating tonight."

"Why do you say that?"

She leans over to tuck Racer in bed. "Because I'm pregnant." She smiles so wide as she looks back at me. "I'm pregnant and Remington is going to be thrilled. Nothing matters more to him than we do. Right, Racer? A little sister, or a little brother?"

"No," he says frowning, sitting up in bed. "My mommy's mine!" He squeezes her. And she laughs and smacks his rump and settles him back down to bed, and nods to Diane.

We take the elevators to where Pete waits with an SUV. And

then we both head out of the hotel, past Central Park and toward the East Side, to the warehouse of the Underground.

There are easily fifteen thousand people present, and Brooke leads me to a row of empty front-row-center seats.

I can smell the metallic scent of blood and sweat and beer and warmth of too many humans together. The sight of the ring so close makes my breath hitch.

"How you do it, I don't know," I tell her as we wait.

She pats my thigh reassuringly. "It gets easier. It's never fun when there's blood."

"There's going to be blood." I exhale, preparing for it.

She nods. "It's the final. They fight for all." She scowls and waves Pete over. "What's the delay?" she asks.

"They're saying Maverick isn't here."

"What do you mean?"

Pete purses his lips in concern. "If he isn't here in a minute, he'll be disqualified."

I glance at Maverick's corner with a sinking feeling in my gut, then I tell Brooke, "Something happened. There's no way Maverick would miss this fight—"

"Reese—" Brooke tries to appease me when the announcer speaks.

"Good evening, ladies and gentlemen . . ."

And Pete glances at Riley, who waves a signal at him, and Pete turns to us with a grin.

"It's on," he says.

And oh god.

It's *on*.

FORTY-SIX

LAST FIGHT

Maverick

Oz is pacing in the back room of the warehouse like an angel of death, hair sticking up, eyes bloodshot, jaw set in determination. "Okay, kid, you better not dump me for anything new and shiny. I'm sobering up for real now."

I look at Oz, smiling to myself.

"This better be fucking worth it." He jabs a finger at my bare chest. "When I get sober, I want to realize I got something good in my life."

"You do, motherfucker. You got me."

He nods. "Now go show Riptide he taught you well."

"I will," I vow quietly, and I let Oz tape up my hands.

"Nah, fuck, it needs to be perfect," he grumbles. He unravels one of them and tightens it up.

I'm pumped up and wired after wondering for a hot second whether I'd even make it to the fight. After Oz, after the run, my veins are crackling with testosterone.

Tate wants a big fight, his last fight.

And suddenly I just want to *fight*.

"He told Brooke this is the best match of his life, and Reese says he means it," Oz says.

"Hell, it's the best match of mine." I look up. "Reese told you that?"

"I talk to Reese sometimes," he says, smirking. He slaps the back of my head. "You were right. I think she's with us."

I exhale, drag my taped hand down my face. Then shove my hands into my gloves.

Because I'm the challenger, I get called out first.

". . . so please welcome our challenger of the night, the fucking underdog of the season. It'll be a miracle if the match lasts past the first round. No rookie EVER has survived that long against our champion. But this isn't just any rookie, ladies and gentlemen, oh no. We give you, here at the Underground, MAVERICK CAGE—THE AVEEEENGER!"

Oz opens the door, and I tap my gloves and head outside, the competitive juices flowing through my veins.

Dozens of lights are trained on the ring. Every single eye in the arena trained on me as I hop inside and jerk off my robe, then wait quietly in my corner as they call Tate.

"Ladies and gentlemen, our defending champion of the Underground, the undefeated KING OF THE RING, we give you, REMINGTON TATE—RIIIIIIPTIDE!"

The crowd comes alive, and Oz cackles in my corner, amused. I scan the crowd for Reese—and my gaze stops on a woman with short dark hair and eyes like mine behind a pair of prim glasses.

Mother.

Her hands are trembling in her lap, and I look at her in apology. *This is why I didn't want you to come before, Mother.*

You're not going to like this one bit.

But she smiles a brave smile, and I cant my head at her in

gratitude for coming. Behind her, Ward gives me the finger and Seneca lifts his fingers in a mocking peace sign.

I glare at them, but I'm glad they're close to my mother. The last thing I want her to feel is alone here, among thousands, with no one cheering for her son.

Tate takes the ring like the king does.

He hits the floor soundlessly.

I stand here. Ready. Waiting.

He turns around. His fans go wild.

I prowl to the other side of the ring as the crowd cheers him. And there, sitting next to Brooke, is the loveliest girl I've ever seen.

She's smiling tremulously, her eyes fixed on nothing—not the ring, not the crowd, not Tate—nothing but me.

My jaw tightens as I try to tame back the wild emotion seeing her here gives me. I put my fist to my chest and her breasts rise a little on a breath, as if she knows what it means.

That's it, between me and her.

She knows.

That I love her. Adore her.

And she knows that I wanted—needed—her to be with me.

And she's there, in her seat in the front fucking row on my left, right where Tate said she'd be.

The referee brings Tate and me together. "When I come in, you step back and stop punching, I want a clean fight tonight."

We both nod in understanding, eyes on each other.

There's respect between us now.

And I know this second that if I lose tonight, I lose to the best.

It begins.

The count . . .

The testosterone is thick in the air. Neither of us likes to go down. We're both too stubborn to go down.

We both hunger for victory. Over each other. Over ourselves.

It's the biggest match the Underground has ever had. My father's departure made people happy, but the fact that word spread about Tate and me developing a friendship created controversy and curiosity. They want to see us—see it to believe it.

We're both aggressive fighters. Though I've learned to defend too, because Tate is also great at defense. While training me, it felt like he wanted to create something better than himself. He taught me everything to look for, things nobody's ever seen because he's never let them close enough. Things nobody else can find but me. I've never been able to beat him. But he's given me every opportunity to find out how.

We tap gloves, both of us trying to gauge each other's strategy for the night. Wear me down? No. He's not playing games with me, and I'm glad he isn't, because we're both here to fight.

Ting ting.

The crowd goes wild as I take the first swing.

He blocks, grins.

He follows me, trying to land a big hit. His knuckles land a clean blow to the head. I react when he opens and bury my glove in his gut. It's like hitting concrete. But I'm strong and, judging by the sound my punch makes, it went deep.

We leap back, then circle.

The crowd alternates between silence and cheers. We're giving them quite a show. A blow that stuns me. He's got the most powerful punch I've ever felt. He's got me against the ropes. He doesn't tell me where I fucked up—hell, I know it already. I put my arms up and block, then lower them and narrow my eyes.

He grins as they stop us and force us apart. I can see it in his eyes—a challenge. Asking me, *Do you think you deserve to be world champion? Champions never fuck up twice.*

I take position.

The crowd stands and starts chanting, "Remy! Remy! Remy!"

I'm waiting for him to look at his wife and take a hit.

And somehow I wonder if he's waiting for me to look at Reese.

Achilles is only as strong as his heel.

And we both have heels.

And we both know where they are sitting tonight.

He takes a shot under the heart, then a hook that shoots my head around. I back away as I recover, Tate becoming the aggressor.

I stop backing up and take a left straight jab. He moves his shoulder, evading, but I see that coming and counteract with another right. Knuckles crush into his temple. The hit stuns him.

The bell for the first round rings.

We keep fighting after the bell, suddenly both of us punching, some landing, some missing, ducking, punching.

The referee yells and slips inside. "Stop! HALT!" he demands.

We ease back and take our stools.

We're back on. The announcer: "Cage is prowling . . . the only fighter this season not in awe of the champion . . . and Tate's up against the ropes! Cage takes a hit. They're getting touchy. Referee cannot break them apart. . . ."

"HALT!" the referee calls again.

"Fucker," Tate says when he steps aside and lets us continue. "Won't let us have any fun," he growls.

"Speaking of fun," I say, chest heaving as I catch my breath. "Checked your wife out yet? She's not looking at you, she's looking at me."

He smacks my face so hard I bounce on the ropes, then I duck and he misses and swings around, frowning *and* grinning. "Fucker. Reese just left. Said to call her when you got better game, pussy."

I swing my left, he ducks and shoots his left out. My forehead catches the blow and my brain jerks inside my skull. I back away, listless.

Things get bloody after that.

I feel a high, a complete rush of adrenaline. Boxing, moving, punching, countering, blocking.

Round four, five, and six—he breaks my rib and I give him a swollen eye. He can only see through one, squinting at me as we fight.

The crowd is overwhelmed. Ringside seats splattered with blood. We're beating each other to a pulp. Throwing punches left and right. We've both got gashes above our eyes, Tate on his temple, and my blasted same cut above my eye has opened again. We are breathing hard, getting Vaseline on our faces when we take our stools, and getting patched up, and wearing down the more we fight.

Round seven, he knocks me to the canvas.

I get up, and the fight keeps going. . . .

Three of Tate's hooks on round eight, and I'm down again.

"Fuck," I growl under my breath, my cheek flat on the ground as my body convulses from the hits.

The countdown begins.

Reese is on her feet, hands to her mouth, crying.

She's with *me*.

My body trembles as I demand more from it than it can give. Everything. I plant my hand down on the ground, and then the other, bring my knees up and stand.

And I look at Tate. One eye is swollen. His coach is cutting it up so the blood can emerge, and he's taping him back.

I look at my gloves. Every mark there on the leather is from me. Fought for by me. I think of my father's message and drag a deep breath. *Guess I'm a real fighter now.*

Tate approaches. He's angry now. Is he disappointed? He looks mad that I haven't given him more. Did he think he wasted his time with me? Is he thinking I wasn't worth it? Like my own fucking father?

Don't want to think he's bigger. More experienced.

He thought I'd give him the better fight.

And I will.

I don't fight for my father.

I fight for me.

I'm the phoenix rising.

I brace my legs, lift my arms, and keep on fighting.

Hungry for victory.

His nose crunches.

He hooks back and busts my face open. I hit the ground and immediately leap up.

My vision's blurred. Legs, arms, nothing responds. I blink and taste blood in my mouth. Pain slowly streaking through me, I force myself forward.

I picture my father. His face. Him fighting me. *You're not good enough. . . .*

Him fighting dirty.

Him fighting Tate.

Him soiling me.

Him letting my mother scrape until her hands were weary.

And I roar and swing out so hard, Tate hits the canvas.

The next seconds are a blur.

Time drains away. The countdown stops, and Tate is still getting his bearings.

My eye's so swollen it's all a blur, but I see something shiny fly at me—and focus on the penny landing at my feet.

The penny I gave Reese when it was all I had. When I had nothing but me.

I scoop up the penny and lift my eyes to Reese. Tears stream down her cheeks, and I inhale and it hurts to breathe, and it hurts to lift my fist and put the penny to my chest, and when she cries harder, and I can't breathe anymore, I look away so she doesn't see the burn in my eyes as the ringmaster grabs my wrist and lifts my arm.

"Your VICTOR, LADIES AND GENTLEMEN! The first rookie ever to win the season championship, to shoot to the top of the fucking stratosphere!"

And for the first time in my life, I hear the crowd. I hear the crowd. And the crowd is yelling at the top of its lungs:

"MAVERICK! MAVERICK! MAVERICK!"

Tate comes to his feet and he looks like shit, and so do I, as he locks his hands behind my neck and bumps his forehead to mine and squeezes the back of my head, grinning until his bloodied dimples pop out. "How do you feel, motherfucker? Is this real enough for you? Huh?"

And the crowd goes, "REMY! REMY! REMY!"

The ringmaster stands between us, lifting each of our arms, and fucking crazy Remington Tate is grinning over the top of his head at me.

The crowd is yelling after him as he leaves the ring for the last time, a legend. Eternal.

But I can't move yet.

For the last few seconds, I stand alone in the ring, bloodied and broken, a winner, the world opening up to me.

But I'm still clutching Reese's penny in my fist like the most precious thing I've got.

I'M ALONE IN the back room.

Hearing the crowd cheer outside.

Oz is patching me up, trembling with adrenaline, sniffing quietly. I stare at the wall. Processing.

There's a knock, and Tate stands at the door. All patched up too. Tape along his temple, his jaw, a lot of swelling spots like my own.

Oz looks at him, reverently pats his back, and whispers something like, "Best fight I've ever seen in my life," and he steps outside.

"Hey." Tate drops on the bench before me. "First time I was up in the ring, I got beat up so hard, I got two ribs broken and my spirit. They both healed though. If it comes to that, yours will too."

I hold my jaw tight as I nod. I want to talk, but I have no words for this guy. My father's greatest enemy, who gave me more attention than my father ever did. My father's greatest enemy, who believed in me more than my own father ever did.

More father to me than my own blood. My mentor. My brother.

"When I started training you," he says, smirking in pride, "I thought you could be great. Hell, I knew you could be great. I knew you could be better than me. And I was right." He jerks his chin toward the door. "Ring's all yours. Own it and never hand it off unless you're stepping down."

"I won't," I vow with conviction, my hands fisting instinctively.

"Good."

He puts his fist out, like his son does. "It's an honor to have fought with you."

I don't know how I can get up. How I can talk. I do both. I meet his gaze with pride and gratitude and admiration and more respect than I've ever felt in my life. I press my knuckles to his, just like I do with his son. And say what I mean. I always say what I mean. "The honor was mine."

EPILOGUE

I'M WITH HIM

Reese

That was the first of many finals for Maverick "the Avenger" Cage. It's been two years, hundreds of matches, and they call him the King of the Ring. People cheer when he's on. The announcers nearly climax when they announce him. "OUR VERY OWN, LADIES AND GENTLEMEN! The most fearless rookie to ever take this ring. The KING, the Avenger, Maaaaverick Caaaaaage!"

He climbs into the ring without glancing at anybody. Then Mav sees me as he disrobes and I look at my phoenix rising and feel so much pride I could burst.

He bought a house in Seattle, near the Tates. They had a baby girl and called her Iris.

Maverick still trains with Riptide several times a week. And every night, before we go to bed, we go for a midnight run.

Because . . . did I mention it yet?

I'm with him.

Every time he steps off the ring, I go stand by Oz, and he comes to his corner. To Oz and me.

I wake up to my mornings with my cheek on his chest and I almost don't know which limb is mine or which is his, except his is harder and tanner.

Mornings, Oz is all business, with a shit-ton of water bottles packed for their daily workout. (Oz has a new girlfriend. Her name is Natasha and now everything wonderful is a Natasha.) "If we're going to be champions *again*"—he rolls his eyes, as if there's any doubt—"you're going to need a coach, a sober one preferably."

Maverick always fist-bumps him now. "That's my man."

And Oz grins, sheepish.

He's met my parents.

I've met his mother.

Maverick and I don't want to be apart. He's determined. He wants me with him.

So, I'm with him.

It's night now. The city of Seattle is quiet. The soft patter of rain died down a few minutes ago, and I'm all set to run as he finishes tying his shoelaces. He straightens and looks at me.

He looks . . .

Like him.

The guy in the darkness coming to the light.

The phoenix rising.

The guy holding my heart.

My love is like a steel weight, but it's nothing compared to the weight of that steel gaze locked on my face like there's no power on earth that will pull those eyes away.

"Ready, Reese?"

A helpless smile pulls at my lips. Love and lust and hope for us twists around my heart. "Always ready to try and beat your ass. Somebody has to."

He steps forward, frowning as he does, still puzzled by my effect on him. "You decimate me, Reese."

I play innocent. "I didn't say anything."

"You say it with these." He touches my eyes, and then he kisses my eyelids. "Hey, I still love you."

"And I still love you."

He still doesn't know that he had me at the penny.

He draws me close now and kisses my neck, and he lifts my head to kiss me on the mouth, and he tastes so right and so hard and so strong, so powerful, my world narrows down to all six-feet-plus inches of my avenger.

On a shuddering breath, my lips part and my eyes flutter shut as he begins kissing my jaw, my lips again. He sometimes smears my lipstick all over his mouth but I don't care. He likes devouring me and I let him. Wild, primitive, his mouth ravages mine, like it does in bed every night.

He tilts my head at the best angle and sometimes he says my lips taste of cherries.

His father's gloves are gone. He has a roomful of fighting gear, everything new, everything his. He's still finding out who he is, but he knows who he *isn't*.

I'm still finding out who I am, and whoever that is, I know that I'm with him.

He has a portrait of that final match with Remy, of that moment—the *moment* where Remy embraces him like a proud father—and he has it in the hall to our bedroom.

He says he never wants to forget what it feels like to fight someone better than him.

He says he never wants to forget that he's not Scorpion's legacy.

And he'll never forget that night despite all the others that have followed.

He's still fighting.

And we're still in love.

Heading out of our home, Maverick pulls on his hoodie and we take to the damp street to run on the wet pavement, where the path feels endless, where we have forever awaiting us.

But we both know nothing is forever, except legends. And except us.

Dear Readers,

Thanks so much for going on the REAL series journey with me. *Legend* is the last of the REAL series books, and although I started writing not knowing which of the men would win the last fight, I wrote as true to the stories as the characters gave me and this is their happily ever after. I couldn't include (because it isn't relevant to this story) that Melanie and Greyson are married, and that Pandora and Mackenna enjoy visits from their daughter, Eve, for entire summers. As you know, Brooke is pregnant and we all hope it's a girl (Iris!). Maverick finally overcame his father's shadow, and Remy officially has passed the torch. A draw for that last fight was impossible, no matter how much I wished for it. Both men fight to win and Remy put all his heart into his mentorship. He taught Maverick to be better than anything he would ever come upon and Maverick delivered. I am so proud of them and so grateful for all your love for my stories and these characters. Thank you for the support you've given us throughout the years.

I look forward to sharing my new and upcoming, amazing series characters with you this year and I hope you all keep your eyes on your own personal dreams and ambitions. Become, in whatever impassions you, a *legend*.

Love,

Katy

ACKNOWLEDGMENTS

Thank you to . . . my husband, my children, and my parents; you are the light of my life!

To Stacey Suarez, the best fitness expert and dearest friend I could have ever hoped for, who has been with me with every step of my writing journey.

To Monica Murphy, for the beta reads, the hours emailing, the laughs, and the friendship.

To Kelli C., my external "ninja" editor, for helping me prep this baby and beautify my words—you are amazing!

To Anita S. for the excellent proofread and extra-gentle touch with my manuscript.

To all the bloggers who have supported me through what is now is my ninth release, I appreciate each and every one of you. Thank you for taking the time to read, review, and promote my releases. Without you it would be incredibly hard for my books to be found.

To my amazing beta readers, for their early feedback and all the chats and book love. Thank you, Monica, Kim Jones, Kati D, CeCe, Angie, Lisa, and a huge special thank-you with a cherry on top to Mara White and her little boy, who was my inspiration for Racer.

This book would not be what it is today without my amazing publisher. My huge thanks to everyone at Gallery Books, including my editor, Adam Wilson; my publishers, Jen Bergstrom and Louise Burke; the art department, copy editors, publishing team, and publicists.

I am equally grateful to all my foreign publishers, who've translated The REAL series in nearly a dozen other countries so far. Thank you!

To everyone at Jane Rotrosen Agency, you are not only amazing people but always manage to make us—your authors—feel like we're family. Thank you! And special thanks to Amy Tannenbaum, my agent, who is not just my agent but also takes on a million other roles like best-advice-giver, relentless cheerleader, and firm Katy-believer. Without Amy, I might quit when the going gets tough, but thankfully when the going gets tough, Amy gets tougher. So thank you, Amy.☺

And most especially, thank you, thank you, *thank you* to my readers. You are as passionate about my characters as I am, you allow them to make you lose sleep like I do, you think about them in the shower and when you're driving like I do, and then you go all out and *love* them like I do. Thank you for all the hours you spend with us. I hope we can continue spending many more.

ABOUT THE AUTHOR

Katy Evans is married and lives with her husband and their two children plus three lazy dogs in South Texas. Some of her favorite pastimes are hiking, reading, baking, and spending time with her friends and family. For more information on Katy Evans and her upcoming releases, check her out on the sites below. She loves to hear from her readers.

Website: www.katyevans.net
Facebook: https://www.facebook.com/AuthorKatyEvans
Twitter: https://twitter.com/authorkatyevans
Email: katyevansauthor@gmail.com